THE *Most to Lose*

THE

LAURA LANDON

The characters and events portrayed in this book are fictitious. Any similarity to real persons, living or dead, is coincidental and not intended by the author.

Published by Montlake Romance
P.O. Box 400818
Las Vegas, NV 89140

ISBN-13: 9781612184784
ISBN-10: 1612184782

To all my readers. You are the best!
Thank you!

Prologue

London, England
May 16, 1852

"You *have* to help me, Jonah. You simply must!

Jonah Armstrong, the second son of the Earl of Haywood, looked at the pleading panic in Melisande's huge blue eyes and felt himself weaken.

He couldn't.

He detached Melisande's clutching fingers from his sleeves and took a step away from her.

"I can't, Melisande. There's nothing I can do."

"Yes, there is! You can take me to Gretna Green. When we return, you can tell Father you've married me."

Jonah fought an overwhelming sense of panic. "I can't marry you. I don't love you. Nor do you love me."

Melisande stomped her dainty blue slipper and glared at him with the fire he was used to seeing when the spoiled only daughter of the Marquess of Kendall didn't get her way.

"I don't love Hadleigh, either, but my father expects me to marry *him*!"

Jonah attempted reason, although he was sure it wouldn't help. It never had with Melisande. "I would think you'd consider Hadleigh a good match. The three of us grew up together. You've known him your whole life."

"Of course I've known him my whole life," she answered, pacing a small area in Lady Camphort's garden. "Which is precisely why Father shouldn't expect me to marry him. He and I aren't at all suited."

Melisande reminded him of a caged animal pacing its too-confining cage. "Hadleigh is a wonderful choice," Jonah said, making an attempt to point out Hadleigh's attributes. "You will never lack for anything. He's intelligent, has an excellent head for investments, and many already look to him for advice on a number of topics. Besides, he's a *duke*. What more could you ask for in a husband?"

Melisande stopped pacing and glared at him with the most appalled expression he'd ever seen on her face.

"Do you think I care a fig whether my husband has an excellent head on his shoulders? Or whether he's intelligent? Or whether he's sought out for advice? Intelligent men make the worst sort of husbands. Everyone knows that."

Jonah studied Melisande for a moment before he asked, "Then what are you looking for in a husband?"

She didn't bat an eye. "Very well, the fact that I would be a duchess is worth something, I suppose. As is the fact that he's relatively handsome, as far as looks are concerned."

"But?"

"You know Hadleigh as well as I. We grew up together. We spent our childhoods together."

"That should be a point in Hadleigh's favor."

Melisande threw her arms up in disgust. "Hardly!"

She paced the tiny area again, the skirt of her expensive gown snagging against Lady Camphort's prize rosebushes.

Jonah heard the glittery material rip with each pass, but Melisande didn't seem to care.

"Please, calm down." He reached out to slow her agitated footsteps, but she slapped his hands away as if she didn't want his sympathy or his understanding. The spoiled female had always had a temper. He and Hadleigh had witnessed it often. But Jonah had never seen her as agitated as this.

"How can I calm down? I've never been more desperate than I am at this moment. I refuse to marry Hadleigh. I refuse!"

"I can't see why," Jonah said again. "You know him better than any other suitor who has asked for your hand."

"That's just the point. I know what he's really like. He's opinionated and domineering, and he'll rule me with an iron hand. Don't you remember how it was when we plotted ways to escape the tutors his father employed to give us an education? We always had to go along with what Hadleigh decided. He wouldn't give up until we did." She paced around a bed of beautiful asters, this time coming perilously close to stepping on the blossoms. "The same was true when we plotted ways to avoid that ugly, bratty sister of his. Hadleigh always decided where we'd hide to escape her, and we had to go along with what *he* said."

"That's because Hadleigh came up with the best idea."

"Oh, leave it to you to stand up for him. You were always his most loyal follower."

Jonah frowned. "I don't understand why you're so repulsed by him. You used to be quite fond of him. And how can you say his sister was ugly? She wasn't. She was simply at an awkward age. Besides, she only wanted to be included, and looking back, even you have to admit we were cruel not to include her."

"We were no such thing!"

Melisande fired her denial in a voice that hardly sounded like the lady Jonah knew she'd been raised to be.

"She was a ghastly brat. She should have been drowned at birth. Serves Hadleigh right. Now he's going to have to find some unsuspecting fool who's blind as well as desperate for her money who will stoop to marry her. She'll never find a husband on her own."

"You can't mean that."

"Can't I? Have you seen her? If I were Hadleigh, I wouldn't even acknowledge her. She's nothing at all to look at."

Jonah stopped. For the first time, he looked at Melisande—really looked at her. When had her thoughts turned so cruel? When had she begun to consider herself so elevated? And everyone else so far beneath her?

"Oh, don't look at me like that," she fired at him. "You thought the same thing. We all did. She's as repulsive as that clumsy, bookish Amanda Radburn you always see her with."

He couldn't believe Melisande had become so hard, that she exhibited so little concern for others. How had this happened?

Suddenly, he knew. The change hadn't just happened.

She'd always had those traits. It's just that he'd never noticed them because he'd been enamored by her incomparable beauty, the same as everyone else.

Tonight, though, she didn't seem nearly so beautiful.

"Why have you chosen *me* to free you from the betrothal agreement your father and Hadleigh signed?"

"Because we're friends. You owe me."

"I *owe* you?"

"Well, perhaps you don't *owe* me," she said, the tone of her voice turning softer, the expression on her face more demure. "But you had to realize that Hadleigh's and my association with you opened doors that wouldn't ordinarily have been opened."

Jonah fought the budding anger inside him. "How did Hadleigh's association with me—or with you, for that matter—open any doors?"

"Oh, Jonah, don't be obtuse. Everyone knows that Hadleigh is rich as Croesus. So is my father. And they come from the finest bloodlines."

"And me?"

Jonah unclenched his fists and pretended Melisande's comparison hadn't affected him like a vicious slap across the face. Even though it had.

"Well, you are only a second son. And your father was never known to invest his money wisely. Which is another reason you should jump at the chance to marry me."

"That would be advantageous, now, wouldn't it?" he answered, his mockery totally unnoticed by her.

"Of course it would. See, I knew you'd see it my way. I knew you'd realize the advantages of marrying me."

"In case I've missed something, though, why don't you spell out *all* the advantages for me?"

She sighed in frustration. "Oh, very well. There's the money, of course. With the dowry my father intends to give the fortunate man who marries me, you'd be able to cover the insurmountable debts your father is amassing every day."

Jonah was shocked. "How are you aware of the debts my father has?"

"*Everyone* knows how poorly your father manages money. Your brother, too. With the money that would come with my hand, you'd be able to make the necessary repairs to your family estate. It's a disgrace, you know."

"Would it be acceptable enough for you to live in one day?"

"Surely you're joking?" Her expression was truly one of shock. "I could never make that my home. It's hardly habitable. I wouldn't dare consider it, not when I've been left a wonderful manor home to which to go when I'm not in London. It's perfect for hosting summer parties. Much better than any place you could provide."

"I see." He settled back on his heels to look at this person he'd watched mature into what he'd considered a beauty of the highest degree.

Unfortunately, her beauty only radiated on the outside. He didn't like anything he saw on the inside.

"Then, of course," she said with a seductive smile on her face, "there's me."

"You?"

"Yes." Her voice held a hint of frustration. "Any man would consider himself most fortunate to have me as his wife. You would be the envy of every man in London."

"And Hadleigh? Doesn't it bother you that he idolizes you? That he's been in love with you forever? That you're the only woman he's ever wanted to marry?"

"Oh, pshaw." She waved her hand in dismissal. "He'll get over his infatuation with me. They all do."

"But he worships you. He has since we were young. He's talked of nothing but making you his wife. He's—"

"He's a boor! He doesn't want to marry me. He wants to *own* me. He wants to tell me every single thing to do and have me jump whenever he gives an order."

She paced again. The tearing sounds as the expensive material of her skirts caught on the thorns of the rose-bushes screamed like irritating scratches on a windowpane.

"He's authoritative and domineering. And he never sees anything the same as I do. Once he makes a decision, he refuses to see any other point."

"In other words, he doesn't let you constantly have your way."

"He's cruel! He's opinionated. He's totally unsuitable!"

"And me?"

Her facial features softened. "You're much more amiable. You always have been. I could always get along with you."

"You mean you could always wrap me around your finger."

She stomped her foot on the ground. "That's not what I meant, and you know it."

"What advantages would *you* have if we married, Melisande?"

"I don't like it when you use that tone of voice. You only talk like that when you're upset with me."

The pout of her full lips and the sad expression on her face were skillful acts she'd practiced to perfection.

"Very well." He softened his voice. "What advantages would you gain from our marriage?"

"You know perfectly well. I'd avoid marrying a tyrant."

"You never know. Maybe I'd be as much a tyrant as Hadleigh."

"No." She shook her head hard enough that several of her golden curls fell from their pins. "You're much more agreeable than he is. Hadleigh is unyielding. He's got such high standards for his wife. No woman could meet them. No one."

"Not even you?"

Melisande laughed. "No, not even me."

There was a look on her face, an odd expression that gave him cause for concern. "Why, Melisande?" He clutched her upper arms. He didn't hold her tight enough to hurt her, just firm enough to let her know he was serious. "Why don't you think you could meet his standards?"

He held her in front of him and looked her in the eyes. But she didn't look at him. Instead, she clamped her lips tight and focused her gaze on the ground to her left.

"You can hardly expect me to marry you without telling me exactly why you would refuse the opportunity to be a duchess whose husband is rich as Croesus and choose instead the second son of an impoverished earl who is one step away from losing the very roof over his head."

"But my dowry could save your father and your estate."

"Why do I think you don't care one fig about my father or the estate, but that you only want to be married? And soon."

"Because I do. And I don't want to marry Hadleigh. I want to marry you. Tonight. Now!"

"Why?"

"Because"—she pounded a dainty fist against her skirt—"because…because I must!"

"Why?"

She paced more rapidly, as if weighing what she was going to say. With a sharp turn, she spun around and faced him.

"Oh, very well. I see you are giving me no choice but to tell you all." She lifted her chin and gave him a defiant look filled with superiority. "I need to marry because I am expecting a child."

To say her words shocked him was an understatement. "You're what?"

"It happens, you know," she said with a noncommittal shrug of her shoulders. "And don't suggest I use one of those potions some magic herb-healer has to rid one's body of an unwanted babe. Women die more often than not." She placed her fists on her hips and glared at him. "And I have no intention of giving up my life to avoid a little scandal."

"So you would choose to marry someone you don't love, and who doesn't love you, rather than marry a man who has already asked for your hand and who in truth already loves you?" He couldn't come up with a logical reason. "Why?"

"You're jesting, am I correct?"

"No." He shook his head.

"Exactly what do you think Hadleigh's reaction would be when he discovered the woman he married is having another man's child? When he discovers his wife is presenting him with the next Hadleigh heir—except the child isn't his?"

"Whose child is it?"

For the first time, Melisande had the good sense to look embarrassed. "That hardly matters now. Let's just say that the brat's father is not in a position to make me his bride."

"He already has a wife."

"Don't make this difficult, Jonah. Of course he has a wife. Do you think I'd give myself to a man who could trap me into marriage?"

He shook his head again, more in disgust than as an answer to her question.

"Now, hurry." She clamped the fingers of one of her hands around the sleeve of his jacket. "We don't have much time. We have to leave as quickly as possible. Father intends to announce my betrothal to Hadleigh tonight."

He shook his head as he pulled out of her grasp.

"Don't be a fool, Jonah. Marriage to me will give you everything you need. Enough money to repair that dilapidated estate of yours. A beautiful bride. Plus, more money than you can ever spend. Surely that's payment enough for any extra baggage I bring with me."

He looked at her in disbelief, then remembered Hadleigh's short temper when he'd last talked to him. "You wouldn't know why Hadleigh thinks there might be something between you and me that he has to worry over, would you, Melisande?"

"Of course not," she answered, but he knew she was lying.

"Melisande?"

"Oh, very well," she said with a wave of her hand. "Perhaps I did hint that something more than friendship had developed between us."

"You what!"

"Well, I had to take the first step in convincing Hadleigh I wasn't worthy to be his duchess."

"Did it ever occur to you that your plan could backfire?"

"Backfire?"

"Yes. Instead of Hadleigh thinking that you might have a character flaw, he's convinced you've been taken advantage of. He's more determined than ever to marry you so he can protect you. And," he added with an anger he didn't bother to hide, "he's convinced that I am now his competition. He's more than a little angry at me, I can tell you."

The word that came from Melisande's mouth wasn't one he'd have thought she knew, let alone used. His opinion of her dropped another level.

"I think you should explain your…dilemma and let Hadleigh and your father decide what is the best way to handle your situation."

Her gaze narrowed, and Jonah saw Melisande's desperation. "Don't you dare become Hadleigh's champion or pretend to give me sage advice. You will get much more from this relationship than I."

"Will I?" He tried to keep the disgust he felt from his voice but knew he failed.

"I'm desperate. Hadleigh is probably looking for me right now so Father can make his grand announcement. Once he finds me, it will be too late!"

"It's already too late," he said, hoping she'd realize that was his answer.

"No! I need your name. I need you to marry me!"

He tried to hold her off, but she grasped him with both hands, showing remarkable strength. Her fingers dug through the material of his jacket and into his arms.

He pried her fingers away and stepped out of her reach. She stumbled backward and tripped over the hem of her gown. She wobbled, overcompensated, and fell to her knees in front of him.

Jonah couldn't leave her on the ground. He reached out to help her to her feet but froze when a loud, angry voice hollered from the top step of the terrace.

"Leave her alone! What are you doing, Armstrong?"

Jonah pulled back.

"It's Hadleigh!" Melisande cried in a hoarse whisper. "No. Oh, no!"

Before he could stop her, Melisande scrambled to her feet and raced toward the wrought iron gate in the garden wall that opened to the street. There wasn't a great distance to travel, but after the argument they'd just had, he knew she was in no condition to think or act rationally. He turned to follow her, knowing he needed to stop her before she did something rash.

"Don't you go near her!" Hadleigh ordered from behind him.

Jonah heard Hadleigh's heavy footsteps race down the flagstone path toward him. Before he could react, Hadleigh's hand grabbed the back of his jacket and jerked him backward.

He turned as Hadleigh's fist met his jaw.

Jonah landed on the ground and stayed there for a second or more until his head stopped spinning.

"You'll answer for this," Jonah's longtime friend vowed as he raced after Melisande.

Jonah couldn't let Hadleigh believe what he knew he must. There was too much at stake. Hadleigh's friendship meant more to him than he could say.

He struggled to his feet, then raced after them. Before he reached the gate that opened to the outside world, he heard it—the sound of horses' hooves as they clattered at a fast pace down the cobbled London street, the warning bellow that came from the carriage driver, the terrifying screams of horses being brought too sharply to a halt, Melisande's cry of alarm cut short, and finally, an agonizing cry of despair being wrenched from deep within Hadleigh.

Jonah staggered to the gate and stared at the sight of Hadleigh kneeling in the center of the cobblestone street, cradling Melisande's broken, lifeless body in his arms.

He clenched his fingers around a wrought iron bar and stared at the horrifying scene. An all-consuming darkness enveloped him that he knew would never lift.

* * *

The Duke of Hadleigh stood with Melisande's family as they lowered her body into the dark, cold ground. Buried with her were all his hopes and dreams. His future. Stolen from him by the least likely person imaginable. By a man he'd always considered his closest friend.

Jonah Armstrong was now his mortal enemy, a man he hated more than any man on the face of the earth. A vile, despicable creature he wouldn't rest until he destroyed.

Hadleigh watched Melisande's father pick up a handful of dirt and drop it onto the beautifully carved box Hadleigh had specially made for the woman he loved.

Melisande's weeping mother was next, followed by Melisande's three brothers. Each dropped handfuls of dirt into the grave.

He wouldn't. He couldn't.

He turned and walked away, not able to watch the mound of dirt cover his beautiful Melisande's resting place.

His vision blurred as he made his way to his waiting carriage. He would be glad to be away from here.

He lifted his foot onto the first step, then stopped when someone spoke from behind him.

"I'm sorry, Hadleigh."

It was Jonah, the man who'd killed his Melisande.

Hadleigh knew he should turn so Jonah could see the full extent of his hatred, but he didn't. He wasn't sure he could refrain from snuffing the life from Jonah's body right then and there.

"If I could undo what happened that night, I would," Jonah added.

"But you can't. There's nothing you can do to make up for what happened."

"No," his enemy answered. "There isn't."

Hadleigh pulled himself into the carriage but held out his hand to stop his driver from closing the door.

He glared into his enemy's eyes. "Someday, when *you* have the most to lose…*I'll* take it all."

Chapter 1

London, England
April 2, 1855

Lady Cecelia Randolph, the Duke of Hadleigh's only sister, reached for another glass of tepid punch and carried it to where her friend Lady Amanda Radburn stood. Thankfully, she'd found a spot near an open window where a slight breeze found its way inside the overly warm Plimpton ballroom.

"I think tonight's affair has the potential to be more boring than the Quinland ball last week," Amanda said, checking to make sure no one was close enough to hear her.

"It can't," Celie said behind the rim of her glass. "Nothing could be *that* boring." She took a small sip. "I tried to get out of coming tonight, but Hadleigh wouldn't allow it."

"Your brother *made* you come?" Amanda smiled. "He hardly ever makes you do anything."

"He did tonight. I even feigned being ill."

"I don't believe it," Amanda said with a giggle.

"It's true. He said this was one of those affairs to which we *had* to make an appearance."

"Do you know why?"

"He made up some excuse that this was one of the most well-attended balls of the Season and we needed to be present."

"But? I can tell you think there's another reason."

Celie released a heavy sigh. "I think what he really means is that this will be heavily attended by the male members of society. He *hinted* on the way over that it's time I concentrated on finding someone to marry."

"Not *that* again."

Celie's grip tightened on the glass in her hand. "He's becoming more insistent every day."

"Why don't you tell him what I tell my sisters when they tell me how old I'm getting and that I'm nearly on the shelf?"

"What do you tell them?"

Amanda gave her a sideways glance. "I tell them the truth, of course."

"Which is?"

"That you and I made a pact and signed it in blood that we would take over for the Chipworth sisters when they died and be the next terrors of London Society."

Celie laughed loud enough to draw looks from the groups closest to them.

The Chipworth sisters laid claim to having royal blood flowing through their veins. They held themselves so far above the rest of society that one word from either of them could ruin a poor girl's reputation.

The first word of warning every young debutante received when she prepared for her coming-out was to avoid the Ladies Maude and Matilda Chipworth at all cost. And above all, not to do anything that might draw their attention.

Although everyone was frightfully afraid of the Ladies Chipworth, Celie and Amanda weren't. Since the two friends were well on their way to becoming spinsters, they no longer cared what either Chipworth sister said or thought, which was probably the reason they got along tolerably well with the two terrors. Their disregard allowed Celie and Amanda to stand back in relative obscurity while the two ladies concentrated on terrorizing the rest of society.

Celie glanced around the room and listened to the music wafting over the din of conversation. "At least the orchestra is passable tonight."

Amanda stopped to listen. "I'll give Lady Plimpton credit for that."

"And the footmen aren't dressed in togas like they were at Lady—"

Amanda's sharp gasp stopped Celie from finishing her sentence.

"Look, Celie. Genevieve Rumpleton is dancing with Viscount Lourey. I thought her father forbade him to go anywhere near her."

Celie turned to follow Amanda's gaze and rolled her eyes. "The fool. From that enamored look in her eyes, she's going to make another embarrassing mistake. You'd think, after her last disaster, she'd come to have more faith in her father's judgment."

"She has nothing lodged beneath that mass of beautifully styled blonde hair to give her the capability of making such astute reasoning."

"Amanda Radburn, I think you're jealous," Celie said in a teasing tone. "I've always known you've had a secret love, and now I know who he is. You harbor secret designs on Lourey."

Her words caused Amanda to choke on her punch. "Drat," she said when she recovered. "You saw through me. I am jealous. I admit it. I've always wanted to be as naive as Genny and attracted to the worst sort of man society has to offer. Instead, I was born with a small amount of common sense and something more than empty space between my ears."

Celie giggled helplessly. "You're terrible, do you know that?"

"Of course I do. I enjoy being this way. My sisters tell me my irreverent sense of humor is why no male invites me for a second dance or a repeat drive in the Park."

"Which sister volunteered to chaperone you tonight?"

Amanda glanced at a group of ladies on the far side of the room. "Mary. I told her the family would be better served if they kept a closer watch over Stephen, since he is far more likely to be involved in a scandal than I am."

"Is he in trouble again?"

Amanda breathed a heavy sigh. "When isn't he? I don't know what it is this time, but I can always tell when he's gotten himself involved in something he doesn't want me to know about. He avoids me."

"He's avoiding you now?"

Amanda nodded. "Oh, I wish Mother and Father wouldn't have been taken from us so early. Stephen needs Father's influence."

Celie saw the wetness in Amanda's eyes and gave her friend's arm a gentle squeeze. "It's frightfully warm in here," she said. "Should we step out onto the terrace?"

"All right. Maybe we'll happen on some unsuspecting lovers who've gone into the shadows. That's always interesting."

Celie took one step toward the open French doors when Amanda's grip tightened on her arm.

"Don't turn around," she whispered in Celie's ear. "Whatever you do, don't...turn...around."

"Why ever not?" Celie said. She was desperate to do just that, but she didn't. If there was one trait she'd come to admire in Amanda, it was her basic instinct to make the right decisions. It had gotten them both out of any number of delicate situations.

"You aren't going to believe this."

"What?"

"*I* don't believe this!"

"What!"

"All right. Get ready to turn around, but don't react. And whatever you do, don't scream."

Celie rolled her eyes. "I won't scream. I *never* scream."

"You might when you see this."

"What are you talking about?"

"I'm saying that Lady Plimpton has just made the largest, most disastrous faux pas of the century."

Celie wanted to turn. In fact, she was doing everything in her power to do exactly that, but she couldn't. Amanda still had too tight a grip on her arm and she couldn't move.

"Let me go," she said, pulling out of her friend's hold. "Whatever it is can't be *that*—"

Celie turned, then followed everyone's lead as they stared with mouths agape at something that had drawn their attention to the top of the ballroom stairs.

She lifted her chin and her gaze locked onto the tall figure standing there.

He stood ramrod straight for several long, tension-filled seconds, allowing the guests gathered below him the time they needed to take note of his presence.

One by one, the crowd turned and stared. The cacophony of voices quieted until the only sound one heard was the discordant strains of the waltz the orchestra struggled to play.

It was him.

Celie's breath caught in her throat and her heart skipped a beat.

It was him. Jonah Armstrong, the Earl of Haywood.

His shoulders were as broad as Celie remembered, his hair as dark. And he was as handsome as he'd been in every dream she'd had of him since she was young.

No, she thought as she studied his features, *he was* more *handsome.* Except his looks had hardened from how she remembered him. There was a rugged handsomeness to him now that added to his magnificence. No doubt the time he'd spent fighting in the Crimea had done that. No doubt everything he'd experienced had toughened his features and erased any hint of softness he'd had when he was younger.

Even from this distance, Celie could see his high, chiseled cheekbones and the sharp angle of his jaw. He wore his hair in the same style he always had, an inch longer in the back than her brother wore his, just long enough that it touched the top of his collar. He parted it on the left and combed it to the side, no doubt to tame the wave that always wanted to fall over his high forehead. The wave she'd often brushed from him in her dreams.

His lips were full, and she'd often wondered what it would be like to…

Celie stopped her imagination from running rampant. Or from remembering how often she'd imagined the feel of his lips against hers. Even though he'd never kissed her. Even though he never would. Even though the passion they'd shared had only been in her dreams.

Her blood heated as it rushed through her veins.

Suddenly it wasn't his looks that consumed her but the speculation of what would happen when her brother realized Haywood was there.

Celie tore her gaze from the figure at the top of the stairs to search for Hadleigh.

It didn't take long to locate him, and when she did, she locked onto the black expression on his face. Her brother's riveting glare wasn't exactly deadly, but it held a threatening warning. A warning anyone who'd ever dealt with him knew to be wary of.

"What do you think your brother will do?" Amanda whispered.

"I don't know."

Immediately after Melisande's death, every hostess in London took great pains to avoid including both the Duke of Hadleigh and Jonah Armstrong on their guest lists.

The first time Jonah showed up at an affair where Hadleigh was, Hadleigh bade his hosts a premature farewell and informed them that he found it impossible to stay in the same room with Jonah Armstrong. In the blink of an eye, Jonah became a pariah in London Society.

But circumstances were different now. Jonah was no longer the second son of an impoverished earl, but he carried the title. As the Earl of Haywood, he was an important member of society. He'd also returned from the Crimea a decorated war hero who'd been commended by the Queen herself. That alone made him someone every hostess wanted in attendance at her event.

"Your brother won't be able to repeat his actions of three years ago. If he bids our host and hostess a premature farewell because the Earl of Haywood is here, I'm afraid Lady Plimpton will wear a smile as she sees your brother to the door. Haywood's presence will give any event he attends the stamp of success."

"I know," Celie agreed. "I overheard Lady Warring tell the Duchess of Portsmouth that everyone had invited the Earl of Haywood to their affairs, but so far, he'd refused them all."

"Well, his presence tonight has given everyone something to talk about."

Everyone in the room remained focused on the Earl of Haywood as he walked toward the edge of the stairs to begin his descent.

"Have you noticed how he favors his left leg?" Amanda asked. "I heard he was injured. His wound must have been quite serious if he's not yet completely healed."

Celie struggled with the concern that consumed her. The two years and four months Jonah was gone were the longest, most worrisome years of her life. She spent more time than she could remember praying that he would stay safe, praying that he would return to England alive.

And he had.

He'd been injured, but he hadn't been killed. And he was here tonight to announce to everyone that he intended to take his place in society.

Celie felt an overwhelming sense of elation, knowing the courage this took.

"Did you know he would be here?" Amanda asked, her voice a hushed whisper.

Celie shook her head. "I'm glad he is, though."

Amanda stepped closer. "If your brother makes a move to cut him like he did three years ago, don't be surprised if I do something very unladylike."

Celie shifted her gaze to Amanda's face. What she saw made her smile.

Her best friend wore the most serious, determined look of resolve Celie had ever seen. She looked like a soldier poised to go into battle.

"You're that determined to protect the Earl of Haywood?"

"No, I'll let you protect him, if you'd like. I'm determined to save your brother the embarrassment of making a fool of himself. Perhaps he might even avoid being the topic of ridicule in every salon tomorrow morning. His foolish mourning has gone on long enough."

Celie couldn't agree more. Everyone knew the Duke of Hadleigh should have gotten on with his life years ago.

Celie turned back to the top of the stairs and let her eyes settle on Jonah Armstrong, Earl of Haywood. A warm blanket wrapped around her heart as she watched him.

The crowd was quiet, but the murmur of whispered comments grew with each step he took toward the bottom, where Lord and Lady Plimpton stood.

He held his head high and kept his back straight, but there was a stiffness in his gait, as if the wound he'd been rumored to have suffered still pained him.

His legs were long and muscled, and he took each step with determination, as if he couldn't wait to reach the bottom of the stairs to make a place for himself. He was exquisite. Perfect in form—as perfect as he'd been the last time Celie had seen him.

As perfect as he was each night in her dreams.

He wore an expensively tailored black evening jacket that was buttoned handsomely over a waistcoat of shimmering burgundy satin. He had donned an elaborately tied cravat and a dress shirt that shone a blinding white.

Her brother was handsome, but the Earl of Haywood was magnificent. His effect on her was like a piece of the sun that had broken off and rolled around in her chest. When it wrapped its warming glow around her heart, her chest tightened with emotion before the warmth invading her chest plummeted to the pit of her stomach.

She'd tried to fight the growing attraction she had for him, reasoning that she only felt this way because he'd been her older brother's closest friend. Because he'd been a frequent visitor at their home. Because he'd been her first love.

But that wasn't it. She knew that now. This was the first time she'd seen him in more than three years, and the same unquenchable yearning ached inside her with greater ferocity than ever before.

A growing heat warmed her cheeks, spread through her chest, then rushed down to her stomach, where it swirled like a bubbling whirlpool. Her unsettled emotions made it unquestionably clear that she wasn't simply infatuated with him.

Lady Cecelia Randolph, who'd known from the day she'd first seen him that he was the only man she would ever love, felt gentle fingers hold and caress her heart. She loved the Earl of Haywood more today than she ever had. She ached with the pointlessness of it.

How stupid she was. How utterly, totally, unequivocally stupid. Her brother was Haywood's mortal enemy. Why would he give someone who would come with such baggage a second look?

Haywood reached the bottom of the stairs and conversed with his host and hostess for several moments. They seemed inordinately pleased to see him. Not at all surprised. As if his presence had been anticipated, as if he'd been an *invited* guest.

Then he turned and entered the ballroom.

The welcome he received from the guests was very different tonight than it had been three years ago. The crowd parted to allow him to enter, then closed the circle to greet him as they would anyone who had been absent for such a long time. Anyone who'd returned from the war a decorated hero.

Celie tried to tear her gaze away from him, wished his towering form didn't stand out so, wished she could lose him in the crowd. But she couldn't. He was nearly a head taller than most of the other men in the room, his coffee-rich hair glistening beneath the flickering candles above him.

Everything about him drew notice. Especially the notice of every female in the room.

Celie looked from one group of gaping debutantes to another. They huddled in small circles like vultures, deciding the best way to gain an introduction to the newest prospect in the marriage mart. The Earl of Haywood was known to be lacking in funds, but for the wealthier females in the hunt for a husband, that didn't matter. Not when the newcomer was as diabolically handsome as Jonah was.

Celie ached with a pain she knew would never go away. The thought of him paying court to any one of them was agonizing.

She tried to avoid watching him, but she couldn't. A crowd of men who probably wanted to hear firsthand accounts of the war monopolized his attention.

She was sure reliving what he'd gone through was undoubtedly the last topic he wanted to discuss. She wanted to interrupt their conversation and draw him away. She wanted to have him to herself instead of sharing him with everyone else.

Celie gave herself a mental shake and called herself several unflattering names. He hadn't given her a second glance when he and Hadleigh had been best friends. What made her think he'd want to make her acquaintance now? Especially when her brother was his most hated enemy? Unless, of course, he intended to pursue her for her dowry.

Perhaps, for him, she'd overlook her vow not to consider any man who'd offered for her because of the dowry that would go with her.

Celie cursed her pride. She'd rather spend her life a spinster than know her money and her brother's lofty title had purchased the ring on her finger—even the Earl of Haywood's ring.

She pulled her gaze away from where he stood. The crowd had grown larger. "I'm terribly warm," she said to no one in particular, yet Amanda heard her and followed her toward the open doors that led out onto the terrace.

She couldn't bear to watch every female in the room make spectacles of themselves as they fawned over the earl.

She couldn't watch him pull one female after another into his arms and twirl them around the dance floor.

She couldn't stand the hurt when he graced another female with the heart-stopping smile she'd dreamed would someday be meant for her.

She couldn't stand the pain of knowing she'd fallen in love with someone who wouldn't love her in return.

Chapter 2

Celie walked to the far side of the terrace and placed both palms atop the cool cement balustrade. This was the third time she'd escaped the ballroom so she wouldn't have to watch every eligible female under the age of sixty make a fool of herself to gain the Earl of Haywood's attention. She stared out into the flower garden as if she were interested in the prize roses Lady Plimpton was so fond of growing.

Actually, Celie wasn't interested in anything right now except going home. All she wanted was to be someplace quiet where she could close her eyes and ease the ache that pounded in her head. Except she knew closing her eyes wouldn't erase the images that were indelibly ingrained in her memory—the Earl of Haywood dancing a waltz with Darceline Covingdale, the Earl of Haywood talking with the three Rummery sisters while each one flirted more brazenly than the other, the Earl of Haywood gracing Penelope Witherspoon with a smile more brilliant than sunlight, the Earl of Haywood…

Celie doubled her gloved hand and slammed her fist down against the unyielding cement railing.

It hurt more than she'd anticipated it would. But she didn't care. It felt better than anything else she could have done except issuing a string of words she wasn't supposed to know.

"I hope I don't know the intended target of that angry gesture."

"Oh!" Celie squeaked as she spun around to see who had caught her exhibiting such an unladylike display.

Her breath caught in her throat, and she stared in awed wonder at the man who'd consumed her thoughts the entire evening.

His voice was deeper than she remembered it being, low and rich and enticingly smooth. His face as he came near her was even more ruggedly handsome than it had been when she'd looked at him across the ballroom. And the smile on his face, when directed at her, tugged at a spot deep inside her that sent hundreds of butterflies soaring in flight.

"I'm sorry," he said, taking another step toward her, then another. "I startled you."

"No…uh…I…uh…I was…"

Celie couldn't find her tongue. Actually, she couldn't find any of the social graces that had been ingrained in her since birth. She'd suddenly turned into a blabbering idiot.

The Earl of Haywood took several steps closer, then stopped. He kept himself a comfortable distance from her.

"I'm not sure what is proper here," he said, placing the glass he'd brought with him onto the flat railing so both his hands were free. "Ordinarily, I'd beg an introduction from a mutual acquaintance to give you the opportunity to refuse acknowledging me."

"Except we are already well acquainted with each other and have been for years. At least you were acquainted with my brother."

His brows lifted. "But that was in the past," he corrected.

"Yes, but it wasn't a part of *my* past."

Even though there wasn't enough moonlight to see the expression in his eyes, Celie thought there was a hint of humor on his face.

"No, it wasn't. But it's a well-known fact that your brother no longer considers me a close friend."

Celie wanted to laugh. "That's probably the understatement of the year."

"Then perhaps I need to ask if you share his opinion."

"If I do?"

"Then I will excuse myself and leave you alone to enjoy this beautiful evening."

She wished the deep timbre of his voice wouldn't stir a myriad of emotions that settled heavily in the pit of her stomach. She wished she wouldn't find herself mesmerized by the broad expanse of his shoulders. But most of all, she wished she hadn't repeatedly dreamed of being alone with him without a prettier female competing for the handsome Lord Haywood's attention.

Being here with him was almost a dream come true.

"Evenings like this are meant to be enjoyed by everyone. I'd be very selfish indeed if I tried to monopolize Lady Plimpton's terrace," she said. "I'd enjoy your company."

He smiled and leaned a hip against the balustrade.

He was taller than Hadleigh, but only by a little, and Celie imagined that if she stood next to him, the top of her head would come to just below his chin. Standing even this close made her feel small and delicate, something that was totally alien to her.

"I have to tell you how surprised I am to see you here, Lord Haywood."

"From the looks of disbelief on the faces of Lady Plimpton's guests, you weren't the only one who couldn't believe their eyes."

"The night Melisande died changed futures for several people."

"Then Lady Plimpton is to be commended, don't you think? For daring to invite both of us to the same event?"

Celie turned her head and looked at him with an expression that said she thought Lady Plimpton's ingenuity was more deeply rooted. "I've known Lady Plimpton for several years, and she's never struck me as the sort of person who would take the initiative to invite two enemies to the same function simply to see what happened."

A broad grin lifted the corners of Lord Haywood's mouth, and the openness of his smile sent a warm rush to the pit of her stomach.

"Are you suggesting that someone may have encouraged the good lady to create an opportunity to bridge the gap that has separated your brother and me for the last three years?"

Celie considered what he suggested for a few minutes, then shook her head. "No, Lord Haywood. I doubt healing the hostility between you and my brother had anything to do with Lady Plimpton's reason for inviting you. I think the reason is much more substantial."

"Do you?" Haywood smiled, then lifted his glass to take a sip of his drink.

"Yes, and since you have just returned from the war, I think that something happened during the time you served that prompted her to take such a risk."

Haywood's arm halted in midair.

"Did you know Lady Plimpton's nephew also returned from the war recently?" she asked. "Now that I think on it, I believe he arrived around the same time as you."

"Really?"

"Yes. He was injured quite severely. Lady Plimpton remarked that he survived only because of the heroic actions of his commanding officer."

The Earl of Haywood took a swallow from the glass he'd brought with him. When he lowered his hand, he was at a perfect angle to look directly into her eyes.

"Do you know what I think?" she said more pointedly.

He didn't speak but simply held her gaze.

"I think it's possible that you and Lady Plimpton's nephew served together. That you were, in fact, the commanding officer who saved Lady Plimpton's nephew's life." She looked directly at him. "Would I be correct?"

When he didn't answer, she continued. "I think Lady Plimpton issued you an invitation to repay you for saving her nephew." Celie took a deep breath as the magnitude of his sacrifice hit her. He could have been killed attempting to save another human being. A fellow soldier was alive because of his bravery.

She swallowed hard. "Remind me to thank Lady Plimpton before I leave," she said, surprised at how husky her voice sounded.

The Earl of Haywood rested his hip against the cement balustrade and steadied his gaze on her.

"What?" Celie asked when he continued to study her.

"When we were young, I often thought Hadleigh underestimated you. Now I'm convinced of it. You are far more intelligent than he ever gave you credit for being."

"Does that frighten you?"

"Frighten?"

"Yes. I've been told my outspokenness frightens people."

A smile brightened his face. "I think a better term might be *intimidation*. I think your understanding intimidates people."

"Are you intimidated?"

"No." He took another swallow from his glass. "Actually, I'm impressed."

"Oh."

When she didn't say more, he tilted his head slightly and frowned. "You're thinking again, but holding your tongue because you're not sure if you should express your thoughts."

Celie was startled by how adept he was at reading her. "Yes, I wanted to say how glad I was that Lady Plimpton risked inviting you. Even though it could have ended badly."

"But didn't."

"No, thankfully, it didn't." Celie paused for a moment. "I don't blame you for taking such a chance and coming tonight."

"You don't?"

"No. You are no longer a second son, but the Earl of Haywood. You need to take your rightful place in society. Lady Plimpton's events are always well attended. Tonight will provide you the perfect opportunity."

Haywood smiled and sat back against the balustrade. "So, if Lady Plimpton's events are known to be so well attended, why do I have the feeling you wish you weren't here?"

Celie tried to look surprised. "I don't know what makes you think that."

"I think that because I believe I saw you ask your brother more than once if he was ready to leave."

Celie could hardly tell him the truth, but wasn't comfortable telling a lie. "Would you believe me if I said I had a headache?"

"No. But I would believe you if you said you weren't enjoying yourself. If the truth were known, I don't believe you particularly enjoy attending the continuous round of parties and balls that everyone in society is supposed to crave."

Celie let the soft sound of the orchestra wash over her as she looked out over Lady Plimpton's garden. "It isn't that I am not fond of society's gatherings. There are times when I enjoy myself as much as anyone. There are times, however, when a quiet evening at home with a good book is more appealing. Or a night at the opera."

"May I say, then, that I'm glad you felt obligated to come tonight. I enjoyed seeing you again after all these years."

Celie smiled. "It has been a while, hasn't it?"

"Yes. If I remember correctly, you were no more than eleven or twelve the last time you tried to tag along after your brother and me."

"I was nearing my thirteenth birthday and an adult in *my* mind. I couldn't understand why Hadleigh wasn't as eager to have me join him as he was to have you and Melisande for companions."

Haywood laughed a deep, sincere laugh. "No brother wants his sister to know everything he does."

The smile on his face caused her heart to somersault several times.

"Besides," he continued, "I'm sure Hadleigh was just protecting you from the trouble in which he and I always seemed to find ourselves."

"You're being kind, my lord. We both know that Hadleigh didn't want me anywhere near because he considered me a child. If I remember correctly, both of you referred to me as a brat several times in my hearing."

This made Haywood laugh even harder, and the effect of his laughter was a thousand times more powerful than his smile.

"Well, no one can call you a brat now," he said, keeping the smile on his face. "Nor is it possible to consider you a child. Not when you've grown into such a charming woman."

A shiver raced down Celie's spine. He'd said she'd grown into a charming woman. Not a beautiful woman, which would have been an obvious lie and dropped her opinion of him by several notches. Not a lovely woman, which would have caused her to wonder what need he had to falsely flatter her.

But a charming woman, a description that had nothing to do with her looks and everything to do with how she appeared to him.

"I have yet to extend my sympathies on the deaths of your father and your brother. I'm sure their deaths took you by surprise."

"The news of their passing was not welcome, but it didn't take me by surprise. Did it you?"

Celie couldn't find an answer except…"No."

Haywood locked his gaze with hers and smiled a sad smile. "I knew you would give me the truth. Thank you for that.

"The lives both Father and Charles lived had bordered on the edge of disaster for several years. That they should both die so tragically came as a shock to no one."

"I didn't know your brother well. He and your father only visited Hadleigh Estate once or twice." Celie turned to Jonah and studied his expression. "You don't remind me at all of him."

Haywood smiled. "Thank you a second time."

"No, I meant—"

His raised hand stopped her from explaining that she'd meant in looks. Charles had been as fair as Lord Haywood was dark.

"I know what you meant, but I want you to know I'm not like Charles in actions, either."

Celie let her shoulders drop. "I know you're not, but I should have made myself clearer from the start. Hadleigh constantly tells me my mouth will get me into real trouble someday."

"Do you believe it will?"

Celie shrugged. "Probably. But there's no help for it. It's in my makeup."

Haywood laughed.

"What plans do you have now that you've made your return to society? Are you going to stay in London?"

"For a while, yes. I have some matters to take care of."

"Yes," Celie answered reluctantly. "I overheard some gentlemen remark that the first thing you need to do is begin your search for a bride."

His eyebrows arched. "Did they?"

"Yes. You have responsibilities now, and properties. You will need an heir to secure them."

Haywood gave a hearty laugh. "Let me first tell you that it's not always wise to believe everything you hear."

"Then you didn't come tonight to begin your search for a bride?"

"I came tonight to take my place as the Earl of Haywood. If I happen to meet someone with whom I might wish to continue my acquaintance, then I will do so. But not because my goal is to leave Lady Plimpton's ball having selected the woman I want as my wife."

Celie wasn't sure if she was relieved or disappointed. After a second's thought, she decided it was best if she didn't put too much thought into it.

He crossed his arms over his chest and shifted enough to face her. He was so near to her she could feel the heat of his leg through the skirts of her gown.

"Do you wish me success?" he asked, but Celie wasn't sure why he needed her approval of the risk he'd taken tonight.

"Of course I do. You're the Earl of Haywood now and deserve to be here."

"Thank you, again."

For several long seconds, he did not shift his gaze, but kept it locked with hers. The herd of butterflies low in her stomach rustled their wings and took flight.

The effect he had on her was transfixing. She found herself drowning in the ebony depth of his captivating gaze and knew she couldn't allow him too close a look into her eyes. She was afraid he'd see far more than she wanted him to.

Celie took a step away from the railing. "I need to return," she said. Being alone with the Earl of Haywood was a dream come true, and she needed to leave before something happened to ruin this perfect moment. "I'm glad things turned out like they did, Lord Haywood. You will make a fine earl."

Celie walked toward the open doors that led into the ballroom. His voice stopped her before she could escape.

"Did you mean what you just said, Lady Cecelia? That you are glad I attended tonight and approve of my plan to enter society?"

"Of course I meant it."

He pushed himself away from the balustrade and stepped toward her. "Would you consider helping me?"

She couldn't help but frown. "Helping you?"

"Yes."

Lord Haywood stepped close enough to her that they were just beyond the open doorway, far enough so no one could overhear their words, yet exposed enough so they were in full view of the guests in the ballroom.

Celie was aware that they were being observed.

"Would you do me the honor of accepting my invitation to go for a drive tomorrow afternoon? Say, about five?"

Celie couldn't hide her surprise. "Are you sure?"

"More than sure. Unless, of course, you are concerned about your brother's reaction."

Celie debated what answer to give him. She knew Lord Haywood wasn't really asking *her* because he wanted to spend time alone with her. She knew that, in all likelihood, he'd asked her to accompany him to downplay the feud between the Earl of Haywood and the Duke of Hadleigh, to convince society that the feud was, if not over, at least not as explosive as it had been three years ago. Being seen in her company would do much to stop any rumors of an ongoing battle from flaming.

Her brother had plans for tomorrow afternoon and wouldn't be home to object to her going. If she was lucky, he might not ever find out that she'd spent the afternoon with the Earl of Haywood, although with rumors traveling like they did in society she didn't hold out too much hope for that. At least, though, he wouldn't find out until it was too late for him to do anything about it.

And she would have one more opportunity to tuck away another special memory of the man who'd always occupied a special place in her heart.

"Thank you, Lord Haywood. I'd be delighted to accompany you tomorrow."

His face lit in a relaxed smile, as if he were truly pleased that she'd agreed to go with him.

"You've made me the happiest of men," he said with a slight bow. "Until tomorrow, then."

"Yes. Tomorrow."

Celie entered the ballroom amid the curious stares of the onlookers who'd seen her talking to Lord Haywood. A sudden rush of pleasure warmed her. Let them think what they wanted. The illusion that a handsome nobleman was courting her was a fantasy she enjoyed.

She suddenly felt years younger than her three and twenty years. For the first time in longer than she could remember, she was almost giddy with a strange sense of excitement.

Celie had always prided herself on keeping her feet planted squarely on the ground—even when her head floated in the clouds. She wouldn't let her emotions run wild. She wouldn't allow herself to imagine anything more than what was obviously the purpose behind Lord Haywood's attention toward her, which was to curb any talk of a renewed battle between her brother and the Earl of Haywood. That was the reason he'd turned to her first. That and nothing more.

Celie searched the crowd for Amanda. Instead, she came face-to-face with her brother.

"What did he want?" Hadleigh's angry glare followed Haywood as he made his way back through the ballroom.

"To say hello."

"Stay away from him, Cecelia. I'm warning you."

Celie turned her head and looked into her brother's hostile countenance.

She graced him with a smile she far from felt. "I refuse to argue with you here, Your Grace. I'm ready to go home. Are you?"

He nodded sharply, then offered her his arm.

Celie placed her fingers on his rigid muscles and walked with him toward the door. He'd seen her alone with Haywood, and he was furious.

Celie couldn't keep a smile from her face. The euphoric feeling engulfing her wouldn't allow a hint of regret to surface.

Whether her brother approved of her being with the Earl of Haywood or did not held no consequence tonight. Not when she felt so young and free and…pretty.

Celie accompanied her brother out of the ballroom. They bid Lord and Lady Plimpton farewell, then waited while their driver brought their carriage round.

The drive home was silent. Hadleigh sat in the corner of the carriage with his hands crossed over his chest in an unyielding grip and sported a scowl on his face. Celie had no intention of telling him that she'd accepted an invitation to go for a drive with Lord Haywood. She knew better.

He confirmed her decision when they alighted in front of their town house.

"I hope you don't intend to make a habit of associating with Haywood," he said, in a tone similar to that of an order.

"Unfortunately," she said, giddy with a bravado that still lingered from earlier, "I'm past the age where you can tell me with whom I can or cannot associate. And if you knew me even a small bit, Sterling, you'd know that the surest way for me to do what you *don't* want me to do is to tell me that I can't do something."

Celie turned on her heel and stepped away from her brother before he had a chance to respond.

The smile she wore refused to fade as she made her way up the stairs and to her room.

Chapter 3

❦

Jonah arrived at Hadleigh's town house shortly before five and carefully stepped down to the cobblestone street. He handed the carriage reins to a waiting footman, then took a few seconds of feigned interest in the impressive stone structure to allow the pain in his side to ease.

He was paying for the hours he'd been on his feet last night. But the end result had been far better than he'd feared it might. He'd received several invitations today and seemed to be well on his way to taking his rightful place in society.

He leaned the slightest bit to the right to stretch the tight skin around the healing saber wound in his left side, then made his way up the short walk that led to the entrance. Hadleigh's butler, Fitzhugh, opened the door before he could reach for the knocker.

"It's a pleasure to see you again, Lord Haywood," Fitzhugh said in greeting.

Jonah looked into the familiar face. He'd once been a frequent guest of Hadleigh's, but that had been a lifetime ago, before Melisande's death. Before he'd left for the war in the Crimea.

Before his life had been permanently altered.

"My sympathies on your father's and brother's deaths," Fitzhugh said, taking Jonah's hat and gloves.

"Thank you, Fitzhugh. I only regret that I wasn't here for them in the end."

"All of us here at home appreciate the contribution you made for your country."

"Thank you, Fitzhugh."

The butler nodded, then stepped to the side. "Lady Cecelia will be right down. If you'll follow me."

Fitzhugh led Jonah to a room off the hall. The room was done in rich shades of burgundies and had a homey feel to it. Jonah felt comfortable here. But he always had. When he'd been a welcome guest.

A marble fireplace took up a large part of the far wall, and he slowly made his way across the room. A large portrait hung above the mantel, and Jonah locked his hands behind his back and stared at the painting of a young Sterling, a younger Lady Cecelia, and their parents, the former Duke and Duchess of Hadleigh.

It was obvious that Lady Cecelia had inherited her mother's wheat-colored hair and vibrant blue eyes. The duchess's coloring was identical to Cecelia's. Even her features resembled her mother's.

They were both blessed with the same high cheekbones and small upturned nose, but the most remarkable similarity was the sharp, intelligent gleam in the duchess's eyes. The artist had captured it to perfection.

Lady Cecelia had that same intelligent gleam.

Jonah doubted that Hadleigh and his father had ever gotten away with even the tiniest of lies. The all-knowing look in the duchess's eyes said she probably realized what her husband was up to before he attempted it.

"They were a remarkable couple," Lady Cecelia said from behind him.

Jonah slowly turned to watch her enter the room.

She wore a deep-lavender gown and a matching bonnet. The color accented the shimmering gold in her hair to perfection. Her gloves were a light gray and so was her parasol.

She was beyond lovely. She was beautiful. Meeting Lady Cecelia had been one of the most pleasant surprises of his life.

He'd expected an older version of the gangly, pesky girl she'd been the last time he'd seen her. Instead, he found her to be a sharp-witted, intelligent young lady who possessed a certain confidence he admired, as well as a strength of character he found refreshing.

He looked at her and smiled. He should have realized any sister of Hadleigh's would never be demure or lacking in spirit. Hadleigh would eat such a weak female alive.

Perhaps that was why she was still unmarried. Perhaps her strengths frightened off suitors. Well, she didn't frighten him. Although he wouldn't call himself a suitor. To be honest, he wasn't sure what he was. He wasn't brave enough to consider what he wanted his relationship to Lady Cecelia to be.

He wasn't sure he'd like himself if he did.

Jonah tore his gaze away from her and glanced back to the portrait on the wall. "You look a great deal like your mother."

Celie answered with a mocking laugh. "I only wish. My mother was a striking woman."

"You don't think you are?"

The slight roll of her eyes indicated she was convinced her looks weren't an advantage.

"Unfortunately, other than the color of my hair and eyes, I inherited far too many of my father's traits."

"I remember your mother and father well," Jonah said.

"I had just celebrated my twelfth birthday when they died. I remember Hadleigh waking me from my sleep to tell me there'd been a carriage accident and Mother and Father wouldn't be returning home.

"Hadleigh tried so hard to be brave, but I knew he hurt as much as I did. I couldn't seem to stop crying, and he told me not to worry, that he'd always take care of me. I told him I knew he would, because he had to. He was the duke now."

Her voice seemed thicker, and Jonah looked down as she stared at the portrait. He knew without asking that she was remembering another time.

"What did he answer?"

She looked up at him with a smile on her face and the glimmer of tears in her eyes. "He said, 'No, not because I'm a duke. Because I'm your brother.'"

"Becoming the Duke of Hadleigh was a huge responsibility for someone so young."

"Yes. Hadleigh was only eighteen when he inherited the title. His personality changed overnight."

Jonah hesitated. "I remember."

"Before then, he had such a zest for life." She laughed. "Do you remember a country party Hadleigh planned for his eighteenth birthday?"

Jonah smiled, knowing the hunting week Celie was talking about.

"Hadleigh informed Mother that he'd invited some friends for a week of hunting. She asked to see the guest list, thinking that by 'some friends' Hadleigh meant a half dozen or so. When he handed her the list, she nearly fainted. I remember her asking him if there was anyone in London who hadn't been included. Hadleigh thought for a moment, then answered he didn't think so, but he'd check to make sure."

She laughed. The rich sound of her laughter affected him in ways he couldn't explain.

"The two of you were inseparable," she continued. "I wish you still were."

"Perhaps we will be again someday," Jonah answered, but knew that was unlikely. "Are you ready to leave? It's too lovely out to waste being indoors."

She placed her small hand on his jacket sleeve, and they walked to his open carriage. He helped her up, then gave the reins a gentle flick.

"Has Hadleigh shown interest in anyone since Melisande's death?" he asked after they'd made their way through the wide gate leading to Hyde Park.

Celie shook her head. "He still idolizes her memory as if she were a paragon of virtue."

Jonah was shocked by Celie's comment. "You don't share his opinion?"

"I'm sorry," Celie said. Her expression was filled with genuine embarrassment. "I didn't mean for my comment to give that impression. It does no one good to speak ill of the dead."

"But you didn't consider her perfect?"

Lady Cecelia paused to nod a greeting to two young ladies approaching them. "No one is perfect. It's simply that death seems to erase the imperfections and leave immortalization in its wake."

Jonah looked at Celie with raised eyebrows. "Has anyone told you how wise you are, Lady Cecelia?"

She gave him a lax shrug and twirled her parasol. "Oh, yes. Hadleigh tells me that constantly. Except he doesn't call it wisdom. He uses the terms *outspoken* and *ill-mannered*."

Jonah smiled. "He doesn't appreciate your directness?"

"Heavens, no. He's quite stuffy, you know. He was much more understanding before he became a duke. As you know, he was even known to have a sense of humor."

Jonah laughed. "That's because he didn't have such responsibilities then."

"You're still his champion, aren't you?"

"Still?"

She lowered her parasol and lifted her face to the sun. "You always saw the best in Hadleigh and ignored his faults. You even allowed him to blame you for Melisande's death."

His breath caught. "You don't consider that in some way I was responsible?"

"Of course not. No one was responsible except Melisande herself."

Jonah leaned back against the seat and allowed himself the first relaxed breath he'd taken in longer than he could remember. She was good for him, like a soothing balm that took away the stiff shards of guilt and regret that plagued him.

"What a remarkable woman you've grown into."

He lowered his gaze and enjoyed watching her cheeks turn a delightful shade of pink. He had a feeling she wasn't overly used to receiving compliments and wondered why.

She turned back to study the path in front of them. A frown deepened on her forehead. "Lady Cushman and her daughter Charlene are coming this way. I'm sorry, but by this evening, all of society will know you asked me for a drive."

"Does that bother you?"

"No, except I'm afraid they will read more into your invitation than you intended."

"I won't let that bother me if you promise not to, either."

He knew she intended to say something but didn't have an opportunity. He brought the carriage to a halt as the approaching carriage came even with theirs and stopped. Lady Cushman was the first to speak.

"Cecelia, my dear. What a pleasant surprise."

"Lady Cushman. Charlene. Have you come out to enjoy this beautiful day?"

"Yes," Charlene answered. "I told Mother it was simply too lovely to stay indoors."

"I agree," Celie answered. "Have you been introduced to the Earl of Haywood, Lady Cushman? Charlene?"

"Not since he's assumed the title," Lady Cushman acknowledged. "I was acquainted with him before he went to serve so gallantly in Her Majesty's service."

Celie did the honors. When she introduced Miss Charlene, the young lady fluttered her lashes in a demure yet blatant form of flirtation.

Celie stiffened in the seat beside him.

Jonah smiled, unable to keep the humor from his face. "Lady Cushman," he greeted. "Miss Charlene. It's a pleasure to meet you."

"And you," both ladies answered.

"I heard that you returned to us injured," Lady Cushman said. "Have you fully recovered?"

"Yes. I have received excellent care since my return."

"Oh, I'm so glad." Miss Charlene followed her enthusiastic response with a shy look of embarrassment. "I would hate to think of you enduring even the slightest pain."

"Then you have nothing to worry over. I am completely healed."

The young lady lowered her gaze in the practiced art of flirtation and sighed softly.

On his left, Cecelia's grip tightened on her parasol until he feared the handle might break.

He nearly laughed out loud. She was obviously unimpressed by Miss Charlene's concern over him.

They conversed with Lady Cushman and her daughter a few more minutes, then took their leave, each heading in opposite directions.

"Miss Charlene seems a charming young lady. Is she spoken for?"

"Obviously not, or she wouldn't have flirted so shamelessly with her mother seated only inches from her."

Jonah tilted back his head and laughed harder than he'd laughed in years. His sudden movement caused a sharp pain to slice through his side. He stiffened and pressed his arm tight against his ribs and waited until the pain subsided.

"Why, Lady Cecelia," he said when he could speak, "one would almost think you were jealous."

Cecelia looked at him for a second or two, then lowered her gaze to her lap.

He wished he could take back his comment as soon as the words left his mouth. From the expression on her face, he'd said the worst possible thing he could say. Her words confirmed it.

"I'm sorry, Lord Haywood. My comment was totally uncalled for. I don't have the right to give the impression I am jealous."

She was nervous, and Jonah hated that he'd made her so uncomfortable.

"Charlene Cushman is the epitome of grace and refinement," she continued in a rush. "She comes from one of the best families in society and will bring with her a very handsome dowry. She will make some fortunate man the perfect wife."

Jonah leaned back and let the horses move at a slow, steady pace. "Is that what you think I am doing?"

He glanced down and noticed that she was rubbing the material of her gown between the thumb and first two fingers of her free hand. He smiled at the nervous habit.

"You are the Earl of Haywood now. It is your duty to secure your title."

A thought struck him that sent a wave of unease down his spine. "Is that why you think I invited you today? Did you think my purpose was to use your name and position to gain an introduction to society's eligible young females?"

Her slight hesitation was answer enough for him.

"It is a wonder you agreed to accompany me," he interjected before she could come up with an answer to give him. "Why did you?"

She turned her head and lifted her chin. The expression in her eyes was filled with steely courage, and Jonah admired her more in that instance than he thought possible.

"I agreed to accompany you because I wanted to," she said, her voice containing not a hint of fear. Or intimidation. "I took your invitation as a compliment, partly because you had the courage to ask me, even though you knew what my brother's reaction would probably be, and partly because there are any number of other females you could have asked, but didn't."

Something shifted inside his chest. "Now, would you like to hear the real reason I invited you?"

They paused long enough to nod to a passing carriage that contained two young couples. When they were alone again, he continued.

"I invited you because, after meeting you last night, I wanted to spend an hour or so in your company."

She didn't lower her gaze, but the look in her eyes changed.

"You don't believe me, do you?"

She hesitated again, and Jonah realized that even though she was a very strong-willed person, there was a softness to her that wasn't comfortable with confrontation.

"I don't lie, Lady Cecelia."

"Yes, you do," she said so quietly he wasn't sure he'd heard her correctly.

Jonah's heart jolted inside his chest. He maneuvered his carriage to the nearest turnoff, then pulled the horses to a halt. "Would you care to explain that?"

He turned in his seat, placed his index finger beneath her chin, and turned her face enough that she was forced to look him in the eyes.

She breathed a heavy sigh that lifted and lowered her breasts. The movement drew his attention, even though he didn't want to be attracted by such a movement.

"What lie do you think I have told you?"

She tried to turn her head, but he kept his finger against her cheek, making it impossible for her to look away from him. She breathed another sigh, then gave up her attempt to look away. When she spoke, the tone of her voice was filled with resignation.

"Very well," she said. "I see you are going to force me to be painfully honest with you."

"It is the only way it should be between two people who are destined to become friends."

Her brows furrowed. "Destined?"

"Yes, destined. But I'll not have you avoid answering my question by asking one of your own. I would first have you explain what lies I have told."

"Actually, there have been two…that I've noticed."

He couldn't hide his surprise. "Two?"

"Yes. The first was last night when you asked me to accompany you today because my presence would help ease your way back into society."

"You consider that a lie?"

"Your presence is already assured, Lord Haywood."

"Jonah. Please, call me Jonah."

"Very well. Jonah. The truth is that your place was assured when you arrived at Lady Plimpton's ball. You are a nobleman, the Earl of Haywood, and a decorated war hero. When my brother didn't turn his back on you or make a premature departure, as he did three years ago, your entry was assured. The statement his actions made to society was that, even though the two of you may never be on friendly terms, the Duke of Hadleigh will at least tolerate your presence at society's social affairs."

Celie moved her gaze to scan the perimeter of Hyde Park. She seemed focused on something in the distance that he'd wager wasn't there.

"I would also venture," she continued, "that your butler has been busy all morning answering the door to collect the invitations that are arriving at an alarming rate. None of society's hostesses will pass up the opportunity to invite to her upcoming event a wounded war hero as well as a most eligible bachelor."

She lifted her gaze, and Jonah found himself looking into the warmest, yet saddest, smile he'd ever seen on anyone's face.

"And the second lie?" he asked, unable to argue with anything she'd said thus far.

"The second lie you told just a few moments ago when you told Lady Cushman and Charlene that they had nothing to worry over. That you were completely healed."

Her expression filled with compassion, and Jonah felt his blood turn warm.

"You're not healed. In fact, you're in a great deal of pain right now. The way your breath caught and you pressed your arm to your side earlier evidenced it."

"You're very observant," he commented, leaning back against the leather cushion to relax.

"Hadleigh tells me the same," she said with a smile on her face, "but he never means it as a compliment."

"What makes you say that?"

"Surely you know that no man is impressed with a woman who proves that there's something more than air between her ears."

Jonah laughed again. "I've never considered that. I've always admired women who could think for themselves."

She looked surprised. "Do you know how progressive that makes you sound?"

"Is that a point in my favor or against?"

"That, Lord Haywood, de—"

"Jonah," he corrected her.

"Jonah. Yes, well, that depends on whom you ask."

Jonah studied her for a moment and was struck by her thoughtfulness. She was not at all shallow, like most of society's other females. Like Melisande had been.

The moment she noticed him watching her, she changed.

"Perhaps we should continue on our way," she said. "Or do you need a moment more to rest?"

"I'm fine."

A glimpse of doubt clouded her eyes.

"Truly, I am. It's only every once in a while that my wound refuses to be forgotten."

"How did it happen?" she asked after he'd flicked the reins against the horses' rumps and turned them around to continue through the park.

"Not very heroically, I'm afraid. I didn't move fast enough when an enemy charged."

"But you moved fast enough to put yourself between the enemy and Lady Plimpton's nephew."

Jonah saw the concern on her face and prayed he did an adequate job of hiding the terror that still engulfed him when he relived that event. "We were both fortunate that day."

"Does it bother you to talk about it?"

Jonah was stunned by her question. No one asked him that. No one cared. They only wanted to hear every bloody, gruesome detail concerning the war.

The problem was, no one who had experienced war's horrors ever wanted to relive one moment of them.

If the other men fortunate enough to return from the war were like him, they did enough remembering every night when the nightmares started; enough remembering when their screams woke them and they bolted upright in bed, soaked in perspiration; enough remembering when, even in the depths of an alcohol-induced sleep, they could hear their comrades' screams of agony and pain. Along with their own.

For Jonah, the earth still trembled beneath him as the enemy's mammoth horse bore down on him, its rider brandishing a once-gleaming deadly saber, now stained with the blood of an untold number of dead and dying.

Jonah closed his eyes for the briefest of seconds but could not afford to keep them closed. If he did, he'd hear the swishing sound of the saber as it sliced through the air, feel the steel as it separated his sinewy flesh, sense the lifeblood flowing from his veins as the strength drained from his body.

Jonah pressed his hand to his side as he'd done that day in a vain attempt to keep the blood from rushing out, then dropped his hand beside him on the seat.

He hoped Celie hadn't noticed.

"The war was a lifetime ago," he said as flippantly as he could manage. "It's easy to forget the worst of it once you return to the peaceful surroundings in England."

She smiled at him, but her eyes spoke volumes. "And that, my lord," she said as she snapped her parasol open in a queenly manner and rested it against her shoulder, "is the third lie you've told in less than one day's time."

She'd tipped her chin upward and let the sun shine on her face. No wonder her face had a hint of bronze to it. She didn't practice the same abhorrence to the effects of the sun as the rest of society.

"Perhaps my statement was a slight exaggeration. But not intended as a lie."

"I'm sure it wasn't. It was probably only intended to be a statement to keep people from knowing how deeply you were affected by the tragedies of war. So far, all your lies have been barriers you erect to keep people from getting too close."

For a few seconds, they drove on in silence; then, in a soft voice that held a great deal of strength, she said, "I can't pretend to ever understand what you went through during the war, but if you ever feel the need to talk to someone, I would be more than willing to listen. Even Hadleigh admits I'm passable as an adequate listener."

Jonah couldn't believe the effect of her words. The moment she finished speaking, he felt as if an unbearable pressure had been lifted from his chest.

A gentle hand wrapped around his heart, easing the raw pain that had been his constant companion since he'd returned. So few understood what everyone who'd fought in the war had endured. Even fewer cared.

But Lady Cecelia did. She cared how he felt, both physically and emotionally.

He couldn't explain what that meant to him.

He looked ahead as another carriage approached them. He and Celie nodded in greeting, but he didn't pull up to talk to them.

"You should have stopped," Celie said, glancing at him. "That was the Marchioness of Portwood and her daughter Lady Felicity. Lady Felicity is extremely eligible and quite sought after."

Jonah looked down on her and smiled. "Why would I want to waste time talking to the marchioness and her daughter when I have the perfect companion sitting next to me?"

He couldn't stop the laughter that wanted to erupt from him. The surprised expression on her face was priceless.

He turned his attention to the horses and gave them a gentle nudging to pick up their step. They had been traveling one of the paths frequented by the members of the *ton* who wanted to avoid being seen. Suddenly, he wanted to be where *everyone* would see him. He turned onto the main thoroughfare.

He wanted to let everyone know that Lady Cecelia Randolph had agreed to accompany him…

And that he considered himself the luckiest man in London.

Chapter 4

❦

Celie squeezed through the crowd milling around Lady Cushing's music room and made her way to the empty chair Amanda had saved for her. There was still time before the musicale began, but she'd wanted to arrive early to get a seat near the front. Tonight's entertainment promised to be superb, and everyone would want to be as close to the performer as possible.

"Have you ever heard Miss Zunderman sing?" Celie asked when she took her seat next to Amanda. She scanned the crowd and saw that almost everyone who was anyone was here.

"No. I can't believe the famous Miss Zunderman agreed to sing for Lady Cushing in such an intimate setting. Rumor has it she only agrees to stage performances."

"Hadleigh said Lady Cushing and Miss Zunderman were acquaintances in their youth. He said that—"

Amanda turned toward Celie and grabbed her hand. "Enough of this trivia, Celie. Tell me about your drive with Lord Haywood yesterday afternoon while we still have some privacy to talk."

Celie took note of the empty chairs surrounding them and scanned the area to make sure they couldn't be overheard. "It was very pleasant. I had a wonderful time."

Amanda's eyes opened wide and her mouth dropped a few inches. "That's all you have to say? It was very pleasant and you had a wonderful time?"

"Well, yes. What more would you like me to say?"

"Did he ask to take you driving again? Did he say he would like to call on you? Did he say when?"

Celie tried to keep her expression emotionless as her gaze met Amanda's. The two of them were best friends, and Amanda could read her like an open book.

Amanda's gaze narrowed. The sky-blue gown she wore matched the color of her eyes to perfection. Combined with her creamy, smooth complexion and the perfect curves of her body, Amanda was an absolute beauty.

Truth be told, Celie couldn't figure out why Amanda didn't have to fight off suitors, although losing her best friend to matrimony wouldn't be easy to bear. Amanda was far prettier than half the females in society. Only the glasses she was forced to wear detracted from her otherwise perfectly delicate features.

Perhaps she wasn't wed already because she was as expert at discouraging suitors as Celie was. More than one suitable male had asked for Amanda's hand, but she'd always declined their offers. Fortunately, Amanda's brother hadn't forced her to accept anyone—yet.

Celie considered for a moment the possibility that Amanda was perhaps in love with someone already and filed that possibility in the back of her mind. That was a question she'd have to ask her friend when they were alone.

"Well?" Amanda asked again. "Did he say anything that might indicate his feelings?"

"No. He simply said…" Celie paused.

"Said what?"

Amanda leaned closer, anxious to have Celie tell her what Jonah had said.

"Well, we both know Lord Haywood only asked me to accompany him at the fashionable hour to gain introductions to society's most eligible females."

"No," Amanda answered, pulling her hands away from Celie's and dropping them into her lap with a heavy sigh. "We don't know anything of the sort. At least, *I* don't know anything of the sort. It's *you* who's come to that conclusion all on your own."

"Because it's true," Celie added.

"Well, we could argue all day on that point, but right now, I'm more interested in what Lord Haywood said."

Celie's cheeks warmed and she found herself embarrassed to admit to her best friend what he'd said. "Nothing that held any significance. It's simply that, when I saw Lady Portwood and Felicity drive toward us, I told him to stop so I could introduce him to Felicity. Felicity will, after all, come with a huge dowry, and that is exactly what Lord Haywood needs."

"Did he stop?"

"No, he only greeted them with a polite nod."

"What did he say, Celie? Hurry, tell me," Amanda demanded with an excited giggle.

"He asked why he should waste time talking to the marchioness and her daughter when..."

"When what?"

Celie found repeating Jonah's compliment very embarrassing.

"What? Hurry!"

"He said something about stopping would be a waste of time when he already had the perfect companion sitting next to him."

Amanda clamped her hand over her mouth and muffled a squeal of delight. "Did he say if he would be here tonight?" Amanda scanned the room in search of him.

"No, he won't be here. Lord Haywood is aware of Hadleigh's love for music. Haywood knows he's sure to be here. It was one thing for them to ignore each other's presence at Lady Plimpton's ball, but another altogether to have to tolerate each other in such an intimate setting."

"Did your brother say anything after Lady Plimpton's ball? Everyone saw you speaking to the earl on the terrace."

Celie shook her head. "I expected him to fly into a rage, but he didn't mention it. Not even at breakfast the next morning."

Amanda's eyes opened wide. "And he allowed you to accompany Haywood for a drive?"

Celie smiled, knowing she had a Cheshire cat grin on her face. "I didn't tell him I'd accepted Haywood's invitation, and he wasn't home when Haywood arrived. Although I can't believe he hasn't heard by now."

"Oh, Celie," Amanda said with a giggle. "You're amazing."

"No, I'm just very independent. Haven't you realized that by now?"

"Yes, but I wasn't sure your independence was a match for the hatred Hadleigh harbors toward the Earl of Haywood." She paused with a frown on her face. "Do you think he isn't quite so bitter anymore?"

"One can only hope. Perhaps if Jonah goes slowly and doesn't force Hadleigh to accept him immediately, he might have a chance."

Amanda paused, then rolled her eyes heavenward. "Then I predict the earl doesn't have a prayer of succeeding."

Amanda's voice had a doleful tone to it and the furrows between her eyes grew deeper as she focused her gaze on something over Celie's shoulder.

"What is it?" Celie asked, refusing to turn around. From the worried expression on Amanda's face, Celie was sure she already knew what she saw. The prickling of the tiny hairs on the back of her neck confirmed it. "Tell me Haywood isn't here," she demanded, clutching one of Amanda's hands.

"Very well. Haywood isn't here."

"Now tell me you aren't lying."

"Very well. I'm not. But that would be a lie."

Amanda's eyes were like large blue orbs, and when their gazes met, Celie saw more than a hint of worry on her friend's face.

"What are you going to do?" Amanda asked.

"Me?"

Amanda hesitated. "Oh, very well. What are *we* going to do?"

Celie breathed a sigh that lacked any semblance of surety. "I don't know. What's happening now?"

She couldn't bring herself to turn around. Instead, she sat ramrod straight in her chair and waited for Amanda to warn her when disaster was about to befall them.

"Lord Haywood is talking to Viscount and Lady Remmington."

"How does he look?"

Amanda shrugged. "Stunningly handsome. But you already know that."

"I don't mean how does he look," Celie said with a hint of frustration. "I mean, how does he *look*. Does he seem nervous?"

Just then, a group of guests at the back of the room laughed. She recognized Jonah's laughter.

"No. I wouldn't say he's nervous. In fact, I would say he is having a most pleasant time."

"Perhaps he doesn't realize Hadleigh is here."

"Then he'd have to be blind." Amanda gave Celie another worrisome look. "Your brother is standing not ten feet from him."

"How does Hadleigh look?" Celie asked. "And don't say he's stunningly handsome. He's my brother. I already know that he's passable."

"Passable?"

"Very well. Stunning. But how does he look?"

"You mean, does he look angry enough to run a sword through Lord Haywood?"

Celie swallowed. "Yes."

"Yes, but I don't think he'll do murder."

"Oh, good."

"At least, not here—not tonight. I'm sure he'll wait until morning."

"You mean challenge him to a duel?" Celie became more nervous by the second.

Amanda looked thoughtful as she studied the two men at the back of the room. She pried Celie's fingers from her hand, then patted her in a consoling manner. "I don't think there's cause to worry that there will be a duel."

Celie breathed a sigh. "Oh, good."

"Hadleigh would never stoop to dueling. I think it's more likely he'll simply hire an assassin to do the deed for him."

Celie wanted to hit her. That last comment was so absurd she knew Amanda had been stringing her along the whole time. "Ooh," she said through clenched teeth. "How could you?"

Amanda giggled. "How could I not? You are so pathetically obvious."

"Obvious?" Anger slowly replaced the worry. "Obvious about what?"

"Your feelings for Lord Haywood."

Celie sat back in her chair and folded her hands in front of her. "I don't have feelings for Lord Haywood. I simply want to avoid a repeat of what happened three years ago. Wanting to stop a feud before it starts doesn't mean I have feelings for Lord Haywood."

"Then why have you been calling him Jonah?"

Celie stuttered. "Well…because he asked me to."

Amanda smiled that familiar grin she wore when she had some news to impart. "Which means that he must have feelings for you, too."

"No," Celie said in a hushed whisper. "It means no such thing. He only feels a friendship because he and Hadleigh were childhood friends, so he feels comfortable around me. The only reason he asked me to accompany him was because he is in desperate need of a wealthy wife. Someone who will come to him with a large enough dowry to pay the bills his father and brother amassed in staggering amounts, if the rumor mills can be believed. He simply thought I could assist him in that."

"What if he considers you to be his choice?"

Celie shot Amanda a look that said they'd discussed this topic before and Amanda, more than anyone, should know Celie's determination that she would not be chosen for her dowry.

"Don't look at me like that, Celie," Amanda said with an all-knowing expression on her face. "Just because Lord Haywood is an extremely handsome man—"

"Who could have his pick of any one of a dozen beautiful females who are tripping over each other to gain his attention," Celie interrupted. "Do you think just because Lord Haywood asked me to accompany him one afternoon that I'm foolish enough to believe he's considering me for his bride?"

"There *is* that possibility," Amanda ventured tentatively.

"There most certainly is *not*."

Celie looked around to make sure no one had taken any of the seats close enough to them that they could be overheard. "Even if there were, do you think that I'd allow myself to become so besotted that I'd throw caution to the wind and consider marrying a man who was my brother's mortal enemy? That fact alone should eliminate him from consideration."

"Should, but will it?"

"Of course it will. Lord Haywood has no interest in me."

"Then why did he ask you to accompany him?" Amanda demanded.

Celie lifted her chin in determination. "To test the water, so to speak. To give society the impression that the war between the two of them has come to a cease-fire. I'm positive there won't be a repeat of yesterday afternoon's invitation. Lord Haywood accomplished his goal. He can now proceed with his mission to find a wife in a way that will not include an association with me."

"Are you sure?"

Celie rolled her eyes heavenward. "Of course I am. In fact, I'm sure Haywood is already looking over the gathering of young ladies here tonight and deciding with whom he'd like to spend the evening."

"I imagine you're right," Amanda answered, releasing a heavy sigh. "In fact, now that you mention it, I'm sure that's exactly what he's doing. Or has already done."

Her words caused more pain than Celie wanted to admit. Even though she realized Jonah had asked her to accompany him for no reason other than to stamp down any unnecessary gossip concerning him and Hadleigh, she couldn't help but feel the slightest bit hurt that she'd performed her purpose. He was now free to continue his search for a wife with the perfect dowry.

But that didn't mean she wasn't interested in which females garnered his interest.

"What is Lord Haywood doing now?" she asked, not quite sure she wanted to hear all the details.

"He's stopping to speak with Lord and Lady Puttnam."

"Is Chastity with them?"

"Of course. She's *always* with them. As their only child, they dote on her." Amanda paused. "Lord Haywood seems quite taken by her. Even though she's only the daughter of a viscount, she's the daughter of a very *wealthy* viscount, and one day she'll be a very wealthy woman."

Celie felt her heart plummet to the pit of her stomach. She could think of nothing to disqualify her. Chastity would make a perfect wife for Jonah.

"Oh," Amanda said, grabbing Celie's arm none too gently.

"Oh, what?"

"Oh, the earl must have another target in mind. He's already abandoned the Puttnam circle."

"Where's he headed?"

"There's a gathering of debutantes on the side of the room next to the open terrace doors."

"Who of note is in it?"

"No one," Amanda said with a nonchalant shrug, "except…Oh, no!"

Celie grabbed Amanda's hand and squeezed her fingers.

"Ouch," Amanda said. "That hurt."

"It was meant to. Stop torturing me. Who has he focused on now?"

"The Bedman sisters."

Celie breathed in a gasp. "No. Surely he's been warned that they're not suitable. Everyone is aware of their reputations."

"Perhaps he hasn't heard."

Celie fought the concern building inside her and made a promise that, the next time she saw Haywood alone, she'd tell him to avoid the Bedman sisters at all cost.

"Is he still there?"

"No," Amanda sighed. "He's walking away from them."

"Good," Celie said with a sigh of relief. "Now where's he going?"

"Are you sure you wouldn't rather watch him yourself?"

"No. I don't want him to think I'm interested in whom he chooses."

"But you are."

Celie rolled her eyes. "But I don't want him to *know* I am."

"Oh, very well," Amanda said, discreetly looking around Celie's shoulder.

"Oh."

"Oh, what?"

"I think he's made his final choice," Amanda said, ducking back so Celie blocked her from being seen.

"How do you know?"

"He's walking like a man with a purpose. He just walked past several groups of guests without stopping to talk, and his gaze is focused on someone in particular. I'm certain he's made his choice."

"Who is it?"

"Oh, no, Celie," Amanda said, lowering her gaze as well as her voice. "This is even worse than the Bedman sisters."

Celie's nerves stretched taut. It was one thing to know Jonah had found someone he wanted to get to know better. It was another to know he'd made a terrible choice.

"Who, Amanda? Who has he chosen?"

Amanda kept her eyes lowered and shook her head, as if the person Jonah was targeting were too horrible for words.

"Turn around and look, Celie. You have to see this for yourself."

"I can't. I don't want to see who he's chosen. Just tell me."

"Very well. But you aren't going to like it."

Celie's stomach roiled. "She can't be *that* bad. No one can be *that* bad."

"This one is. She's without a doubt the most undesirable female here."

"Who is it?" Celie said much louder than she intended.

Before Celie could demand Amanda tell her, her friend lifted her gaze and placed the warmest smile Celie had ever seen on Amanda's cherub-looking face.

"Good evening, ladies," Jonah's deep, rich voice said from behind her.

"Good evening, Lord Haywood." Amanda's voice brimmed with innocence. "We were just talking about you."

"Were you?"

Celie wanted to die. She wanted to fall through a hole in Lady Cushing's floor and disappear. She wanted to physically hurt Amanda. Instead, she slowly turned in her chair and lifted her gaze.

Her gaze locked with his and her heart skipped a beat when he smiled.

Celie found herself staring into a face even more handsome than she remembered from their drive.

"Good evening, Lady Cecelia."

"Lord Haywood," she greeted softly.

Amanda cleared her throat to draw attention. "Cecelia was just telling me how much she enjoyed herself yesterday afternoon."

"I'm glad." His smile broadened. "I enjoyed myself as well. It was a lovely day, and I was blessed with the perfect companion."

"I'm so glad," Amanda interrupted, "because I hear the weather is supposed to be perfect tomorrow, too. I'm sure—"

"Amanda," Celie warned.

"What?" Amanda feigned a convincing look of innocence. "I'm simply telling you that the weather tomorrow is predicted to be perfect for a drive, too."

Celie shot daggers in Amanda's direction. "How can you possibly know what the weather will be like tomorrow?" She growled her words between her clenched teeth. "Do you have a crystal ball to look into?"

"I don't need a crystal ball. I have Hodgkiss."

Celie couldn't believe her ears. "Your *butler*?"

"Yes, his knees always tell him when it's going to rain, and he told me as I left tonight that he felt so limber he was certain he could do a jig."

Celie stared in disbelief. The very devil danced in Amanda's eyes.

"In that case," Lord Haywood said, "perhaps we should take advantage of tomorrow's guaranteed weather as well, Lady Cecelia."

Celie's cheeks blazed with embarrassment, but she had no choice but to accept. "Thank you, my lord. I'd be delighted."

Amanda cleared her voice again. "Do you have plans to sit with anyone else tonight?" she asked, leaving Celie to flounder in a sea of discomfort. The devilish gleam in her friend's eyes shone brighter.

"No, I was just going to find a seat."

Celie held her breath. It was hard to tell what Amanda would do next. But it didn't take long to find out.

"Please, we'd love to have you join us. Wouldn't we, Celie?"

Celie stumbled over the words tripping her tongue. "Yes, please."

"Then I'd love to. Is this seat taken?" he asked, indicating the chair next to Celie.

"No," Amanda answered for her. "In fact, Lady Cecelia just mentioned that she hoped you'd honor her with your company."

"Did she?"

"Oh, yes," Amanda said, looking around Celie with a broad smile on her face. "She said she enjoyed conversing with you yesterday ever so much."

"As I enjoyed conversing with her."

Celie wanted to die of embarrassment. He *had* to know Amanda was conniving to throw them together, that she was making up her tale as she went, and Celie thought she would die of mortification.

She tried to speak but couldn't find her voice.

She tried to kick her friend in the shins to shut her up, but she couldn't wade through her layers of skirts to reach her.

She tried to pretend she wasn't helpless against Amanda's efforts to humiliate her, but she had no choice but to suffer in silence.

Celie fanned her burning cheeks. They were on fire, nearly as heated as her rising temper. Lord Haywood drew her attention back to him.

"I haven't mentioned that you look especially lovely tonight."

"Thank you," Celie managed. "And I am glad you decided to attend the musicale. Miss Zunderman is reportedly one of the finest vocalists of our time."

"So I've heard, which is why I came. I could hardly miss such an opportunity."

He smiled again, and even though it was evening, Celie felt like the sun had come out to shower down golden rays. "I recall that you and Hadleigh enjoyed going to the opera when you were in Town," she said.

"I'm surprised you remember such a minor detail."

"Oh, Celie has an excellent memory," Amanda interrupted. It was obvious she wasn't about to leave well enough alone. She took great pleasure in Celie's discomfort.

Celie turned her head and focused a hostile glare in Amanda's direction. "Yes, I do," she said through clenched teeth. "An excellent memory. Which might be a wise point for you to remember."

The sly grin on Amanda's face said she was enjoying herself entirely too much to be worried—yet.

Celie clenched her teeth, then gave Amanda the deadliest glare she could muster. "My flawless memory is why you can trust me to remember the oath I took a few minutes ago."

A frown deepened across Amanda's brow. "Oath? What oath?"

"The oath I took to make you suffer a thousand deaths for embarrassing me."

Chapter 5

Lord Haywood laughed.

The sound was rich and deep, and filled with sincere humor. Celie felt every pair of eyes turn to stare at them, but she didn't care. The warmth that rushed through her evaporated any embarrassment she might have felt.

She turned to Amanda. "Why don't you get something to drink, Amanda? Some hemlock, perhaps? Arsenic?"

Amanda shifted in her chair and lifted her chin. She tried to look affronted, but failed. "You know very well that, if I leave now, I'll lose my chair."

"There is always that possibility," Celie said, giving Lord Haywood a half smile so he knew their comments were light banter.

"Do you see what kind of personality our Lady Cecelia has, Lord Haywood? No wonder her brother, the duke, has given up trying to reform her."

"Who says I've given up?" a deep voice said from behind them.

Celie's breath caught, and both she and Amanda darted looks in the direction of the voice. Only Haywood didn't seem affected by the Duke of Hadleigh's presence.

"Hadleigh," Lord Haywood greeted after he'd risen to his feet.

"Haywood. Lady Amanda." The Duke of Hadleigh acknowledged them with the dignity befitting his title, but his voice contained a great deal of stiffness.

The two enemies glared at each other for several tense seconds before Hadleigh spoke. He directed his question to Celie even though his intense stare didn't shift from the Earl of Haywood's face. "You realize you've attracted the attention of the entire room, Cecelia, don't you?"

Celie stopped herself from glancing around the room. Their joking banter, as well as Jonah's laughter, may have drawn a bit of attention, but nothing compared to the attention Hadleigh drew by joining his sister and the Earl of Haywood.

"I believe, if I'm not mistaken," Celie said with a cordial smile on her face, "that you and Lord Haywood glaring at each other as if one of you might issue a challenge are attracting more attention than if I'd scream at the top of my voice. Perhaps both of you might be interested in taking your seats. There's an empty chair to Amanda's left, Hadleigh."

Celie took several breaths, praying that the tension around them would dissipate.

It seemed to take forever before her brother made the first move. Only then did Haywood follow suit.

"May I?" Hadleigh asked, indicating the chair beside Amanda.

"I would be pleased," Amanda answered.

The duke sat in his chair as if he were chiseled from stone. He held his back regally straight and folded his arms across his chest.

They sat in silence.

Celie waited as long as she could stand the uncomfortable quiet, then leaned forward and whispered, "I just told Lord Haywood that, when I was younger, I remember watching the two of you leave for the opera."

Without indicating he'd heard her, Hadleigh answered, "How can you say that? You were just a child."

She and Amanda simultaneously turned their heads to glare at him. "Your Grace," she said, knowing the use of his ducal title would gain his attention, "I am only six years your junior. By the time you'd reached the advanced age of eighteen, I was a young lady of twelve. In case you doubt me, I can recall several other incidents that happened when I was that age. Some of which you might prefer I not mention in public."

"Your sister's always had an excellent memory, *Your Grace*." The chiding tone of Amanda's voice drew Hadleigh's attention equally as sufficiently as Celie's had. "I might suggest you dissuade her from recalling her *childhood* memories. Some of the incidents could well be embarrassing."

The shocked look on the Duke of Hadleigh's face was as entertaining as anything Celie could remember. She nearly burst out laughing.

Amanda had always enjoyed making remarks concerning Hadleigh, always commented in a teasing manner about his pompous air, his stiff demeanor, and his total lack of a sense of humor. But never had she been so forward as to challenge him to his face.

"Are you suggesting that there's something in my past I wouldn't want revealed, Lady Amanda?"

She lifted her eyebrows in a questioning gesture. "Are you suggesting that there's *nothing* in your past you would rather not have remain there?"

Celie wanted to applaud Amanda's bravery. She wanted to congratulate her on successfully engaging Hadleigh in a conversation that didn't revolve around all the mundane topics of the decisions being made in the House. She wanted to give her friend a hug to thank her for putting a combative glimmer in Hadleigh's eyes she hadn't seen for three years.

She wanted to shout for joy.

Instead, she giggled silently and turned her head in the opposite direction so neither Hadleigh nor Amanda could see the laughter she couldn't stop. What she saw when she looked away from them, though, was equally as mesmerizing as the couple to her left.

Lord Haywood wasn't even trying to hide the amusement he found in the situation. He sat relaxed in his chair with a wide grin on his face.

When Celie turned, he met her gaze and broadened his smile.

Her heart did a rapid somersault and the blood flowing through her veins warmed to a soothing heat. He sat close enough so she could see several golden flecks in his ebony eyes, and a glimmer of something to which she couldn't quite put a name stared back at her.

"I think your brother's met his match," he whispered, low enough that he couldn't be overheard.

"The two of them have never been what you'd call *compatible.* Amanda thinks Hadleigh's too full of himself. She enjoys nothing more than emphasizing his human failings, as well as what she considers his errors in political judgment."

"And Hadleigh?"

"Oh, he's convinced Lord and Lady Mattenden made a fatal error by not drowning their youngest daughter at birth."

Jonah tipped his head back and laughed.

"Plus," Celie added, "he's convinced an even more serious error was made by allowing Amanda use of their library. She's far too knowledgeable to fit into Hadleigh's mold of the perfect society female, far too outspoken to conform to his expectations of demureness and refinement. He's certain Lady Amanda will never make any man a suitable wife."

"And what about you? I'm surprised he allows you to associate with Lady Amanda."

"Oh, he'd forbid it if he thought I'd listen to him."

"But you wouldn't?"

"Of course not. I simply allow him to blame all my shortcomings on Amanda's influence and continue our friendship."

"And does Hadleigh consider you to be headstrong?"

"Of course. I'm not at all the soft-spoken, malleable female he thinks I should be."

His smile broadened. "Good."

Celie felt her cheeks warm and looked away from him before he noticed her embarrassment.

The room was full now, every chair occupied. Thankfully, the noise level was high enough that their voices could not carry. The bustle of excitement from the guests anticipating the performance did nothing, however, to ease the tension building inside her.

The emotions roiling inside her from sitting near Haywood were more powerful than anything she'd ever experienced before. The heat that wrapped around her when he looked at her unsettled her nerves. The emotional pull she experienced was so alien she almost couldn't fight it.

She almost cried out in relief when Lady Cushing called for quiet and began her introduction. She wasn't sure how much longer she could sit this close to Haywood before her nerves stretched to the snapping point. Every inch of her body tingled in alertness. Then Elthea Zunderman stepped to the front of the room and began her first selection.

Celie came alive the moment the mezzo-soprano sang the first note. It seemed impossible for such a petite woman to put out such a huge, rich sound, but she did. Celie was mesmerized, as was every other person in the room.

The gathering sat enthralled, hanging on to every lilting sound, anticipating every note, immersed in the experience of knowing they were listening to one of the greatest vocalists of the age.

Miss Zunderman finished her first selection, and for several long moments, no one moved. No one dared even breathe. Every guest in attendance sat spellbound. Her finishing note reverberated in the room, leaving an echo of perfection.

In unison, the audience released a sigh, then broke out in resounding applause.

The experience was spiritual, affecting one's soul as effectively as it affected one's emotions. Celie took a gasping breath, then wiped her gloved fingers over her damp cheeks. She hoped Lord Haywood hadn't noticed how she'd been moved to tears, but the clean white handkerchief he held out to her said he had.

Thankfully, Miss Zunderman began her next selection before Celie was required to speak. She doubted she could have found words to express her feelings, doubted she could have found her voice to express her thoughts.

She risked a sideward glance to the man sitting next to her, then sat back against her chair and prepared to let the gifted angel transport her to the stars.

Life had suddenly turned perfect.

* * *

Celie remained in her chair when the performance was over. The front of the room was too congested to get anywhere near the talented Miss Zunderman.

"Would you care to take a stroll through Lady Cushing's garden?" Lord Haywood asked when the crowd closed in on them. "Or should we make our way forward to offer our congratulations to Miss Zunderman?"

Celie looked to where Amanda and her brother stood talking to some acquaintances. They were engulfed by a sea of people and weren't able to move in any direction. The crowd surrounding the vocalist grew deeper by the second. Celie shook her head. "I intend to offer my congratulations, but not now. I'll speak with her after she's had a moment to catch her breath."

Haywood offered her his arm, then ushered her through the crowd to the open French doors that led onto the terrace. The moment they reached the silence outside, she realized how loud and uncomfortable it had been inside.

"Oh, this is wonderful," she said, taking in a deep breath.

"You enjoyed the performance," he said as they walked across the veranda and down the three steps that led into Lady Cushing's garden.

"It was remarkable. I don't remember the last time I heard such talent. I enjoyed every moment."

"And I don't remember the last time I enjoyed watching anyone as much as I enjoyed watching you."

Celie stopped, then turned to look into his face.

The moon was full and bright, providing more than enough light to see his expression clearly. She could see the smile on his face and the look in his eyes, although she wasn't sure she was reading his look correctly.

She couldn't be, she told herself, for there was a hint of something she could easily mistake for interest. Or perhaps admiration.

"May I ask you a personal question?" she said, knowing this probably wasn't the time or the place for such an inquiry, but needing to stop her imagination from dreaming of more than might ever be.

"Why do I have a feeling I need to be sitting for this question?"

She smiled at him in an effort to hide her nervousness. "Because you probably do."

"Very well." He scanned the area. When he located a wrought iron bench placed on a cement pad beneath a huge shade tree, he led her to it.

Celie sat down and he sat beside her.

"Very well, Lady Cecelia. I'm ready for this serious question that you've wanted to ask since I asked you to ride with me through Hyde Park."

Celie couldn't hide her surprise. "What makes you think I've wanted to ask you a question since then?"

"Do you deny it?"

She hesitated, then answered, "No."

"I thought not." He smiled.

For the first time in her life, she had a feeling she'd met someone who could see through her—perhaps too well.

"You're thinking too hard. Relax and ask your question."

Celie stared at her hands clutched in her lap while she thought how to phrase her question. She suddenly realized how important his answer was and how afraid she was that it wouldn't be the answer she wanted to hear. But she had no choice. Nor could she afford to allow matters to go further if…

Well, she couldn't.

She gathered her courage and let the words rush from her mouth. "Why have you concentrated so much energy on spending time with me?"

"Have you found my attention distasteful?"

Celie swallowed hard. "Please, don't answer my question with a question."

For the span of two of the longest seconds Celie had ever endured in her life, he said nothing. When he spoke, his voice was void of its former humor and sounded as serious as she'd ever heard him.

"Very well, I will answer your question, but you may not hear everything you want. First, though, I would like you to answer a question of my own. Do you find my attentions distasteful?"

"You know I don't. I enjoy your company…very much."

"I'm glad."

He paused, and Celie imagined she heard him release a breath he must have been holding. Before he spoke, he pushed himself to his feet and took a step away from her.

"It wasn't by accident that I sought you out that first night. It was intentional."

He stopped, but Celie couldn't let it rest there. She finished his sentence for him. "You sought me out because of my brother, didn't you?"

He locked his hands behind his back and looked at her. "Yes, because of your brother."

She wasn't sure how his admission should make her feel. She thought perhaps angry, but that wasn't the emotion that settled over her. She remained silent and waited.

"I want you to know that meeting you was a surprise. I expected to like you." He smiled. "I had from when you were a young girl tagging after Hadleigh and Melisande and me. You were so determined to be a part of our threesome. Even though Hadleigh and Melisande were determined to keep you at arm's length."

His smile broadened, and Celie couldn't help but answer it with a smile of her own.

"But I never anticipated feeling as I did when we met," he added.

"How was that?"

"As if I'd known you forever."

Celie's cheeks warmed, but she refused to lose herself in his flattery. She lowered her gaze and asked the question she dreaded hearing the answer to the most. "What purpose did you have in wanting to meet me? Was it because you expected Hadleigh to become furious and you wanted to repay him for some of the anger and frustration you'd endured because of him?"

"What makes you think I've been angry?"

"How could you not be? Hadleigh was the reason you were ostracized by society. He was the reason you went to war and came home injured. He was the reason you weren't here when your father and brother died."

He took a step toward her and sat. He turned to face her and placed his hand over hers. "I didn't speak to you that first night because of any hidden agenda to take revenge on your brother, nor to get even with him for anything that happened. He didn't *force* me to enter the war. I chose to go. I needed to separate myself from what had happened that night with Melisande as much as Hadleigh needed me to be gone so he could heal."

"And the fact that you weren't here when your father and brother died?"

He shook his head. "My father and brother had been traveling down a path toward destruction for years. Each made one fatal decision after another. Each failed to live productive lives years before their physical deaths."

"Then why?"

He released her hands and leaned back against the bench. "I warned you that you would not like everything I had to say, and this will be something you'll like the least. I sought you out that night because when I came back to

London after the war, I came back as the Earl of Haywood." He took a breath. "My intent was to take my rightful place in society, and I could hardly do that if your brother was still intent on forcing everyone to choose between the two of us."

He rose to his feet and clutched his left hand to his side. Celie could see his side still pained him, no doubt because he'd been on his feet for so long.

"When your brother did not turn away from me, I decided I would carry my plan one step further."

"You wanted to see what he would do if you introduced yourself to me?"

"Yes."

"What did you think to do if he objected?"

"I told myself I would handle that problem if and when it arose."

Celie breathed a sigh. The Earl of Haywood had accomplished his goal. He'd been accepted back into society and had spent an adequate amount of time with her to convince everyone that any rift between the Duke of Hadleigh and the Earl of Haywood had been bridged. Though she'd dreamed that there might have been a more personal reason he'd singled her out, she'd been nothing more than the vehicle he'd used to take his rightful and necessary place.

That knowledge shouldn't pain her, but it did. She'd watched the bitterness her brother harbored toward his longtime friend eat away at him for the last three years, until she feared for his health and mental well-being. She should be glad that Hadleigh's healing process had begun and that she'd played a part in it. But it hurt to know that the man she'd secretly loved all these years felt nothing for her. That he'd only used her to gauge Hadleigh's feelings.

So this was how it would end.

Her instinct told her that the role she'd played in Haywood's attempt to regain his rightful place was finished. She closed her eyes and prayed he wouldn't ask that she still remain his friend. She didn't think she could survive that.

She cloaked her heart with the impenetrable armor she was so adept at putting in place, the same shield she erected each time a suitor attempted to court her, knowing it was her dowry they wanted instead of her; as she watched one childhood friend after another meet the man of her dreams, then marry, knowing the man of her dreams didn't even know she existed; as she attended wedding after wedding and smiled at the happy bride and groom as if their happiness didn't cause an empty ache that never went away.

She refused to let Lord Haywood think she'd been foolish enough to expect—no, dream of—more than friendship, dreamed that, one day, he would ask her to be his bride. She possessed too much pride to let him think she thought it possible for a man to want her enough that he'd overlook the ill feelings between himself and his wife's family.

No, she would handle this with the same indifference that she handled every disappointment.

"So now you can continue with your agenda." She lifted her gaze and gave him a bright smile. "You can begin your search for a wife. Or have you already?"

He looked her in the eyes. "Yes, I've already begun."

"I see," she answered.

A part of her died a little, but she would not allow him to see it. She took a fortifying breath. She refused to have him feel sorry for her, refused to let him pity her. Refused to let him realize how much she hurt.

"Aren't you going to ask if anyone has attracted my attention?"

Celie kept the smile on her face even though it hurt to keep it there. "No, Lord Haywood. I think I prefer to watch your story unfold."

"But I value your opinion, Lady Cecelia. I'd like to discuss my choice with you and gain your opinion."

"I'd prefer not, Lord Haywood. Perhaps when you have narrowed your choices, I'll offer an opinion, but not yet."

Their gazes locked for what seemed an eternity. When it hurt too much to look at him, she broke the contact and moved to rise. "If you're ready, I think we'd better go back."

She needed to escape, needed to make her way someplace where it would be quiet and she could be undisturbed for a while.

She took his outstretched hand, grateful that he realized they'd spent enough time alone and needed to return before they were missed.

She rose to her feet and made a move to step away from him, but he held her fast.

"Perhaps I would do better to show you my intent," he said when she stood next to him. "As I said, it's important that you are aware of my intentions."

She started to object, but before she could separate herself from him, he stepped closer and cupped his palm to her cheek.

He smiled, then lowered his head and pressed his lips to hers.

Their kiss was short, tender, and without a doubt, the most emotional experience of her life.

"I surprised you," he whispered, pulling back slightly. "I'm sorry. I should have asked your permission first."

She opened her mouth to speak, but no words came out.

She'd been kissed before. Not often, but at least a few times—but never had the experience been so…wonderful.

"Have I offended you?" he asked, the expression on his face part humor and part concern.

He smiled when she shook her head. "You have a question. I can read it on your face. What is it?"

She swallowed. "Why?"

"Why did I kiss you?"

"Yes."

"Because I wanted to. And I thought you wanted me to as well." His expression turned serious. "Was I wrong?"

Celie thought to lie, but couldn't. "No," she answered softly.

"Good."

Before she could think what he meant, he lowered his head and kissed her again.

His mouth covered hers. The feel of his lips atop hers was as warm and tender as before, only this kiss was different. There was nothing simple in their contact, nothing shallow. Nothing that hinted at *friendship*. Even the way he held her emphasized a possessiveness she'd never experienced before.

His arms wrapped around her, pulling her against him, holding her tight, and her body ignited with a burning sensation that shot to every extremity. Suddenly, even though he kissed her with more passion than she'd ever been kissed before, it wasn't enough.

She wrapped her arms around his neck and held him to her. She stretched out her fingers and let them glide through his hair.

The feel of it was silky and soft, yet thick and heavy, as strong and robust as the arms holding her. The flames inside her intensified at such an intimate gesture. And he deepened his kiss even more.

Each second slowed, then seemed to stop while her balance shifted at a dizzying pace. She'd lost control several minutes ago. She no longer knew how long he'd held her in his arms, or how long he'd kissed her with such fervor, or when her knees had turned to butter beneath her. All she knew was that she couldn't breathe on her own but needed him to help her, couldn't stand on her own but needed him to support her, wasn't complete on her own but needed him to make her whole.

His mouth opened atop hers and he urged her to follow his lead.

She did.

Celie knew at that moment she'd follow him to the ends of the earth if he took her there. And go willingly.

He deepened his kiss, demanding more and taking all she gave. Then, as suddenly as he'd begun his kiss, he lifted his mouth and released her. Thankfully, he didn't drop his hands from her, but pulled her closer to him and wrapped her in his embrace.

Celie placed her cheek against his chest. His heart thundered beneath her ear. His chest heaved as rapidly as hers, and she knew their kiss affected him as much as it did her.

"Jonah?"

"Shh," he whispered, cupping one hand against her head and the other around her shoulders to keep her cocooned in the shelter of his arms. "Don't say anything yet. It's…too soon."

Celie did as he asked, even though she was desperate to ask him what had just happened to her. She'd give anything to be more worldly, to have more experience in the art of kissing. Was this the way it always was when two people kissed? Had the effect of the kiss they shared been the same for him?

If it had, no wonder people enjoyed it so much.

"Are you steady enough to make it back to the house?"

She nodded, and he loosened his hold on her so she could test her shaky limbs. "Jonah," she began after they'd taken the first few steps back through the garden.

His arm around her shoulder tightened, and Celie stopped speaking.

"Tomorrow, Celie. We'll talk tomorrow. After I've had a chance to sort things out."

Celie nodded, and they made their way back to Lady Cushing's music room.

She would have to wait until tomorrow…

But it wouldn't come fast enough.

Chapter 6

Jonah sat in the darkness and stared at the flames that whipped in the fireplace. His emotions roiled inside him with a fury that matched the flames. Each pop of the burning logs snapped at him like a harsh reprimand for tonight's foolish behavior.

Why the hell had he kissed her? Doing something so stupid had never been part of his plan. Now he'd jeopardized everything.

From the moment he received word that he was the new Earl of Haywood, he'd had one goal—to keep from losing Haywood Abbey. That was when he'd laid the foundation for what he had to do to pay the staggering debts his father and brother had left him.

An image of how Haywood Abbey looked before his father had allowed it to fall to ruin flashed before him. The grandeur of his family home when his grandfather was still alive tugged at him with affection. He loved Haywood Abbey more than his father or brother ever had and was desperate to bring it to its former glory.

He breathed a deep sigh. There was only one way to save the estate he loved. He had to marry someone who would come with a dowry massive enough to pay his astronomical debts.

But that someone was *not* going to be anyone related to the Duke of Hadleigh. It was *not* going to be Lady Cecelia Randolph. Paying court to her had never been part of his plan. Never!

He took a larger sip of the whiskey in his glass. If only he'd never given in to the temptation to exact a small amount of revenge the first night he'd seen her. If only he hadn't followed her outside the night of Lady Plimpton's ball. If only he hadn't talked to her and glimpsed how special she was.

His strategy from the beginning had been so simple and straightforward. He would make his way back into society. He would find and marry a bride who came with a large enough dowry to pay his debts. He would devote the remainder of his life to making Haywood Abbey profitable. His plan was perfect. Its success was guaranteed.

Until he'd met Lady Cecelia Randolph.

Approaching her had never been part of his plan. The less he had to do with the Duke of Hadleigh or anyone connected to him, the easier his life would be. Then he'd seen Hadleigh's sister leave the ballroom, and his desire to strike out at his enemy made him do something he knew would infuriate Hadleigh.

There wasn't much he could do to irritate his nemesis, but he had two things in his favor that he hadn't had three years ago: he wasn't a second son any longer, but was now the Earl of Haywood, and he'd returned home a war hero. Even Hadleigh's ducal influence couldn't force society to turn their backs on someone the Queen herself had decorated.

So, in an impulsive move, he followed her onto the terrace.

Of course Hadleigh would know he had. His enemy had followed every move he'd made all night.

Jonah remembered smiling inside when he thought of how furious Hadleigh would be when he realized that the man he hated more than anyone in the world was alone with his sister. He remembered how pleased he'd been when he found Lady Cecelia alone and started talking to her. How full of himself he'd been because, for the first time ever, he had the upper hand over Hadleigh.

But meeting Hadleigh's sister wasn't what he'd anticipated. He hadn't expected Lady Cecelia to be so intelligent and personable. He hadn't expected her to be so thoughtful and understanding. He hadn't expected to feel a connection to her and want to spend more time with her.

The afternoon they'd gone for a drive had been the most enjoyable afternoon he'd ever spent. And the most disturbing. The ease with which they conversed caused him to yearn more for her company. But when he left her at the Hadleigh town house he vowed he'd never seek her out again. He knew if he didn't stop the forward progress of this ill-fated relationship, her friendship would ruin everything. Hadleigh would see to it.

Then tonight he'd kissed her.

He rested his head on the back of the chair and called himself every kind of fool imaginable. What was wrong with him? Didn't he realize he'd lose everything if he allowed his emotions to control him? The feelings that erupted inside him when he held her in his arms, when he kissed her, were more intense than he thought any emotion could be.

Pursuing her was guaranteed to destroy him. And his plan to save Haywood Abbey.

He couldn't allow himself to continue down this path. If he did, he'd risk everything he needed to accomplish.

There was a limit to the harm Hadleigh could inflict as Jonah went forward with his goal to marry well and restore his family estate. But there was no limit to what Hadleigh would do if Jonah continued to pursue his sister.

Jonah didn't doubt Hadleigh would do everything in his power to destroy him. He'd vowed he would, and Jonah didn't doubt for one minute that he'd go through with his threat.

If only he could erase the memory of Hadleigh's sister from his mind. But how could he, when the time they'd spent together in Lady Cushing's garden earlier was the most memorable experience of his life? He only wished he hadn't lied to her, but he could hardly admit that seeking her out that first night had been a perfect way to repay Hadleigh for embarrassing him in front of the *ton* three years ago. He could hardly make the boast that he knew how much it would infuriate Hadleigh if he spent time alone with his sister. That he couldn't stop his desire to make him pay at least a little for the night he'd turned his back on him and the rest of society had followed suit.

But nothing after that had been planned. He'd kissed her tonight because the desire to kiss her had been as strong as the desire to take in air to breathe. He'd kissed her tonight because he could no more walk away without holding her and kissing her than a starving man could walk away from his next meal.

He closed his eyes and relived the kiss they'd shared. He'd kissed many willing women before, but their kisses had never been as powerful as Lady Cecelia's. The feel of her lips pressed to his rocked him to his very soul. He told himself he needed to walk away from her now, but feared it was already too late.

He sat in the darkness for several long minutes remembering the feel of her in his arms. Reliving the way she wrapped her arms around his neck and pulled him closer to her. His body reacted as violently as it had earlier in the evening.

He growled in frustration, then sat forward in his chair and listened to the voices in the foyer—loud voices, angry voices.

He waited.

The door slammed against the wall with a loud thud, and the Duke of Hadleigh stormed into the room.

"The Duke of Hadleigh to see you," Bundy said in a gasping voice. "I told him you weren't receiving—"

"And I told your butler I didn't give a damn," Hadleigh roared.

"How like you, Hadleigh," Jonah said, rising to his feet. "Come in. I've been expecting you."

Jonah nodded at his former sergeant—now butler. "Light some lamps, Bundy, then you may retire for the evening. I'll see His Grace out."

Bundy issued Hadleigh a severe glare, then lit several lamps and left.

The minute the door closed, Hadleigh took three menacing steps into the room. "You leave my sister the hell alone," he growled. "I don't want you anywhere near her."

"I'm sure you don't." He paused. "Unfortunately, your sister has indicated she doesn't feel the same way you do."

"I don't care what you think she's indicated. I don't want you near her."

"If you feel so strongly about this, perhaps it's your sister you should be talking to."

"Damn you!"

Jonah couldn't help but laugh out loud. "It must be terrible to have a sister as strong willed as you are. I imagine you find her nearly impossible to control."

"I'm warning you, Haywood—"

Jonah slashed his hand through the air. "Enough! You're done warning me. And I'm done listening to you. You've done your worst. There's nothing more you can do to me."

Hadleigh glared at him for several long, silent moments, then sucked in an angry breath. "You're doing this on purpose, aren't you? You're using my sister against me, trying to take Cecelia away from me just like you took Melisande."

A rage more intense than Jonah could control pummeled him from every side, and he threw his glass into the flickering fireplace. Glass shattered against the stones, and the whiskey flashed into wild, violent flames. "You fool! You were always blind where Melisande was concerned and still are!" Jonah glared at his enemy. "Taking your sister away from you would be fitting, though, wouldn't it? Courting her, then marrying her. There would be a certain amount of justice in repaying you for what you did to me three years ago."

Hadleigh's face reddened. "You'll never marry her. I'll never allow it!"

Jonah smiled. He couldn't help himself. "I hear Lady Cecelia comes with an amazing dowry."

"Then you hear wrong. My sister only comes with an amazing dowry if *I* approve of the man she marries. If I don't give my stamp of approval, she comes with *nothing*. *Nothing*! Do you hear?"

Jonah walked to the window and stared out into the ebony darkness beyond. "That does pose a problem, then, doesn't it, Your Grace? The question becomes what I consider more important. Marrying someone who will come with a massive enough dowry to pay my father's debts and save Haywood Abbey? Or sacrificing Haywood Abbey to marry Lady Cecelia? But one never knows. I might consider taking your sister from you repayment enough for what you did to me three years ago."

"What *I* did to *you*?"

Jonah spun from the window and faced Hadleigh. "Yes, what you did to me! You made me an outcast in society. You left me with no choice but to leave England because I was no longer welcome here. Because of you, I was gone when my father and brother died. Now, it's possible for you to get a small taste of my revenge." He paused to let Hadleigh realize the strength of his anger. "What would you do, Your Grace? What decision would you make if you were in my shoes?"

"Damn you, Haywood!"

"You've damned me enough, Your Grace. You've ruined enough of my life. It's time you realize what it was like to have all the choices taken from me, to have the power to do nothing except react to what your enemies do to you. I have spent every day since I returned trying to repair the damage *you* caused me and my reputation."

The two adversaries stared at each other for several tension-filled moments. Hadleigh's angry glare held countless unspoken threats that would have frightened anyone else to death. But Jonah knew him too well. He'd already lived through the worst his enemy could do to him. He'd never yield to his dominance or his threats again.

"Was there anything else you wanted to discuss with me?" Jonah asked, making sure his voice held a note of disinterest. "If not—"

"This isn't finished, Haywood. You haven't heard the last from me."

"Another threat, Your Grace? What more do I have for you to take?"

Another long silence stretched between them. Jonah refused to be the first to shift his gaze from his enemy's intense glare.

The Duke of Hadleigh finally broke the silence. "Stay away from my sister," he ordered through clenched teeth.

"I will if Lady Cecelia requests I do so. If not..." Jonah finished his thought with the shrug of his shoulders. "Now, I'm sure you can find your way to the door."

"You'll regret this, Haywood. I'll see that you do." With those words, the Duke of Hadleigh spun on his heel and left the room.

Jonah waited for the front door to slam shut and wasn't disappointed. He slowly made his way to his whiskey decanter and filled his glass. Bundy came into the room.

"Do you think it was wise to anger the duke like you did, Cap'n?" he asked.

Jonah took a large swallow and let the whiskey burn a path down his throat. "Probably not, Bundy. But the duke's hatred is like a powder keg with a lit fuse. His hatred for me is what keeps him alive."

"That's what worries me. What's going to keep *you* alive?"

"The most valuable lesson I learned from the war was not to let your enemy determine the time or the place to wage an attack. Hadleigh's going to attack. I prefer to make the decision as to when and where."

"How will you do that, my lord?"

"I won't, Bundy. Lady Cecelia will."

Jonah carried his glass to his chair and sat. "Go to bed now, Sergeant. I'll take care of things down here."

"See that you do, my lord. See that you do."

* * *

Hadleigh leaned forward and lifted the edge of the heavy velvet curtain at his carriage window. Its weight was designed to keep out the chill and prevent him from being observed as his carriage made its way across London. He stared out into the bleak darkness and watched the rain fall from the sky in huge drops. The heavens were weeping for his Melisande as they had time and again since her death.

Haywood had reentered his life to inflict more misery—as if he hadn't caused enough pain.

A dreary dampness covered the streets and collected in the gutters. The night fit his mood. It helped him plot his revenge. Haywood would pay for what he'd done. And this time, his payment would cost him everything.

Hadleigh let the curtain fall back into place. He regretted he couldn't drink a toast to celebrate Haywood's demise, to the complete and total annihilation of everything

Haywood held dear—the estates, his home, his reputation, and his future. Everything but his life.

He should want Haywood dead, but he didn't. He wanted his enemy to live. To live an empty existence. To live without hope for a future. To live without love.

The blackguard thought he stood a chance of winning Cecelia's heart. Well, he didn't. Cecelia was no doubt only enjoying his company because he'd once been a friend and she was too kindhearted to cast him off—although he was surprised she'd accepted his attentions as long as she had. She usually cast aside every male suitor long before now. But she would soon. She'd react to his suit the same as she reacted to every other man's attentions. She'd ignore him as if he had the plague. She'd put him in his place the moment she realized his intent.

Until then, though, perhaps he could use her to assist him in his plan to ruin Haywood.

He sat back against the squabs and smiled. Perhaps he should encourage his sister to continue her association with Haywood until he could lure the bastard into his trap.

His mind suddenly wrapped around a plan, and all the pieces fell into place. All he had to do was make sure his sister didn't cast Haywood aside for a few more weeks. All he had to do was make Haywood think he was making progress with his sister.

Hell, he might even enjoy watching the scoundrel think he was gaining ground in his attempt to get a wife with a large enough dowry to pay the staggering amount he owed. Of course, he wouldn't for one second seriously consider Haywood as his future brother-in-law.

He wanted to laugh at the thought. There was no way he'd give Cecelia into that murderer's hands. But if Haywood thought there was a chance…

Hadleigh outlined every possibility, considered every detail that could go wrong. In the end, though, Haywood's total demise outweighed any risk he would take. Only Cecelia's involvement gave him the slightest pause.

He suffered a twinge of guilt at the thought that she might discover how he'd used her. But she was the perfect pawn. Haywood had already made his intentions known. And for some reason he didn't understand, his sister hadn't rejected Haywood as quickly as she rejected other suitors. But she would. If he weren't so sure she would tire of Haywood, he wouldn't consider using her in his plan for revenge.

But in the meantime, he'd watch over her to make sure she didn't get hurt. When she discovered Haywood only wanted her for her dowry, she'd thank him for interfering in her future. She'd be grateful that he'd saved her from ruining her life. She'd agree that Melisande's murderer needed to be destroyed.

Chapter 7

"Do you think Lord Haywood will be here tonight?" Amanda asked when Celie met her amidst the crowd of operagoers. The crush of people moved slowly as they began their ascent up the winding staircase to take their seats in the upper boxes.

"Yes, he'll be here because I told him we were going to attend tonight."

"That doesn't mean you'll see him or get to talk to him," Amanda said, searching the latecomers walking through the entryway with the same diligence as Celie.

"Yes, it does. I've invited Lord Haywood to join us in Hadleigh's box."

The shocked look on Amanda's face caused the butterflies in Celie's stomach to flutter nervously.

Before she could say anything in her defense, Amanda's expression turned serious. She none too gently grabbed Celie's arm and led her to one of the alcoves tucked into the wall at either end of the long hallway beneath the stairway. "You didn't!" she said, pulling Celie down beside her on the paisley-cushioned bench. "Does your brother know?"

"No, and unless you tell him, he'll probably never find out." Celie smiled nervously. "He had an important committee meeting to attend and said he wouldn't be able to make it to tonight's performance."

"You don't think he'll hear about it?" Amanda asked.

Celie tried to ignore the frustration she heard in her friend's voice. "Of course he'll hear about it. But by the time he does, it will be over and there won't be anything he can do about it."

Amanda gave a loud guffaw. "You know your brother better than that, Celie. It will never be too late for him to react to something the Earl of Haywood does. And this is definitely something that will cause him to take action."

Celie tried to watch for Haywood, but Amanda had the view blocked.

"Is he here yet?" Celie asked, feeling a little more nervous than she had earlier in the day when she'd convinced herself she was finished allowing her brother to control where she went and who she saw.

Now she wasn't so sure this was the wisest move she could have made. Especially after the argument they'd had earlier and Hadleigh's demand that she avoid the Earl of Haywood.

Amanda looked at the entrance as the door opened and closed to admit any newcomers. "Not yet. But if he intends to come, he'll be here soon, or he'll miss the first act."

"He'll be here. He sent a note saying he would."

"You're pretty sure of him, aren't you?"

"I have no reason not to be," she answered. She was sure of him, in more ways than even Amanda realized.

"The two of you are causing quite a stir, you know. Not only because of the long time the two of you spent alone in Lady Cushing's garden the other night, but you've been seen riding through Hyde Park together nearly every afternoon since. Then, last night, everyone noticed he chose you as his dinner partner at Lady Rossely's ball."

Celie tried to avoid looking Amanda in the eyes. She knew if she did, her best friend would see more than Celie intended.

Her tactic didn't work.

"Celie, look at me."

Celie hesitated, then slowly lifted her chin.

"Oh, blast it all." Amanda's eyes were as round as saucers. "How could you?"

Celie was shocked. "How could I what?"

"I mean, we're not talking about just anyone, you realize. We're talking about the Earl of Haywood."

"Just what is wrong with the Earl of Haywood?"

Celie was prepared to be angry with her best friend, but couldn't when she replied, "Nothing. Absolutely nothing, except…"

Celie waited for Amanda to continue.

"Except, what?"

"Celie, he's your brother's most bitter enemy. Nothing good will come of an association with him. Besides, I thought there was a secret love you've always dreamed you'd—"

Amanda's eyes opened even wider. "Oh," she whispered as if she had a difficult time saying even that much.

"Don't read anything into this, Amanda. I simply enjoy Lord Haywood's company. I simply—"

"You've fallen in love with him, haven't you?" Amanda peeked around the corner of the alcove to make sure no one was close enough to overhear their conversation.

"I haven't fallen in love with him," Celie started to deny, but Amanda stopped her from finishing.

"Of course you haven't *fallen* in love with him, because you've always *been* in love with him."

Celie cleared her throat. "I admit I've always considered Lord Haywood very appealing."

"That's an understatement considering the way you've always talked about the man of your dreams. And now I know why!"

"You think he's special, too, don't you?"

"I think he's *very* special. So special, in fact, that your association with him may cause your brother to disown you."

Celie wanted to tell Amanda that Hadleigh would never do that—except she wasn't sure. She wanted to tell Amanda that she thought Hadleigh had changed since Jonah had returned—except the opposite seemed to be true. She wanted to tell Amanda that she didn't care if her brother disowned her—except she did. She had to… because her dowry was probably the only reason Jonah was paying her such attention.

Everyone knew his father and brother had left him a staggering amount of debts. Rumors circulated since he'd returned that his first order of business, as soon as he was well enough to leave his bed, was to find a bride with a large enough dowry to save him from losing all his entailed property. Who was there in all of London with a larger dowry than she?

"Hadleigh will never disown me," she said with a greater amount of confidence than she felt.

"He probably won't," Amanda said, leaning forward for a better view of the operagoers entering the theater, "because one of them will be dead after the duel they'll fight when your brother arrives to find Haywood alone with his sister."

"Oh, don't be ridiculous," Celie said, praying that wasn't a possibility. "Hadleigh won't be here, and even if he comes, I won't be alone. You'll be there."

Amanda rolled her eyes. "Oh, that will certainly help. He's always considered me your partner in crime. All that's saved me from being banned from existence is that he can't quite figure out which one of us is the mastermind behind all our schemes."

"Yes, he can," Celie said, trying to add a little humor. "He knows it's you."

"Well, if he does..." Amanda said, peeking around the opening once more. She gave a little squeal, then pulled back inside and pressed her back against the wall. "If he has any doubts as to which one of us is the worst, then neither of us is likely to survive the night."

Celie swallowed hard. Amanda's eyes filled with terror and her lips pressed tight as if clamping them together was the only way she could hold back her scream. "Why?"

"Because your brother is here," she said, pulling back into the alcove. "He is standing in the middle of the lobby talking to Lord Riverton and his wife."

"Damn!" Celie sucked in a shaky breath. "He told me he wouldn't be here."

"Well, he is." Amanda looked back out to the lobby. "And so is Lord Haywood. He's right behind him."

"Oh." Celie clamped her hand over her mouth to stifle a moan. Or a scream of horror.

"Now what?"

"How should I know?" Celie said as the panic inside her bubbled until she thought she might be ill.

"I suggest you go out to face the music," Amanda said.

Celie tried to come up with a solution that would keep her from having to face the two at the same time. If she could just get Hadleigh off by himself, she might have a chance to plead with him to behave and not cause a scene. But she didn't know how she could manage that if the two were in the lobby together.

No, on second thought, she might stand a better chance if she told Hadleigh she'd invited Lord Haywood while His Grace was surrounded by the esteemed members of the *ton*, several of whom he'd have to face in the House tomorrow morning. She would rely on his pride to stop him from making a scene.

Celie took a shaky breath and rose to her feet. "All right. Let's go."

"What's this *let's* term? If you think I'm going to accompany you—"

"Of course you're going to accompany me. You're my best friend. You're my—"

"*I'm* going to visit the retiring room. I'll probably need to be there for at least thirty minutes. Or until the shouting stops."

"You wouldn't!" Her desperation must have been transparent because a harsh breath rushed from Amanda's mouth and her shoulders sagged in resignation.

"All right. But you owe me, Celie, and I'm going to collect someday!"

"Yes. Yes! Now let's get out there. You just divert Hadleigh. Keep him from killing me. And from killing Lord Haywood."

Celie couldn't believe the word that came from Amanda's mouth when she walked out of the small alcove. Someday she'd have to ask her what that particular term meant.

They walked through the lobby toward where Hadleigh and Jonah stood. They were barely an arm's length away from one another.

Celie knew this was going to be one of the longest nights of her life. She prayed all of them survived until morning.

* * *

Jonah had assumed when Celie invited him to sit in their box for the opera that Hadleigh either wouldn't be in attendance or that he knew about it and she'd somehow forced him to agree. But one glance at the surprised look on Hadleigh's face when they entered the theater at the same time told Jonah his presence was not only a surprise but an unpleasant one.

Jonah envisioned the sight of Cecelia and him together was as pleasant as salt poured onto an open wound. A nagging sense of doom settled over him as he swore under his breath and prepared to endure a torturous evening.

Until it was over, he'd take pleasure in the fact that his presence had the power to put a scowl of immense magnitude on Hadleigh's face tonight.

He stepped forward when he saw Celie and her friend walk toward him from the other side of the lobby and smiled.

There was nothing insincere about his smile. Celie did that to him—turned his insides warm. Bloody hell, but she was unique. Every time he looked at her, he wanted to touch her, hold her. Kiss her.

"Lady Amanda. Lady Cecelia. Good evening."

"Good evening, Lord Haywood," Lady Amanda and Celie said in unison.

"Hadleigh."

"Haywood, I wasn't aware you were joining us tonight."

Jonah arched his brows in what he hoped was a condescending gesture. "Weren't you?"

"No, I wasn't." He cast a severe look in his sister's direction.

"Have you seen *La Traviata* before, Your Grace?" Lady Amanda said, forcing Hadleigh to shift his glare from his sister.

Facing his sister's friend did little to improve his disposition.

"No, but I am familiar with Verdi's works. I attended his *Rigoletto* last year when I traveled to Italy."

Hadleigh turned back to his sister to make another comment, but Lady Amanda prevented anything he intended to say by asking him another question.

"Were you as impressed with *Rigoletto* as the rest of Europe seems to have been?"

Hadleigh gave Lady Amanda an aristocratic look of boredom that would have sent most young ladies in society running for cover, but it didn't seem to bother Lady Amanda in the least.

"Actually, no. I wasn't impressed. I find Verdi far too emotional for my taste."

Lady Amanda gave him a smile that didn't at all resemble humor, but something near to condescension. Her words confirmed it. "Why doesn't that surprise me?" she said in what didn't seem at all to be a question.

Jonah sensed a fury building in Hadleigh. It was obvious that Lady Amanda was diverting Hadleigh's attention intentionally, and the idea that she was playing mediator struck him as humorous. How very brave of her. Or foolish.

"Did you enjoy *Rigoletto,* Lady Amanda?" Jonah asked, admiring her courage.

"Actually, I did. Very much. I find certain of his arias heart-wrenchingly passionate. But then, I've been told the fact that I have a heart exposes me to such emotions."

"As opposed to people who supposedly don't have hearts?" Hadleigh growled between clenched teeth.

Lady Amanda's face lit in a gleaming smile. "I think you understand perfectly."

The two men glared at each other for several long seconds; then Hadleigh turned his gaze to Amanda. She simply shrugged her shoulders and smiled. Jonah wanted to laugh out loud but knew such a reaction would only add more fuel to the explosive situation.

Hadleigh quickly returned his attention to Lady Amanda as if he refused to allow her the last word. But it was already too late. Celie's friend was expounding on the beauty of Verdi's other works.

Jonah chose to ignore the hostility emanating from the two. Why should he waste any of his energy worrying about the Duke of Hadleigh when he had the opportunity to spend several hours sitting next to Celie?

"May I escort you to your brother's box?" he said, extending his arm for her to take.

She smiled and placed her hand atop his.

His heart did a somersault before settling back into place.

"I should probably explain about my brother," she began, but he stopped her.

"There's no need. I've known him equally as long as you and am as aware of what drives his emotions as anyone."

"You mean Melisande," she said, looking back to where her friend still had Hadleigh trapped in conversation.

Jonah followed her gaze back to Hadleigh and Lady Amanda and thought that the discussion between the two looked as if it were turning more…confrontational.

"Yes, Melisande."

"Everything always returns to Melisande, doesn't it?"

"Yes, somehow she's able to reach out from the grave and cause trouble."

"Speaking of Melisande," she said. "I intended to warn you about something."

Jonah paused en route to the staircase. "Warn me?"

"Yes, concerning Melisande's mother. If you happen to attend the same function, please take care to avoid her. Since Melisande's death, she's lost her grasp of reality."

He regretted hearing that. Lady Kendall had idolized Melisande as much as Hadleigh had. He didn't doubt that she had difficulties adjusting to her daughter's death.

Celie continued. "At Lady Farthington's ball, she insisted Melisande had come with them and refused to leave until Melisande was ready to go home. Lord Kendall finally convinced his wife that Melisande had already left."

A heavy weight pressed against his chest. So much had happened as a result of that night. So many people were still affected by Melisande's actions. Jonah wondered when it would end. *If* it would ever end.

"Thank you for the warning," he said. "I appreciate your concern.

She smiled at him, and he led her across the lobby, then up the winding staircase.

Several people took note of them as they made their way to Hadleigh's private box. It was impossible to avoid the stares.

"Does it bother you that people watch us," Jonah asked, feeling her fingers tighten against his arm.

"No. Does it you?"

Jonah laughed. "No. Why would it bother me?"

"Because I'm sure everyone is questioning why you are with me."

"Why would anyone question that?"

She was uncomfortable, and Jonah knew she was struggling to find the right words.

"Everyone knows there are many other eligible females who would come without the problems associated with me."

"You mean the problems associated with your brother."

"Yes. Everyone is aware of the hostility between you." She paused. "Up ahead," she said, keeping a smile on her face that hid the seriousness in her voice, "are Camile and Rosalind Attkisson. They are both very beautiful and will come with huge dowries when they marry."

"The reason you are telling me this is because?"

"Because they are confused as to why you are with me instead of one of them."

"Should we approach them so I can explain my reasons for preferring your company to anyone else's?"

Her eyes opened wide as if she weren't sure whether or not he was serious; then she hurried her steps toward Hadleigh's box. She obviously didn't want to take the chance that he was.

"I take it your answer is no."

He opened the door, and she rushed inside. He followed after her.

"Do you realize," he said, stopping her from going past the velvet curtain that separated the entryway from the padded chairs at the front of the box, "that tonight is the second time you've questioned my motives for wanting to be with you."

"Oh, I'm not questioning your motives," she said in a reassuring tone. "It's the rest of society that can't understand why you prefer my company to anyone else's."

"Perhaps they know perfectly well why I want to be with you but are watching in fascination to see if you want to be with me." Jonah took a step toward her, waiting to see if she'd step away from him. She didn't.

"Why wouldn't I want to be with you?"

He stepped closer. "There are many reasons."

Jonah couldn't stop himself. The whole situation was too enticing—the flickering glow of the candles, the murmur of hundreds of voices from the seats below them, the feeling of seeing but not being seen, the danger of being discovered by Celie's brother.

"Remind me to explain them to you. Later."

Jonah braced his foot against the door for a second's warning to keep someone looking for Hadleigh from barging in on them, then lowered his head and kissed her.

She responded quickly and passionately, returning his kiss with an intensity that caused his emotions to soar.

He hadn't kissed her since that first time, and she melted in his arms, pressing her lush form against him.

The moment she wrapped her arms around his neck to give more of herself to him, he knew he wasn't remembering their first kiss correctly at all.

He thought their other kiss had been the most powerful kiss in which he'd ever been engaged, but he knew it hadn't been. This kiss was. Holding her in his arms, feeling her next to him. He'd never experienced anything like it.

Their first kiss hadn't been nearly so overwhelming. Not like this kiss was.

Even though he didn't kiss her nearly as long as he had before, something in their joining was more emotional, more powerful. More remarkable.

Jonah kissed her one last time, then pulled away when he heard Hadleigh's voice outside the doorway.

"Take a chair, Celie. In the second row. That one. We'll leave the front row for your brother and Lady Amanda."

Celie quickly took the chair he indicated, and he watched her struggle to calm her breathing. He was seated in the chair beside her when the door opened and Hadleigh and Lady Amanda entered. Their conversation didn't seem any friendlier.

"Do they always argue like that?" Jonah whispered, leaning close to Celie.

"Yes. I've never seen any two people get along less well."

Hadleigh escorted Lady Amanda to the front of the box but turned back to face Jonah and Cecelia. His expression seemed about as cordial as a wild boar with a sore tooth.

"You shouldn't have come up without us," he said to his sister in a scolding tone.

Cecelia looked at her brother with the most innocent expression Jonah had ever seen.

"Why ever not?" she said. "I was perfectly safe with Lord Haywood."

"Safety has nothing to do with it, Cecelia, as well you know. It's what people will say. From now on, wait until you're properly chaperoned. Now, would you care to sit in front with your friend?" Hadleigh indicated the chair beside where he'd deposited Lady Amanda.

Cecelia shook her head. "I'm quite comfortable where I am, Hadleigh. I wouldn't want to deprive you and Amanda of discussing the opera as it progresses, since you have such varying opinions of Verdi's works."

"I think His Grace and I have reached an impasse as far as being able to agree on Verdi's talents," Lady Amanda said.

The tone of her voice was not at all amiable, and Jonah couldn't help but feel a great amount of humor in the scene.

Hadleigh must strongly dislike Lady Amanda if he preferred to spend the evening in a chair next to Haywood rather than beside Celie's friend.

Jonah nearly laughed out loud. He suddenly realized that, even if *La Traviata* were the worst opera ever performed, he would enjoy it tremendously just knowing that Hadleigh was so miserable.

"We saved you a front-row chair, Hadleigh," he said, settling back in his chair. "Sit down. They're snuffing the lanterns. The opera is about to begin."

Hadleigh had no choice but to take his seat beside Lady Amanda.

Jonah smiled at the perfect positioning of Hadleigh's chair in relationship to where he and Lady Cecelia sat. If the duke wanted to keep an eagle's eye on his sister, he was forced to turn his head in Lady Amanda's direction.

He quickly found out that, every time he did, Lady Amanda turned toward him, and their gazes locked, each flashing with fiery anger.

Hadleigh chose to watch the performance.

Jonah smiled as he placed his arm across the back of Celie's chair.

The evening was perfect.

Chapter 8

Last night's opera had been perfect. He hadn't been able to escort Celie home, but he'd spent several pleasant hours in her company. The knowledge that Hadleigh hated every minute of the evening made the night even more special.

Jonah sat alone at the table in the club he'd recently joined and considered the events of the night before. He shouldn't take such pleasure in Hadleigh's irritation, but he couldn't help it. Hadleigh's discomfort eased a little of the anger that appeared every time the two were in close proximity.

Jonah relaxed into his chair and let a peaceful calm settle over him. This time of day was usually quiet here, and he found he preferred it to the more fashionable hours when most of the tables were full. He could think more clearly, could sort through the confusing path his life had taken.

So many things had happened that would have been impossible three years ago.

When he'd first applied for membership, he wasn't sure he'd be accepted, but his position was different now. Not only did he hold a title, but he'd returned from the war with a reputation of sorts. It was also possible that word of his close association with the Duke of Hadleigh's sister helped pave the way for him. He wondered what would happen if and when he no longer paid her court.

He tipped the full bottle that sat on his table and put a small amount of the exquisite brandy in his glass. He took a long swallow as memory of the kiss they'd shared replayed in his mind. He hadn't anticipated Cecelia to affect him like she did. The reaction from her kiss had been a thousand times more powerful than he'd anticipated it would be. His body's reaction took him completely by surprise.

When he'd felt her fingers skiff through his hair, he thought he might lose control. He'd wanted her more at that moment than he'd ever wanted any woman before in his life. He still wanted her more than he'd wanted any woman before. His greatest fear was that this feeling wouldn't lessen, but increase with every day that passed.

He took another swallow of brandy, then shifted uncomfortably in his chair. He needed a cold bath. "Hell," he muttered beneath his breath. He needed a woman. He'd been without one too long. That's all that was the matter with him.

Perhaps when he left here, he'd seek out one of Madam Genevieve's most expensive girls. Maybe afterward, remembering the kiss he'd shared with Cecelia wouldn't seem so life altering.

He set his glass down on the table and breathed an agonizing sigh. He wouldn't seek out one of Madam Genevieve's girls. What made him think a stranger could make what he'd shared with Cecelia any less earth-shattering?

He moved his glass from left to right as he considered what was happening. His plan wasn't going at all like he'd thought it would. He'd intended to pay her court once or twice—just often enough for Hadleigh to take note and demand he never approach his sister again. His intent had been to irritate Hadleigh, then abandon his pursuit of his sister in search of a bride with a large enough dowry to provide him with the money he needed to cover his debts.

Finding a bride who would come with a large dowry was essential. Unfortunately, for as much as Lady Cecelia consumed his dreams both day and night, a future with her wasn't possible. Hadleigh would never allow anything to develop between them. And if they went against his wishes, Cecelia would come to him penniless.

He shoved his glass away from him and sat back in his chair. He was destitute. As things stood now, he didn't know how much longer he could support himself, let alone a wife. Let alone a lady, the daughter of a duke and duchess.

He swallowed the last of his brandy, then slid back his chair to leave.

"Sit down, Haywood. We need to talk."

Jonah slowly lifted his gaze to meet Hadleigh's firm glare. Neither moved for several long moments, then Jonah slid closer to the table. "I didn't know you were a member here, Hadleigh. If I had, I wouldn't have—"

"I'm not. I'm here to see you."

Hadleigh pulled out a chair. When he was seated, a waiter placed a glass in front of him and filled it with brandy. Hadleigh slowly lifted the glass and drank.

Jonah stretched his long legs out in a relaxed manner and waited. There was obviously something on Hadleigh's mind, but Jonah wasn't going to beg to hear what it was.

The duke took another swallow, then set his glass down. "I want to know your intentions."

"Intentions? Are you talking about Lady Cecelia?"

His gaze narrowed. "You know damn well that's who I'm talking about. How long do you intend to let her believe you enjoy her company?"

Jonah let a broad smile cover his face. "Do you find it so impossible that I find it pleasurable to be with her?"

"Don't play me for the fool, Haywood. The only reason you take pleasure in being with her is because you know I find your attentions to her disgusting. You wouldn't give her a second glance if she weren't my sister."

"Oh, Hadleigh. What a low opinion you have of your sister."

"The only person deserving my low opinion is you, Haywood. You have poisoned my sister's mind the same as you poisoned Melisande's. If I allow you to associate with Cecelia, you'll destroy her the same as you destroy every woman with whom you associate."

A bolt of rage shattered inside him. "What happened to Melisande has nothing to do with my association with your sister."

Hadleigh's glare turned more irate. "Everything you think, everything you touch, every action you make is connected to what happened to Melisande and will have the same fatal results."

Jonah met Hadleigh's glare and held it. He refused to be the first to look away. Refused to be the first to yield. He was tired of being blamed for what happened that night.

Except he knew Hadleigh would never believe the truth.

With his gaze still leveled with his enemy's, he lifted his glass. "Why are you here?" he demanded, looking over the rim.

"Why do you think I've come?"

Jonah took a swallow, then lowered his glass. "My guess is that you are here to see me because you attempted to forbid your sister from seeing me and she refused." Jonah pushed his glass on the table as if it were a chess piece. "What's your next move, Hadleigh?"

Jonah felt the growing anger and bitterness build inside Hadleigh. Loathing and resentment swirled around him like a living, breathing monster. The hatred that had been a part of his life for so long was so intense Jonah doubted Hadleigh was able to think without animosity souring his thoughts.

Finally, Hadleigh loosened his tightly fisted hands and leveled Jonah with a narrowed glare. "I've already lost Melisande. I refuse to let you take Cecelia from me, too."

"I took no one from you," Jonah said through clenched teeth. "Melisande alone was responsible for what happened that night. And if you lose Lady Cecelia, it will be because of your own doing."

Hadleigh pressed his lips together as if he didn't trust what words might pass through them if he opened them. Jonah wondered what profanities would spew forth if he did. Enough time finally passed before he could speak.

"I have chosen to give Cecelia enough time to see your true colors for herself. I've chosen to let her discover your dark nature on her own. Like you said, she's an intelligent individual. It won't take her long to discover the wretch you are."

Jonah evaluated Hadleigh's words. He tried to accept them at face value, but that was difficult. Hatred had bound Hadleigh and him together for so long that Jonah found it inconceivable to think his archenemy was offering his sister such an open rein. That he was offering Jonah a truce of sorts. He hated him too much.

"If you lose your sister, it won't be because of anything I do."

"If I lose my sister, it will be because you have stolen her from me. It will be because you think so little of her that you will use her to exact your revenge upon me. Nothing is beyond what you will do. You've already proven that. But I am warning you..."

Hadleigh leaned forward. The fury written in his eyes would have caused a weaker man to stagger backward.

Jonah answered his glare with one of his own.

"If you so much as cause my sister one minute of heartache, there will be no lengths to which I won't go to destroy you."

Jonah clamped his teeth together so hard his jaw ached from the pressure. It was all he could do to keep from leaping across the table and knocking Hadleigh to the floor. It was all he could do to keep from pummeling his fist into Hadleigh's smug, condescending expression. All he could do to keep from beating his archenemy to a bloody pulp.

"Don't you dare threaten me, Hadleigh. You have no power over me."

"No, but I do over Cecelia. Or at least what you can gain by pursuing her."

Jonah studied the sadistic expression on Hadleigh's face.

"You think my sister is the answer to your problems, but she isn't. You are penniless, Haywood. Your father and brother spent every pound on which they could lay their hands. They left you without even a solid roof over your head."

Jonah tried to keep the edge of fury from his voice but knew he'd failed. "My finances, or lack thereof, are my concern. Not yours."

"They're mine when you involve my sister in your misbegotten plan to save what your father nearly lost." Hadleigh lowered his voice when he spoke. "You are destitute. All of London knows it. You have no choice but to marry a female who will come with a large enough dowry to cover your debts and repair your dilapidated Haywood Abbey."

Jonah's temper burned hotter. "Is that why you're here? Do you think you can offer me enough money to cut my association with your sister?"

Hadleigh focused on the brandy in his glass for several long moments. With an unsteady hand, he picked it up and took a drink. "You have no idea how I wish that's exactly what I could do," he said when he'd lowered the glass. "But Cecelia would hate me forever when she discovered I paid you to abandon her. And she *would* find out. I'm not enough of a fool to think she wouldn't. I have no choice but to pray that, in time, Cecelia will discover what kind of wretch you are for herself."

Jonah leaned back in his chair and crossed his arms over his chest. "Just how do you intend to do that?"

"By giving you exactly what you need."

Jonah tried to look relaxed, but he wasn't. His insides churned with confusion. Then with rage. "I don't remember having asked for anything. And if I needed something, believe me, you would be the last person I would turn to."

"I don't doubt that is true, but in this, you have no choice. I refuse to allow the person with whom my sister is foolishly enamored to owe every merchant and gaming establishment in London massive amounts of money. I am tired of hearing the comments that my sister means nothing more to you than the means to pay your debts. I will, therefore, take care of any debts you owe so that particular belief discontinues to circulate."

A tidal wave of rage raced through Jonah. "I won't take money from you."

The muscles twitched in Hadleigh's jaw. "You will. Because if you don't, it will only be a matter of hours before every creditor to whom you owe money is pounding on your door. I will see to it that they are. And that they continue to do so until you are so publicly humiliated that you can't show your face."

The rage inside Jonah intensified.

"You will also begin restoration on Haywood Abbey—immediately. If by some remote chance Cecelia does not realize what a poor excuse for a man you truly are, I refuse to think that she might be forced to live in a home as dilapidated and in need of repair as your country estate."

Jonah felt such furor inside he wasn't sure he could control the emotion. He wanted to tell Hadleigh to take his pompous self-assurance with him to the grave—but he couldn't. He, too, had overheard the comments that the only reason he paid attention to Cecelia was because of the dowry that would come with her hand. He'd heard the rumors that suggested he didn't find anything remarkable about her but had *settled* on her because of her worth. And because paying court to her infuriated Hadleigh more than anything he could do.

The first time he heard the rumors, he was filled with rage. How could anyone not realize what a unique female she was? Or that they could believe he would use her for revenge? It angered him that no one saw how special she was.

Because of his association with her, he was being handed a golden opportunity to save everything his father had almost lost. He'd be a fool to allow his pride to refuse Hadleigh's offer.

But something stopped him from agreeing too readily. A little voice deep inside him warned him that Hadleigh's offer was too good to be true. That although there didn't seem to be a price tag associated with his offer, there was. And the cost would be more than he could pay. That, in the end, he would lose everything.

"Why are you doing this?"

Hadleigh laughed. "Don't look to find anything noble in my offer. You won't. Just the opposite. I am hoping my sister will come to her senses and realize what a poor choice you are. If that happens, any amount of money I throw in your direction will have been well spent. Until she does, however, I have no choice but to give you and your pursuit of her at least a small amount of credibility."

Jonah thought of what he was being offered and wanted to jump at the chance to begin anew. Paying his creditors would be a huge weight off his back. Several of them had already sent their bills with threatening notes attached. If he didn't accept Hadleigh's offer, the threats and demands would only get worse.

Yet Hadleigh was the last person from whom he'd accept anything. Even food if he were starving.

Thankfully, when he opened his mouth, his pride controlled his words. "Take your money and go to hell, Hadleigh. I want no part of it—or of you."

Jonah knew Hadleigh as well as anyone. He was prepared to hear Hadleigh rant at his foolishness, then watch him storm from the room. That's what the friend he'd grown up with would have done. The man sitting across the table, however, simply leaned back in his chair and smiled.

"I have to admit you surprised me, Haywood. I expected you to jump at the chance to cover your debts."

"Then you underestimate how badly I want to avoid being in your debt. I have no desire to have anything to do with you or with your money."

Hadleigh's malicious smile broadened. "I'm afraid you're going to be very disappointed, then." Hadleigh reached into his jacket pocket and pulled out a stack of neatly folded papers. With deliberate care, he unfolded them and slid them across the table.

Jonah's initial inclination was to ignore them, as if Hadleigh hadn't so painstakingly placed them before him. But he'd never been one to turn away from oncoming danger. And no one was more dangerous than the Duke of Hadleigh.

Jonah picked up the papers and turned them in his hand. There were several of them, each sheet containing long lists of business names with an amount next to them. At first, he didn't realize what they were, but upon closer scrutiny, he recognized them as the creditors to whom his father and brother owed money.

"You aren't showing me anything I haven't already seen, Hadleigh. I know who these men are and how much I owe them."

"*Owed*, Haywood. These are the debts I have already covered for you. There are more, of course. Your father and brother were quite practiced at purchasing items for which they couldn't pay. My man of business is in the process of collecting the remainder of your debts and will take care of those in the next few days."

Jonah saw red. "You bloody bastard," he growled, slapping the papers onto the table. "You had no right."

Hadleigh leaned forward, the haughty disdain in his gaze enough to turn Jonah's stomach. "I didn't do this for you," he hissed through clenched teeth. "I wouldn't lift a finger to help you. I did this for Cecelia. I refuse to allow you to embarrass her or me with the string of debts you owe all over London."

"I didn't ask for your help, and I won't accept it."

Hadleigh's gaze turned more livid. "Not only will you accept what I've already done, but you will accept more from me. My man of business has opened an account in your name. You will gather the supplies you need and begin work immediately to restore Haywood Abbey."

Blood pounded in Jonah's head, the thundering crash of his fury more intense than it had ever been. "Go to—"

Hadleigh slammed his fist against the table. "I've had enough of your disregard for my sister, Haywood. Now, I'm giving you a choice. If you respect her at all, you will accept my offer. Either that or you will give up your pursuit of Cecelia and never bother her again."

Hadleigh leaned forward. "You may think my sister will solve your monetary problems, but she won't. The amount everyone speculates my sister is worth will only come with her when she marries if *I* approve of her husband. If I don't approve of the man she chooses to marry, she will bring with her very little in the way of a dowry. Not nearly what you need to pay your creditors."

Jonah couldn't find the words to say. He didn't know what he should say. Nothing seemed adequate.

"My greatest fear is that she'll be blind to the reprehensible creature you are and choose to marry you with or without my consent—with or without her dowry."

He kept his focus leveled on Jonah. "Repairing the dilapidated condition of your estate will at least provide her with a decent home in which to live. Paying off your father's and brother's creditors will provide me the assurance that, in a year's time, my sister will not be living on the street."

Hadleigh's hands tightened to fists. "If you care for my sister at all, you will accept my offer to cover your debts. Doing so will indicate that you are at least a small degree more responsible than your father and brother. However, if you find my gesture so revolting that you cannot accept it, then walk away from my sister and leave her alone. If you do, I'll give you whatever time you need to repay the amount for the debts I covered."

Jonah's heart stuttered in his chest. Blood pounded against his ears. He considered everything Hadleigh was offering him. He thought of how desperately he wanted to save the estate that had been in his family for several generations, how long the tenants working the land had gone without because of his father's gaming and poor management. But even those reasons weren't the most important. What mattered most was the threat of never seeing Celie again. Of never enjoying her company. Of never holding her in his arms, or sitting next to her, or… kissing her.

He wasn't strong enough to walk away from her. He wanted her too badly. If either of them walked away from what was developing between them, she would be the one to make that choice. He couldn't.

Jonah breathed a heavy sigh, then pushed himself out of his chair and walked to a spot far enough from where Hadleigh sat so he could think. He braced his legs wide and locked his hands behind his back. He stared at the burgundy-and-gold stripes on the paper on the walls but didn't really focus on it.

Could he do this? Could he align himself with the man who'd turned him into a social outcast and made his life a living hell? Could he live with himself once he took money from a man he hated nearly as much as Hadleigh hated him?

"Walk away from her now," Hadleigh said from behind him. "Either drop your pursuit of her or accept my help."

Every conceivable outcome raced through his mind. Accepting anything from Hadleigh was the most reprehensible thought imaginable. Giving Celie up was as impossible.

"You'll lose it all without my help, Haywood. You are the last Haywood heir. The Crown will take it when you cannot pay the debts your father and brother amassed."

Jonah dropped his head back and tried to tell himself none of that mattered—but it did. Only not as much as knowing he would lose Celie if he refused.

He took a painful breath and turned. He didn't have a choice, not really. Not if he couldn't give up Celie. Not if he wanted what was developing between them to continue to grow.

Jonah breathed a submissive sigh, then turned. "Inform your solicitor that I expect an itemized list of every pound it takes to cover my debts. You will have it all returned to you with interest."

"My man of business will be to see you when everything is taken care of."

Jonah told himself there wasn't a glimmer of satisfaction in Hadleigh's eyes, but the shiver that ran up and down his spine warned him that he'd walked into a trap Hadleigh had set for him.

Even though he knew he had no choice in what he had to do, the move to accept money from Hadleigh made him sick.

"If you will excuse me," Jonah said, taking a step to the door. "I doubt that you and I have anything more to say to each other."

Without waiting for Hadleigh's final remark, Jonah left his club and walked down the street. He didn't signal for a hack to take him home but walked the several blocks instead. He needed to think. Needed to consider the dangers he'd put himself in by accepting what Hadleigh had done for him.

And he needed to evaluate what it meant that it had been less of a risk to sell his soul to the devil than to never see Cecelia Randolph again.

* * *

Hadleigh remained at Haywood's club long after his mortal enemy left. He filled his glass from the bottle of excellent brandy on the table and drank a toast to his success.

He should experience a hint of remorse for what he'd just done. A twinge of guilt. But how could he? He'd waited three long years to exact his revenge on Haywood and everything had proceeded perfectly.

Hadleigh thought of his beautiful Melisande, the love of his life. He was finally going to fulfill the oath he'd made at her graveside. When Haywood had the most to lose, he would take it all.

He sipped his brandy and smiled. Oh, he intended to enjoy himself. He would pay every note the late Earl of Haywood and his eldest son had left unpaid. He would cover every new bill Haywood amassed in his attempt to repair the dilapidated Haywood Abbey. But he'd *never* let his sister sleep one night beneath its crumbling roof. And he'd *never* consider Haywood as his future brother-in-law.

He wanted to laugh at the thought. There was no way he'd give Cecelia into that murderer's hands. No way he would allow there to be a connection between them. No way he would assist him in saving his estates.

His one regret was that he had to use Cecelia in his plan for revenge. But she was the perfect pawn. Her dowry was what drew Haywood to her. Thinking he would gain control of the astronomical amount that went with her when she married was the reason he'd accepted Hadleigh's monetary offer.

He didn't for one second believe Haywood had feelings for his sister. He wanted to laugh. The thought was ludicrous. Haywood only intended to destroy Cecelia the same as he'd destroyed Melisande.

But he would never let that happen. Haywood would never harm anyone Hadleigh loved ever again.

Chapter 9

❦

It had been more than two weeks since the opera, and Celie could still feel Jonah's warmth as he placed his arm across the back of her chair. She shivered each time she remembered the feel of his jacket against her shoulder and the soft, gentle circles his fingers traced against the flesh above her elbow. A molten heat spread to every part of her body when she recalled the daring kiss he placed on her cheek when he was certain Hadleigh wouldn't see them.

Since then, he'd called on her every afternoon to take her for a ride through Hyde Park, or just to walk with her around the gardens at Hadleigh House. Then, in the evenings, he attended the same functions as she and Hadleigh, making sure to escort her in to dinner, or sit beside her during the musicale, or dance a waltz or two with her.

Society was abuzz with rumors concerning them, but she didn't care. In fact, she reveled in them. She'd never been the topic of speculation before. No one had ever placed wagers on when Hadleigh would announce his sister's betrothal—and to a man her brother still avoided as much as he could.

Celie didn't care about that, either.

Hadleigh had made almost daily hints of disapproval concerning her choice of admirer, but none of his comments forbade her to keep Jonah company, so she'd ignored them. Besides, she didn't care what her brother thought. She didn't care what anyone thought. She was…

In love.

For the first time in her life, Celie realized the power of love. She understood how love could build or destroy empires, could change the course of history, could cause people to do things they'd ordinarily never do. And its power thrilled as well as frightened her.

"Well, if you don't look like someone who is woolgathering, I don't know who does."

Celie looked to her right to see Amanda standing beside her.

"He must not have arrived yet," Amanda said, casting her gaze over Lady Writhington's ballroom.

"No, not yet."

"Maybe he won't come."

"He'll come. He sent a note saying he would."

"You realize you're pathetically in love," Amanda said, hooking her arm through Celie's and walking her toward the refreshment table.

Celie stopped. "Yes. What am I going to do about it?"

Amanda laughed. "You're going to accept his proposal when he asks."

"What if he doesn't ask? I mean, he hasn't mentioned marriage."

"He will." Amanda urged her away from any eavesdroppers. "If I were you, though, I'd be more concerned with your brother's reaction when Haywood asks you to marry him."

Celie followed Amanda to a corner where their conversation couldn't be overheard. "If Jonah asks me to marry him, I don't care what my brother says. I intend to marry him."

"Even if he forbids it?"

Celie hesitated, but not for long. "Yes."

Amanda rolled her eyes. "I'd better stay close to you, then."

"Why?"

"To be your buffer. I'm obviously the only person in London your brother dislikes more than Haywood."

"Hadleigh doesn't dislike you," Celie started to say, then stopped when she realized Amanda would never believe such a lie. "Well, perhaps he doesn't see your admirable traits, but—"

"You might as well stop there, Celie. Dislike isn't close to what your brother feels for Haywood or me."

Celie focused on Amanda's sad expression. "Does it really matter if he likes you or not?"

"Heavens, no!" she protested too heartily. "It's only that it's so very uncomfortable being with you when he's there, too. I've been waiting for the time when he tells me I'm not welcome in your house."

"That will never happen." Celie squeezed her best friend's hand. "You'll always be welcome wherever I am."

"Of course I will. Besides, I'd come anyway. Welcome or not."

Celie laughed at Amanda's honesty and her bravado.

"Come on, let's mingle. Your hero should be here any moment. We'll let him find us."

Celie followed Amanda into the ballroom. But it wasn't Jonah who first found them. It was Hadleigh.

"There you are," he said, the tone of his voice filled with frustration.

"Did you need something, Hadleigh?"

"Yes, Cecelia. Lord Quigley asked to accompany you for the first waltz."

Celie swallowed. The first waltz was Jonah's. "I'm afraid the first waltz is taken."

"If you mean by Haywood, then the waltz is *not* taken. I'll inform Quigley that you'd be delighted to dance with him."

"But I wouldn't be delighted, Your Grace, and you know it."

This was the firmest Celie had ever opposed her brother in her life, but this was an emergency. She intended to dance with Jonah and nothing would stop her.

"That hardly matters. The number of times you allow Haywood to partner you is causing talk. I won't have it. Quigley asked to accompany you, and I'd prefer you'd accept his invitation."

"She can't, Your Grace."

Amanda's statement caused both Hadleigh and Celie to turn their attention to Amanda.

"She can't?" the Duke of Hadleigh mocked.

"No, Your Grace. She can't dance the first waltz with Quigley because he already asked me. Here's my card, if you'd like to see."

The Duke of Hadleigh studied Celie's friend with a murderous glare, but he didn't ask to see her card. To look and be proven wrong would have been embarrassing beyond the pale.

Celie wanted to laugh. If the situation hadn't been so explosive, it would have been funny. What was funnier still was that Amanda didn't flinch when her brother glared at her but returned his look with a narrowing gaze of her own.

The shocked expression on his face indicated that the Duke of Hadleigh couldn't believe a female of such little consequence had the nerve to stare him down.

Celie anticipated several outcomes to the situation between Amanda and her brother, so was thankful when Jonah approached them with a broad smile on his face.

"Good evening, Lady Cecelia. Lady Amanda. Hadleigh." Jonah gave Amanda a courteous nod, then moved to stand by Celie. "May I suggest, Hadleigh, that you remove that ferocious frown from your face and try to smile. You and Lady Amanda are being discussed by every group of gossipers I passed on my way across the ballroom. And, Lady Amanda," he said, smiling at her with a grin to help her look less angry, "I know Hadleigh doesn't inspire humor, but perhaps you could force yourself to look as though you're enjoying your conversation with him a bit."

"His Grace doubts that Lord Quigley has asked me to accompany him for the first waltz."

Jonah arched his brows. "How ungentlemanly of you, Hadleigh."

"I simply suggested that—"

"Apology accepted," Amanda interrupted, leaving the Duke of Hadleigh speechless.

Celie tried to relax, tried to initiate a friendlier environment, but for several long seconds, only Jonah followed her lead.

Finally, after giving Hadleigh a blatant look of innocence, Amanda relaxed her features and smiled. Then laughed.

Her laughter wasn't simply a feigned attempt at humor, but laughter that came from deep inside her.

"Oh, Your Grace," she said, holding her hand over her mouth to stifle the uproarious sound, "you truly are a man accustomed to using manipulation, aren't you?"

"If you define doing what I think is best for the people I care most for as manipulation, then I am guilty."

"Ah," Amanda said thoughtfully. "The fallacy becomes what *you* consider best and what actually *is* best. I'd love to debate that with you, but the orchestra is playing the first waltz, and as you know, I've promised this dance to Lord Quigley."

With that, Amanda gave Hadleigh a regal curtsy that was anything but sincere and turned away from him to walk across the ballroom to where Quigley stood.

Celie had never seen her brother left speechless in his life, but there wasn't another word to describe him. He stared after Amanda, his brows arched in disbelief, his jaw dropped in incredulity, and his first two attempts at speech unsuccessful.

"If I thought you would adhere to my wishes," her brother said, looking at Celie as if he'd like to throttle her—except she doubted she was the one he wanted to throttle, "I would forbid you to have contact with Lady Amanda ever again. She is impossible."

"It's good you realize to make such a demand would be a waste of your breath."

Hadleigh gave her one last glance, then, without a farewell, strode off to find the nearest drink.

But not before Celie noticed he'd turned toward the dance floor to take a final look at Amanda and Quigley dancing the first waltz.

"It seems I'm not the only person who is capable of raising Hadleigh's temper," Jonah said, watching Celie's brother reach for the glass a footman standing behind a reception table handed him, then drinking the contents in one swallow.

"Interesting, isn't it?" Celie said, having observed several peculiar encounters between Amanda and Hadleigh, but never such a volatile confrontation. And never such a display of bravado from Amanda.

"Do you think Quigley's name is on Lady Amanda's card for this waltz?" Jonah asked.

"What do you think?"

Jonah smiled. "I think I owe Lady Amanda a debt of gratitude. Which means," he said, extending his hand, "that I'd best make use of the time she allowed us. Would you care to stroll through the gardens with me, Lady Cecelia?"

"I'd love to." Celie placed her hand atop Jonah's arm and walked with him through the double French doors that led to Lady Writhington's lavish gardens.

"There's something I'd like to discuss with you, Celie." He took her to the far corner of the garden, where a cozy white-latticed gazebo faced a small pond.

Rumor had it the gazebo and pond were small replicas of a larger, more lavish gazebo and lake situated on Writhington's country estate. Celie had never seen it, but she could envision it and, more than anything, wished to have something similar when she had a home of her own.

The atmosphere was perfect. Very romantic.

Celie sat on a bench overlooking the man-made pond and realized how breathtakingly beautiful it was with the full moon shining overhead. Its shimmering brightness glimmered on the quiet water, which caused the scene in front of her to be picture-perfect.

She watched it for several calming seconds before she realized that Jonah hadn't come to sit beside her on the bench, but was pacing back and forth in front of her.

"Is something wrong?" she asked.

"That remains to be seen."

"Very well." Celie clutched her hands more tightly in her lap. "Why don't you explain the reason you need to talk to me before I jump to several conclusions? None of which I want to consider."

He stopped pacing and looked at her. "What conclusions would those be?"

"For one, that you would like to warn me against reading too much into our friendship. That even though you like me, perhaps have even grown fond of me, that you have the need to experience the companionship of other young ladies."

"Is that what you think?"

Celie found the look of incredulity on his face a bit reassuring. But not completely. "Such a thought is not beyond the realm of possibility," she answered.

"Let me assure you that it is."

Celie's heart shifted in her breast.

"In fact," he continued as he sat beside her on the bench, "such an idea is the furthest thought from my mind."

He gathered her hands in his and held them. Molten heat moved to every part of her body.

His hands were strong and powerful. His touch gentle, yet reassuring.

Before she became acquainted with Jonah, her brother was the most formidable man she knew. But he paled in comparison. The difference was that Jonah possessed a quiet strength that left her feeling safe and secure, whereas Hadleigh's strength elicited fear.

Where Hadleigh demanded attention, Jonah deserved it. His calming demeanor, his regal carriage, and his impressive aptitude combined to make him a remarkable person. He'd been a captain in the war, and Celie understood why. He possessed outstanding leadership qualities and an amazing ability to garner trust.

"Is something wrong, Jonah?"

He shook his head. "No, everything is fine. It's just that..."

She waited.

He rose to his feet and paced the small confines of the gazebo. "It's just that..."

He stopped in front of her and looked at her. "It's that I find I am terribly fond of you, Celie. As you know, I introduced myself to you for the purpose of gaining my foothold back into society. I knew Hadleigh would be my biggest obstacle in being accepted by my peers and thought making your acquaintance would help me achieve my goal. I've never lied to you about that."

"And I told you that I understood why you had to do it."

"But I didn't expect to become so fond of you. I didn't expect to admire you so." He paused. "And I didn't expect to want to marry you and spend the rest of my life with you."

Celie struggled to find her voice. "What did you say?"

"I have nothing to offer you." His regal stance reminded her of the officer he still was in many ways. "My debts are enormous. People will say I am marrying you for your dowry."

"Are you?"

He didn't flinch. "In part, yes. I won't lie to you. The debts I inherited when I assumed my title were staggering. I am in desperate need of the money that might someday come with you."

"There are a number of other wealthy females inside that ballroom who would be ecstatic to be your wife. Why didn't you choose one of them?"

"Because I don't want anyone else. I've discovered I only want you."

Celie swallowed past the lump in her throat. She blinked fast to stop the tears from welling in her eyes. Jonah sat beside her and gathered her hands in his. A fresh wave of strength engulfed her.

"If I marry you," she said when she could speak, "people will think you're only marrying me to exact some sort of revenge on Hadleigh."

Jonah smiled. "More than likely, yes. They will also say that you chose poorly. That you could have had any one of a dozen men more deserving to be your husband than me and that you made an unwise decision."

Now it was Celie's turn to smile. "It's more likely they will say that *you* have made the unwise decision and will now have to live with my plainness for the rest of your life."

Jonah ran the back of his fingers down her cheek. "I can think of nothing I'd rather do."

Celie wanted him to kiss her. She wanted to experience the emotions that engulfed her when he held her in his arms and kissed her. She wanted to touch him and feel his warmth beneath her fingertips, but she wanted to feel his flesh without the barrier of clothing. And that thought shocked her.

"Jonah, would you kiss me?"

He smiled. "It would be my pleasure," he answered her, then lowered his head and kissed her.

The myriad of emotions that shot through her as he deepened his kiss caused her mind to spiral in a hundred different directions. Even sitting on a bench didn't prevent her legs from turning weak beneath her. But most disturbing of all was the warmth that settled low inside her stomach. So low she wasn't sure she could put a name to where the liquid heat was located or why only Jonah was able to affect her there.

Jonah opened his mouth, and she matched his movements. She wanted his invasion, ached to submit to his possession, but not in any form of weakness. Only in a combative manner that left them both breathless and yearning for more.

She waited for his tongue to enter, then met his assault with an attack of her own. She confronted him with a boldness she never thought herself capable of. She battled him with the skill of one practiced in the art of kissing. Except she wasn't. She'd had so little experience that she was amazed at where her bravery and knowledge came from.

She only knew that when Jonah kissed her there wasn't anything she wouldn't do or allow.

She leaned into him and wrapped her arms around his neck.

A low moan echoed in the moonlight, but she wasn't sure where it had come from. All she was aware of was the fiery brand his touch caused as he moved over her flesh.

Her arms seared as he slid his fingers from her shoulders to her wrist. Her sides and stomach erupted in flames as he moved up her middle to her breasts.

She knew he intended to touch her there but wasn't sure she'd be able to tolerate the sensation without bursting into flames.

She leaned closer to him, encouraging him to give her what her body was so eager to have. Yet she wasn't quite sure she knew exactly what that was.

Then he deepened his kiss even more and touched her.

Celie made a low moan that echoed against her ears, then nearly shattered into a million pieces.

Jonah began his assault again, but pulled abruptly away when a loud, angry voice shouted his name.

"Haywood! Damn you, Haywood!"

Jonah kept his arm around her shoulder as if he knew she was helpless to stay upright on her own if he let her go.

"Don't move," he whispered. "I'll take care of this."

Celie watched as Jonah slowly turned.

"Did you need something, Your Grace?" he asked.

"I need—no, I *demand* you take your hands off my sister!"

Celie could hear Hadleigh's heavy footsteps pound toward them as he came down the flagstone walk. She could hear the anger in his voice. And she didn't care.

She sat straight, putting a decent degree of distance between Jonah and herself, then smiled when she lifted her gaze and stared into Jonah's battle-ready demeanor.

Jonah smiled back at her, then rose to his feet.

She'd never feared her brother, never been intimidated by him the way people who didn't know him were. Suddenly, she doubted her own sanity. The last thing she should experience was humor, but she did. She found the situation…exhilarating.

She wiped the smile from her face and rose to her feet to stand beside Jonah. He'd taken a step in front of her to shield her, as if she needed his protection from her brother.

"What the bloody hell do you think you're doing?"

"I am having a discussion with your sister. A discussion you rudely interrupted."

"If the scene I just witnessed is any indication of what you think constitutes a discussion, it's a damn good thing I interrupted when I did."

Celie sensed Jonah's exception and placed a calming hand on the rigid muscles that ran up and down his arms. He didn't look at her, but she felt the knots ease.

"I'd be very careful of what kind of accusations you're making," Jonah said in a voice that sounded like the former captain issuing a command. Something Hadleigh was totally unfamiliar having directed at him.

The air sparked with unleashed tension, and Celie could see that the anger Hadleigh harbored for Jonah even after three years still simmered inside him. The elation she'd experienced only moments ago died.

What if Hadleigh refused to allow her to marry Jonah? What if he refused to turn over her dowry?

Oh, she was of age and could marry without Hadleigh's consent. But she was helpless to do anything about the dowry that was to come with her. Hadleigh had control of it. Hadleigh had to approve of the man she married, or she would go to her marriage penniless.

Jonah had already told her that one of the reasons he wanted to marry her was because of the money that would come with her. But if she came with no money…

She was frantic to stop them before one or the other said something that would be irreparable.

"I'm not blind, Haywood. And I'm not stupid. The female you were treating like a—"

"Enough, Sterling!" Celie took a step forward. She stood like a barrier between the two battling men. Jonah stepped close enough to feel the heat of his body radiate against her back. "You will stop this infernal battle of words right now."

The Duke of Hadleigh gave her an angry glare, but Celie didn't back down. She knew if she did, she'd lose Jonah forever.

"You are causing a scene, Sterling," she added, shifting her gaze to the edge of the terrace where several guests had gathered.

Every time the Earl of Haywood and the Duke of Hadleigh were anywhere near each other, all eyes remained riveted to the two of them the entire time. No one wanted to miss seeing a resurgence of the bitterness between the two rivals. Celie knew her brother didn't need to turn around to see that her words were true.

"Please erase that scowl from your face and lower your voice. It's not necessary to provide any more fodder for the gossip mills than they already have at their disposal."

Her brother's shoulders relaxed and he took a step closer to them. At least now, perhaps, the guests wouldn't overhear every word they said.

"Was your intent to make a spectacle of my sister?" Hadleigh said, directing his insult to Jonah.

Celie answered before Jonah had a chance.

"Lord Haywood didn't make me a spectacle, Hadleigh." She paused to let her next words reap their full impact. "Unless you are insinuating that simply by *wanting* to spend time alone with me, Lord Haywood made a spectacle of me."

Her accusation stunned her brother and Celie was glad. He opened his mouth to speak, then closed it again as if words weren't at his disposal.

"You know that isn't what I meant, Cecelia," he said.

"Unfortunately, that is exactly what I thought you meant."

"Then I owe you an apology."

Celie smiled at her brother. This was indeed a consolation. "Apology accepted, Your Grace."

"Perhaps we should return to the ball," Jonah said, taking charge of the situation. He took a step forward until he was even with Celie but addressed himself to the Duke of Hadleigh. "But I would first like permission to call on you tomorrow, Your Grace."

Hadleigh's eyebrows shot upward. "Concerning my sister?"

Jonah turned toward her and lowered his gaze. "Yes. Concerning Lady Cecelia."

Their gazes met and held in the moonlight, and she saw a look she'd only dreamed of seeing in a man's eyes.

Even though she only had a cloudless sky and Lady Writhington's garden lanterns to go by, she saw it plain as if it were daytime. There was a glimmer in his eyes that mirrored the smile on his face and…she'd never seen anything so wonderful in her life.

"I'll expect your visit in the morning," the Duke of Hadleigh replied, then turned to go back to the Writhington ball.

"Don't worry," Jonah whispered to Celie when Hadleigh had walked through the small group of onlookers on the terrace. "Everything will be all right."

It was only when Jonah loosened her rigid fingers that Celie realized her fingers were digging into his arm. "I think they will, too, but I won't feel better until after you've talked to my brother."

Jonah turned to her and held her gently by the shoulders. "Are you sure this is what you want?"

Celie couldn't help but smile. In fact, she was nearly giddy just knowing there was a possibility she would be marrying the man with whom she'd been in love her whole life. "I'm sure. And I'd show you exactly how sure I am if we still didn't have an audience straining to get a glimpse of us in the darkness."

Jonah laughed, then lowered his head and whispered in her ear. "As long as they're watching so intently, it would be a shame to disappoint them."

And he leaned down and lightly kissed her cheek.

Chapter 10

❦

Sterling Randolph, Duke of Hadleigh, watched the Earl of Haywood mount his horse and ride away. He'd given him a complete list of all the debts he'd paid for him. The amount was staggering, but well worth any dent to his coffers. No amount was too much when it came to exacting revenge on the man who'd killed his Melisande.

He wanted to declare victory, but it was too early to celebrate. He couldn't count on anything until Cecelia came to her senses, until she realized what a blackguard Haywood truly was and broke off any association with him. Only then would it be too late for Haywood to escape the trap he'd set for him.

Hadleigh returned to his study and poured himself a glass of the special brandy he'd had brought up from his cellar. He at least intended to toast the progress so far.

Haywood was well on his way to losing it all.

Hadleigh anticipated a few moments of privacy in which to celebrate, but the knock on his door stopped him. He looked up to see Cecelia enter the room.

"Fitzhugh said Jonah was here a short while ago." She rushed across the thick Turkish carpet and stopped a few feet from his chair. There was something different about her. A certain glow he'd never noticed before.

"Yes, he was here."

Hadleigh watched the smile on her face reach her eyes. She wasn't a beauty like Melisande had been, but for the first time, he noticed there was something quite attractive about her.

He tried to remember when his sister's looks had changed but couldn't. Now, though, she had the look of a woman who was…happy.

Surely her feelings for Haywood weren't serious enough to be unalterable?

"Well, are you going to tell me what he came to discuss? Or am I going to have to go ask Jonah?"

He leaned back in his chair. "Come, sit down, Cecelia."

A frown covered his sister's forehead. "You didn't refuse him, did you?"

He'd seen that expression before: the firm set of Cecelia's mouth, the hard glare in her eyes, the pout of her lips. Everything about her was the same as it always was when she was determined to get her way.

"No, I didn't refuse, exactly."

"What do you mean…exactly?"

"Sit down."

He waited until she sat, then rose to close the door. He didn't want any of the servants to overhear their conversation.

"Haywood asked my permission to court you," he said after he sat in his chair. "With intentions of marrying you."

"What did you say?"

"I listened to his offer and tried to keep an open mind. He made some remarks that caused me concern."

"What kind of remarks?"

"Remarks about his intentions concerning the money he will receive upon marrying you."

"Is that all?" The frown dropped from her face and was replaced by a smile. "He needs my dowry to make improvements to his estate. He's told me about them." She paused. "Are you worried he might not use my money wisely?"

"You know his father's and brother's reputations."

"Jonah's not at all like either one of them."

"How do you know? You just met him a month ago."

"Hadleigh, how ridiculous. We've known Jonah our whole lives."

"Yes," he said in a louder voice than he'd intended. "Which is exactly why I'm warning you about him."

"Then you can save your breath. I know all I need to know."

"Really?"

"Yes, really."

Cecelia rose from her chair and walked to the window that looked out onto their mother's garden. "We might as well quit this bantering of words. It's getting us nowhere. Why don't you tell me what it is that you think I need to know about Jonah?"

"I have a question for you first," Hadleigh said. He had to handle this right. He wanted to cast a few doubts in Haywood's direction. Overdoing it would ruin everything.

"Yes?"

"What are your feelings for Haywood?"

"I'm not sure I understand."

"Do you imagine yourself in love with him?"

She laughed and he took great relief in that reaction. Of course she hadn't fallen in love with him. How could she have? She didn't know anything about him. She didn't know how deceitful he could be. How he couldn't be trusted. What little regard he had for anyone.

It was his fault Melisande was dead, and he'd never forgive him for that.

"I knew you couldn't be in love with him," he said, feeling more sure of himself. "You are far too intelligent for that. It's just that it's so easy for people to give him more regard than he deserves."

"Do you think people regard him too highly?"

Bile rose in Hadleigh's throat and he thought he might choke. "Of course people think too highly of him. He's not a bloody hero, you know. He wasn't wounded in a battle, exactly."

"I thought he was," Cecelia argued.

"He wasn't. It was only a minor skirmish. Hardly worth having its own name."

"I see."

"No, I don't think you do."

Hadleigh rose to allow his towering height to place more emphasis on his words. His nearness was bound to make his accusations more effective. He walked to where she stood. "I don't want you to get hurt."

"You think Jonah will hurt me?"

"I think you will be hurt if you make the mistake of falling in love with him."

She seemed to ponder his words. He was glad.

"I see," she answered, pacing the small area in the front of the room. She stopped and turned to face him. "What else would you like to warn me of concerning Lord Haywood?"

"Like you said, Cecelia, I've known Haywood for a very long time, and I'm not sure he's capable of love."

"Capable of love?" she asked. "Or capable of loving me?"

"I'm not sure there's a difference. The man has no heart. I learned that three years ago when he caused Melisande's death."

"Did you refuse his request to see me, then?"

"Of course not. That would have been the surest way of inviting you to defy my wishes."

"What did you tell him?"

"That I would give him six months to court you. That I would not entertain talk of marriage until that time was over."

"Because you think I will come to my senses in that time and realize what a villain he is?"

"Yes. Or that you will at least realize what kind of man he truly is and walk into any connection with him with your eyes wide open as to his faults and the reason he's determined to marry you."

"And that is?"

"Your dowry, Cecelia. Haywood is no different than any other suitor who has asked for your hand. He only wants your dowry."

Cecelia placed her hand on the nearest piece of furniture as if she needed the support it offered. His words had shocked her. His accusations had bothered her.

"You don't think he can love me?"

"Of course he can't love you. He's incapable of the emotion."

Her voice was small, unsteady, and he wanted to celebrate. He'd planted the seeds of doubt, and they'd already taken root.

Today had turned out better than he'd imagined.

"And yet you gave him six months to court me?"

"Yes. I know it will no doubt take you less than half that long, but I want you to believe beyond question that—"

"I won't need the six months, Hadleigh." She faced him with a bravado he hadn't expected to see on her face. "I doubt that it will take me even one month to discover the kind of man he is."

"Only one?"

"Yes. But to make sure of his intentions, I'll accept your six-month stipulation."

Hadleigh held his breath. Oh, he hoped he hadn't done too good of a job discouraging her. Her refusal to continue seeing Haywood would ruin his plan. Haywood hadn't begun work on Haywood Abbey yet.

"Actually, I'm glad you gave Lord Haywood a specified amount of time to court me. You can be assured I will use every moment of that time wisely."

His sister gave him a reassuring smile, then made her way to the door. "Now, if you'll excuse me, Hadleigh, I think I'll take the carriage out to call on Amanda. I told her I would help her decide on the material she selected for a new gown."

Hadleigh sat back in his chair and took a swallow of the brandy he'd poured before Cecelia had arrived. This was indeed a day to celebrate.

He hoped his sister was correct in the length of time it would take her to discover Haywood's true nature. He hated to think of her spending too much time with a man who possessed such a black heart.

Chapter 11

Celie looked across Lady Windemere's crowded ballroom in search of Amanda. She couldn't wait to tell her what had transpired over the last few days. The minute she spied her, she left Hadleigh's side and walked toward her.

"It's about time you arrived, Celie. I've spent the last half hour listening to Lady Ruggers and Lady Coleton explain all their aches and pains and the remedies they're taking to alleviate them."

"It serves you right. I told you we wouldn't be early. Hadleigh was locked in his study all afternoon with his man of business. I was afraid they'd never finish."

"I had no choice. My brother insisted we leave early, and since I wanted to speak to him, I took advantage of the opportunity I'd have when we were confined in a carriage and he couldn't escape."

Celie looked at her friend. "Uh-oh. That sounds serious."

"It is. I spent the afternoon going over the estate books my brother has neglected for the last few months. The accounts weren't encouraging."

"Did you ask him about it?"

"I tried. He always has an excuse as to why things aren't as good as they could be. Mostly, though, the reason is his lack of responsibility and his overspending."

Amanda looked concerned. "Father did Stephen a great disservice by giving him such free rein. But enough of Stephen." Amanda waved her hand in front of her and her frown quickly dissipated. "I want to hear about you. You've got that dreamy look in your eyes. What have you been up to for the last few days?"

Celie couldn't help but smile. "Jonah asked for Hadleigh's permission to marry me."

Amanda squealed in delight, then pulled Celie to a secluded corner. "Did your brother say yes?"

Celie nodded.

The look of shock and surprise on Amanda's face made Celie laugh. "He said yes, but with one stipulation."

"What?"

"That Jonah court me for six months before he gives his approval."

"Why six months?"

"Because he's certain that, in those six months, I'll realize what a villain he is. That I'll come to my senses and see him for the blackguard he really is."

"Then your brother is a fool."

Celie studied her friend. "You don't believe Jonah is only courting me to exact revenge on my brother? Or to gain my dowry?"

"The truth?" Amanda asked seriously.

"Yes. The truth."

"That may have been his initial intent, but that changed after your first meeting. It's obvious to everyone that

Haywood is head over ears in love with you. Everyone except your brother."

Celie smiled. She'd smiled a lot since Jonah had returned home. She suddenly wanted her best friend to experience that same happiness. "Is there anyone special in your life, Amanda?"

"Oh, no you don't! Don't you dare try to play matchmaker with me." Amanda stepped back a foot and let her gaze roam the ballroom. "You and I pledged to remain old maids and replace the Chipworth sisters when they retired. We decided to be the next terrors of London Society. My plans haven't changed. I still intend to follow that course, even though you've abandoned me."

Celie laughed. "Isn't there someone?" Celie encouraged a second time. "And don't attempt to lie. I always know when you're not telling me the truth."

Amanda gave Celie a wrinkle-faced look and turned her attention back to the ballroom floor. "Very well. Perhaps there is someone I consider special."

"Who?"

"Oh, no," Amanda said, "I'm not telling you."

"Why ever not? I've always shared everything with you."

"This is not something to share." Amanda brushed away a speck of imaginary lint from her gown.

"But maybe I can—"

"There's nothing you can do, Celie. There's nothing anyone can do."

Celie saw a glimpse of something she rarely saw on Amanda's face—defeat mixed with a hint of despair. What was even more heart wrenching was that Amanda's voice contained a hopelessness she rarely heard from her friend.

Celie clutched her hands to her middle. "Oh, Amanda. You've fallen in love with someone who's already married."

Amanda didn't deny her assumption, and Celie ached for her friend. Now that she knew what it was like to love someone, she couldn't imagine what it must be like to give your love to someone who could never love you in return.

"Is there something I can do?" Celie asked, knowing the futility of her question even as she asked it.

"Yes, you can erase that maudlin expression from your face so we can enjoy ourselves tonight."

Celie caught sight of Jonah walking toward her, and she couldn't stop the smile from lighting her face. She would always feel Amanda's loss, but nothing could stop the elation she experienced every time she saw Jonah.

Love did that. And her heart overflowed with love for the man walking toward her.

* * *

The waltz ended and Celie took Jonah's arm and walked with him out onto the terrace. A full moon shone above and a gentle breeze blew softly as they made their way down one of the cobbled paths in the garden.

"I haven't told you how beautiful you are tonight," he said, keeping her close to him as they slowly walked through Lady Windemere's garden.

"And you, my lord, are undoubtedly the most handsome man here," she answered in return.

"Then perhaps you will be content with that thought until I return."

"Return?"

"Yes, I have to be gone for a few weeks," he said when they were seated on a small iron bench overlooking a small pond. "I have some estate business to attend to."

"You're going to Haywood Abbey?"

"Yes. The manor house is in desperate need of repairs, and I want to start before winter."

"How long will you be gone?"

"I don't know. Several weeks, I'm sure. Perhaps longer."

Jonah's words affected her in a way she wasn't prepared for. She realized she didn't want to be separated from him for even a few days, let alone several weeks. She turned to face him. "I wouldn't mind spending some time in the country. Would you mind if I accompanied you? I'll take Amanda with me, of course."

A smile brightened his face. "I can think of nothing I'd enjoy more. But do you think your brother will allow it?"

"I'm sure he'll send an army of chaperones along to guard my every move, but Amanda can be a most impressive diversion. I'm sure we'll find at least a little time to spend together."

Jonah laughed. "The thought of having you there to help make some of the decisions is perfect. And no one is more capable of creating a diversion than Lady Amanda."

The sound of his laughter surged through her like molten lava rushing down a hillside. Its blazing warmth filled in every crease and crevice and covered her with an inescapable heat. That's how Jonah affected her. His nearness created an intense sense of need and desire.

"When will you leave?"

"In two days. There are several items the carpenters need that can't be obtained in the village. I'll leave as soon as I get the supplies the workmen need. Will you be able to be ready by then?"

She smiled. "That will give me plenty of time."

Celie lifted her head and her gaze locked with Jonah's. He reached for her hands and held them in his.

"Did your brother tell you I visited him this morning?"

"Yes. He said you requested permission to marry me—which he granted, with the stipulation that includes a six-month waiting period. He thinks I'll come to my senses before the time is over and realize what a bad choice you are."

"Perhaps he's right," Jonah said.

The tone of his voice sounded so serious she was suddenly frightened. "Do you think he is?"

"I pray to God not, but you could do much better. I have nothing to commend me."

"You have more to your credit than you realize. You possess the qualities I most admire in a man. I want nothing more than what you can provide."

She wrapped her arms around his neck and gave herself to him. Even though he'd never said the words, she knew he loved her. Just as she knew her brother loved her, even though he'd never said the words, either.

Jonah deepened his kiss, touching her, possessing her until Celie could barely breathe. She wanted him.

She wasn't sure she could have described that thought; she wasn't even sure she knew where it had come from, but every fiber in her body said she wanted Jonah. And only Jonah.

He kissed her again, then lifted his mouth and pulled her close to him when they heard a noise from somewhere nearby.

She thought she heard him whisper something about the next six months and the longest of his life, but she wasn't sure. "Did you say something?" she asked, listening to his heart pound beneath her ear.

"I was reminding myself that I am the luckiest man on the face of the earth."

"You must have read my mind," Celie said, smiling up at him, "for I was just telling myself that I'm the most fortunate woman alive."

Jonah lowered his head to give her one last, brief kiss, then separated himself from her before someone saw them.

Chapter 12

Celie stood at the top of the stairs and watched several footmen carry one heavy trunk after another out the door and to the waiting carts. From the amount of luggage waiting to be loaded, it was obvious her brother hadn't changed his mind about accompanying her.

She said a silent prayer that they would survive the trip to the country without a fatality. The journey would only take a couple of hours, but that was more than enough time for the atmosphere to become explosive. She was courting danger by confining her brother and Amanda in the same carriage for that length of time, let alone the volatile tension that was always there when he was anywhere near Jonah.

She didn't know how they would arrive at Hadleigh Manor unscathed.

She reached the bottom of the stairs as Amanda walked through the front door. Amanda stopped and surveyed the mound of trunks and baggage.

"I thought we were only going to the country for a few weeks. You didn't tell me it could be years."

"We will only be there a few weeks."

Amanda rolled her eyes. "Celie, please tell me all these trunks are yours and they're not your brother's."

"I…uh…"

Amanda's fists tightened at her sides. "You promised you'd be able to talk him out of going."

"Well, I couldn't. You know how he can be. With Haywood residing at the neighboring estate, he insisted on coming. Then, when he realized that you would be there, too, well…"

"I can imagine. He was thrilled."

Celie stifled a giggle. "Come with me. I've had tea and a tray sent to the morning room. I hoped sending us all off on a full stomach would help our dispositions."

"I don't think there's any help for your brother's disposition once he's locked inside a carriage with his archenemy."

"That's where you will help."

"Oh, no. Not me. I'm not playing buffer between Haywood and your brother. That's like entertaining a death wish."

Celie laughed. "Silly. Come with me. Tea will help."

"Nothing will help," Celie heard her friend mumble behind her. She hoped she wasn't right.

Celie led the way down the hall. "I really thought he might remain in London because he's at the head of so many committees in the House. He's always at one meeting or another. He's the chairman of almost every committee he's on and takes his responsibilities so seriously I was certain he'd stay here to attend the meetings."

Amanda shook her head. "The only reason he's the chairman is because the other committee members find it much easier to put him in charge and let him control the outcome than to try to fight him."

Celie handed Amanda a cup of tea. "Unfortunately, I think you're right. But I was so sure he'd be too busy to leave right now."

Amanda took a sip of tea, then set her cup down. "I think it's time someone stood up to your brother and made his life a little more difficult."

"Oh, no you don't, Amanda. Don't even think of causing trouble. His life has been difficult enough since Haywood's return. Haywood's appearance resurrected the scandal involving Melisande."

"We both know he hasn't allowed himself to *have* a life since the scandal. At least not a life outside his work in the House. I think he needs someone to make his life more of a challenge than the wasted existence he's allowed it to become."

Celie couldn't stop the laughter from escaping. "Well, when you decide how you intend to accomplish that feat, let me know. I want to be there. I just don't want you to implement your schemes just now. For the next few weeks, we *have* to reside with each other."

"Very well. But it would be interesting to see—"

Amanda was about to add something Celie was sure she'd find amusing when the door opened and Hadleigh entered.

"Your Grace," Amanda said in a sweet tone. "What a surprise."

"Surprise? I can't imagine why, Lady Amanda. This is, after all, *my* house."

"Of course," Amanda added with a sweet smile on her face. "I mistakenly assumed you would be out supervising the loading of the luggage."

"I have employees perfectly capable of overseeing that detail. I was more concerned with supervising the loading of the passengers. But since you are both sitting here enjoying tea, it is impossible to assist you into the waiting carriage." He shifted his impatient glare in Celie's direction. "You are blatantly tardy, Cecelia."

"Oh, please, forgive me, Your Grace," Amanda interjected. "The fault is entirely mine."

"Why doesn't that surprise me?" Her brother rolled his eyes. "In what calamity have you involved yourself this time?"

"Not a calamity, exactly. More a concern I had that—"

"Concern?" Hadleigh interrupted in his most arrogant tone. "A concern that had to be handled now?"

"Yes, Your Grace. It is a *personal* matter."

"That only my sister could help you solve."

Celie noticed the sly grin on Amanda's face and knew it was time to change the subject. Unfortunately, she didn't interrupt quite soon enough.

"Of course, Your Grace. Surely you realize how close Celie and I are?"

"How could I forget?" her brother retorted. "I was usually the one who had to rescue the two of you from the schemes in which you involved my sister."

Celie started to object, but Amanda held up her hand to stop her.

"Oh, Your Grace, you give me far too much credit. I would be remiss to take credit for all of our misdeeds. After all, Celie does possess some of the same traits that are so prevalent in *your* personality."

Uh-oh.

Her brother's eyebrows shot up in sharp arches. Celie knew whatever happened next would not be good.

"Such as?" he asked through clenched teeth.

"Well, Your Grace, all of society is well aware of your keen mind. Celie possesses the same sharp wit, except..."

"Yes?"

Amanda took a deep breath. "Perhaps I shouldn't continue."

"Perhaps that would be best," Celie interjected before Amanda had barely finished her sentence.

"Oh, no, Lady Amanda. I insist. I'm sure your opinion of me will be very...enlightening."

"Very well, but be forewarned. I'm often brutally honest when offering an opinion."

The Duke of Hadleigh lowered his head in a regal nod that Celie knew he didn't mean. "I'm sure my skin is tough enough to withstand your comments."

"Well, as you know, Celie also possesses a sharp wit. The difference is, she doesn't use her keen mind to degrade, but rather, to uplift and support."

"Are you insinuating that—"

"Oh, don't misunderstand me. The world needs men like you."

"Like me?"

"Yes, men who possess unwavering confidence and self-assuredness."

Celie breathed a sigh. That wasn't so bad.

"Men who are staunch believers that they are always right. And that anyone who disagrees with them is undoubtedly wrong."

Celie flinched.

"Oh, yes, Your Grace," Amanda continued. "It must be ever so exhilarating to know you are always right."

Celie flinched again.

Her brother's eyes narrowed. "I see. So you think I am inflexible and narrow-minded."

"Oh, you misunderstand me. I wouldn't exactly say you are narrow-minded. Perhaps *relentless* is a better term. Everyone knows of your dogged determination and uncompromising resolve." Amanda sighed as if she were some besotted ninny. "What would we do without leaders like you?"

Celie closed her eyes and said a quick prayer that Amanda would stop now.

She didn't.

"The fact that, once you set your mind on a certain course, there is no altering your opinion is a rare gift."

"You admire my...hardheadedness?"

Amanda feigned surprise, and Celie watched the hole her friend was digging sink even deeper.

"Oh, I wouldn't call you hardheaded, Your Grace. Perhaps *obdurate* would be a better term."

"*Obdurate*." Her brother's gaze hardened. "Oh, yes. That's much better. I can tolerate being obdurate so much better than if you had said I was obstinate."

Amanda ignored his comparison and smiled. "Oh, Your Grace, I can't imagine how reassuring you must find it to be so self-assured. It must be peaceful, indeed."

Hadleigh walked from one side of the room to the other. He reminded Celie of a steam engine that was building steam and was about ready to blow.

"Let's see, Lady Amanda," he said, stopping too near Amanda for Celie's peace of mind. "So far, you've used the terms *obstinate, uncompromising, relentless, narrow-minded—*"

"Oh, no, Your Grace. *You* referred to yourself as narrow-minded. I only said you were obstinate."

"I believe the term you used was *obdurate*."

"So it was."

Amanda smiled one of her most innocent smiles, and Celie realized how much self-control it took for Hadleigh to hold his temper.

"It seems to me, Lady Amanda, that you must think that I am terribly bullheaded."

Amanda clasped her hand to her chest as if she were shocked by Hadleigh's accusation. "Oh, no, Your Grace. I don't think you are bullheaded. In fact, I hardly think of you at all."

After Hadleigh recovered from the blow Amanda leveled at him, he gifted her with another glaring look. "That is the first reassuring statement you've made since I walked through the door."

Amanda placed her finger over her lips as if she were concentrating.

Celie had seen Amanda do this before and knew this wasn't a good sign.

"I'm afraid I've offended you, haven't I?"

Celie suddenly saw a side of Hadleigh she'd never seen before. Amanda had definitely put him on the defensive. That was, without a doubt, a new experience for him. He always possessed the upper hand in any conversation, had control of every confrontation. Except, this time…he didn't.

The realization almost made her laugh out loud. She didn't, though. She couldn't risk adding fuel to an already explosive situation.

"Of course you haven't offended me," Hadleigh answered in a cavalier manner. "I'm simply wondering why you devote so much time to evaluating my uncomplimentary characteristics."

"Oh, believe me, it's totally by accident. My friendship with your sister has provided ample time for me to observe your personality. I'm quite impressed with your astute awareness of society's many inferiorities and your supreme…um…"

Thankfully, Amanda stopped.

"My what, Lady Amanda? Please, go on."

"No!"

Celie jumped to her feet and stepped between the two adversaries. "We really must be on our way, Your Grace. Are you ready?"

Her brother looked at her as if he couldn't quite remember where they were going, then focused his attention on her rather than on Amanda.

"Yes."

"If you'll excuse me, then," Amanda said, rising to her feet, "I think I'll check to make sure my trunks get packed. I'll meet you outside, Celie."

Amanda opened the door and took a step through the opening before she stopped. "I can't tell you what a pleasure it's been conversing with you, Your Grace. I look forward to continuing our conversation. The trip to the country should prove ever so enjoyable."

The Duke of Hadleigh lowered his head in a regal nod that wasn't any more genuine than the last one. The minute

Amanda closed the door, Hadleigh opened his mouth to speak, but Celie pressed her finger against his lips to warn him to remain silent.

He didn't refrain from speaking his mind—that would have been asking too much. But at least when he spoke, he didn't yell his thoughts loud enough to be heard through a closed door.

"That woman is the most insufferable creature God ever created," he hissed through clenched teeth. "How on earth you can tolerate her is beyond me."

"You have to get to know her, Hadleigh. Once you do, you realize how special she is."

"Then I'll never discover her uniqueness because I don't intend to get to know her well enough."

Celie knew trying to convince her brother of Amanda's special qualities was useless, so she changed the subject. "Was there something you needed before we left?"

"Yes, Cecelia. I'd like to make one last attempt to dissuade you from going."

A heavy weight dropped to the pit of her stomach. They'd been over this several times in the last few days, and each time the end result was the same. Her brother didn't want her to go, and she refused to abide by his wishes.

"I know the only reason you want to go to Hadleigh Manor is because Haywood will be close by."

She tried to keep her expression even. She didn't want her brother to see the excitement in her eyes or on her face. "Yes, he's making several improvements to Haywood Abbey, and I offered him my help."

Hadleigh's expression turned more dour. "I don't want you anywhere near him or his estate."

Celie knew she'd run out of time. She had to tell him the one detail she'd kept from him for days. "I'm afraid it's too late for that, Hadleigh. Not only did I offer to visit him several times while we were there, but I also invited him to ride with us."

"You what?"

"I invited him to accompany us. It seemed a waste to take several carriages when one would suffice."

Her brother's look turned murderous. "Did you do this on purpose? Do you think that confining me with that murderer for several hours will erase the hatred I've felt for the last three years? Do you think that being forced to spend endless hours with him will evaporate the revulsion I feel toward him?"

A sense of hopelessness weighed down on her. "No, Hadleigh. I don't expect your feelings for Haywood to change. I know you too well to hope for that. I do hope, however, that for my sake, you will tolerate his presence for the few hours it will take us to reach Hadleigh Manor. And I hope you realize how tragic it will be for both of us if you force me to choose between the two of you."

Her brother's face paled and his eyes widened in disbelief. "Are you telling me—"

"I'm not telling you anything. I'm only asking that you tolerate Lord Haywood for my sake." She rose. "Now, it's time to leave, if you still intend on accompanying us. If you would rather stay here, I'll more than understand and bid you good-bye now."

Her brother slowly rose to his feet. "You leave me no choice, Cecelia. I cannot in good conscience allow you to travel to Hadleigh Manor unaccompanied. And our relationship is too important to me to let my personal feelings destroy our closeness. Even though I cannot abide the man with whom you've chosen to associate, I promise I will be on my best behavior while we are in the country."

This was almost like the brother she used to know. With tears in her eyes, she threw herself at Hadleigh and hugged him tight. "Thank you, Your Grace. You don't know how much I appreciate hearing that."

Hadleigh cleared his throat, then offered her his arm. Together, they walked to the front door and down the stairs to their waiting carriage. When Celie looked up, her eyes locked on the smile on Jonah's handsome face.

The muscles in her brother's arm beneath her hand tightened. The unleashed fury she felt frightened her, but she brushed it away.

She had her brother's promise. And he'd never before broken a promise to her.

Chapter 13

The ducal carriage rolled through the English countryside with amazing speed. The weather was perfect for the trip to Haywood Abbey. Celie was happy beyond words that she and Jonah could spend the time in such close proximity. And, more importantly, Amanda and her brother had survived being confined in such tight quarters for nearly three hours and hadn't killed each other. Although it was obvious Amanda's pointed remarks had tested Hadleigh's patience to the limit.

She let her gaze rest on Jonah's features and smiled. He watched her as he'd done nearly the entire trip. There was something about being so near him that affected her in the strangest way. If the truth be told, she was relieved that she and Jonah weren't alone. Her mind envisioned a variety of experiences she was certain she'd enjoy if they were.

"Are you quite finished making such disparaging remarks, Lady Amanda?" her brother asked in a strained voice.

"My intent is not to disparage, Your Grace. I'm simply stating an opinion."

"And your opinion is that if the choice were left to you—heaven forbid—you would do away with the entire peerage system? That you would do away with our nation's governing system as we know it?"

"Of course not, Your Grace. I'm simply stating that rank doesn't necessarily equal intelligence, or respect. That many of the highest-ranking individuals in society regard themselves so elevated that they consider the working class synonymous to the Turkish carpet in their homes. That both are placed beneath them to be walked upon. Unfortunately, I fear most of the members of society haven't used their brains in so long the intelligence God gave them has atrophied."

"Of all the—"

If looks could kill, Amanda would be reduced to a pile of ashes. Celie smothered another laugh behind her hand.

"Please, don't take my criticism personally, Your Grace."

"But of course not," he mumbled between clenched teeth. "Why would I think your words were intended for me?"

"Well, you *have* indicated on more than one occasion that you prefer to disregard my opinions."

"That's because it is highly unlikely you understand even one of the complex aspects of the measures that are under consideration in the House."

"What is there to understand about the necessity for reform? Poverty and abuse abound. Working-class families are living in abject conditions. Children are starving. Women are forced to sell themselves to earn enough—"

"Enough, woman! Such matters shouldn't even be mentioned in polite company."

"Not mentioning them won't make them go away, Your Grace. How can we expect to change government policies if we leave the idea of reform up to men and they're of the opinion that not talking about the problem will solve it?"

"Reform movements advance slowly."

"Tell that to the hundreds of children who go to bed each night hungry. And the scores of babies who won't live to see the sun rise tomorrow."

Amanda became more irate with each sentence, and Celie knew, for everyone's sake, it would be wise to call a truce. She reached over and squeezed her friend's hand as they made their way closer to the Abbey. "Your points are well taken, Amanda, but do my brother a favor and try not to argue with him any more today. He's had a difficult afternoon."

"Very well," Amanda finally agreed, but not before she gave Hadleigh one last lethal glare. "I'll have pity on him as a special favor to you."

"Thank you. You can resume your bantering tomorrow."

Hadleigh's eyes rolled upward. "That gives me something to look forward to."

Celie glanced at Jonah, and the smile on his face warmed her heart. Before either of the antagonists could issue another argument, the carriage turned into Haywood Abbey's long drive. Celie looked out the window and focused on the house that would be her future home.

"It's beautiful, Haywood."

"It will be one day," he answered. "There is much to be done, however."

Scores of workmen busied themselves at various jobs—replacing windows on the three floors, reinforcing the bricks with new mortar, replacing the tile on the roof.

There didn't seem to be a lack of projects to work on, both inside and out.

The carriage came to a halt, and a footman rushed to open the door and lower the step. Jonah disembarked first and held out his hand.

Celie exited and stopped before stepping away from the carriage to look upward. If things went as planned and Jonah and she married, this would be where she lived.

The brick manor house was beautiful, with six steps leading up to an expansive portico. Four huge pillars supported a gabled roof and shielded visitors from rainy weather.

Four ceiling-to-floor windows framed either side of a monstrous front door, and several servants waited in line to assist the earl's guests. The only person she recognized was Jonah's London butler, Bundy.

"Are you terribly disappointed?" Jonah whispered before he released her hand.

"Oh." She breathed a deep sigh and gave him the warmest smile she could offer. "Not at all. I have just fallen in love with your home. As I fear I'm likely to do with its master."

He paused, then brought her fingers to his lips and kissed them. "You have no idea how happy you make me."

"That is my intention, my lord."

The gentle pressure of his fingers sent heated waves rushing to every part of her body. Hadleigh's harsh voice, however, doused her emotions.

"Cecelia, you are blocking the exit and I'm in desperate need of a breath of fresh air. I've spent enough time trading insults with your friend."

Celie and Jonah both laughed, then stepped away from the carriage to let her brother step down. Jonah moved to assist Amanda, probably because he was afraid Hadleigh wouldn't perform the honors. But years of training came to the forefront and Hadleigh did the honors.

"Welcome to Haywood Abbey," Jonah said when they'd exited the carriage. "Much needs to be done to restore the Abbey to its former grandeur, but as you can see, it won't be long before it will be a home of which I can once again be proud."

Another rush of warmth settled over her, but as before, her brother put a damper on her feelings.

"All I can say, Haywood, is that it's a good thing Hadleigh Manor is close by. I would hate to think of the four of us having to stay here overnight. With so many workmen making such incessant noise, I doubt it's habitable."

"I agree it will likely be quite noisy, but I assure you it's not so bad that we won't be able to enjoy ourselves while we're here."

A palpable tension arched between the two men, and Celie stepped forward in an attempt to ease the situation. "Well, I, for one, cannot wait to see your home. Will you take us inside?"

She reached for Jonah's arm and walked with him up the paved walkway that led to the steps. She assumed Hadleigh would escort Amanda, then thought better of her assumption and turned around to make sure.

She wasn't sure what happened next, but without warning, a muffled pop echoed behind her. Jonah pulled her to the ground as a sharp sound whistled past her ear. She heard a crackling thud against the bricks at the front of the house, then experienced a sharp bite, as if she'd just been stung by a bee.

She tried to grab at her arm, but she couldn't reach it. Jonah had her confined beneath him.

"Are you all right?" he whispered in her ear.

"Yes, I think so."

"Then get ready to move. When I release you, get up as quickly as you can. I'm going to pick you up and carry you into the house."

"I can run myself, Jonah."

"No. I need to keep you in front of me. It's the only way I can protect you. Hadleigh," Jonah ordered, "can you see to Lady Amanda?"

"Yes."

"Ready?"

"Yes."

"Now!"

His weight lifted off her, and she rose to her feet as fast as her bulky skirts would allow. In one swift motion, Jonah swung her into his arms and ran with her up the steps and into the house. Hadleigh and Amanda followed on their heels. Before Jonah set her on the floor, Bundy slammed the door shut.

"Did you see anything, Bundy?"

"Some movement to your right, in those trees. But they weren't close enough to see them clearly. There's nothing moving there now. Looks like maybe they're gone already."

"Take some men with you and see if you can find anything."

"Right, Cap'n."

Bundy and three workers raced through the door.

Jonah slowly lowered Celie to the floor. The minute her feet hit the marble stone in the foyer, her knees buckled beneath her and everything went dark.

"Celie!"

Chapter 14

Jonah sat close to the sofa where Celie lay and watched her eyes slowly open. He was never so relieved in his life as he was the moment she showed signs of regaining consciousness.

"What happened?"

He leaned forward and took her hands. "You fainted."

"That's ridiculous. I never faint."

He wanted to laugh at her fierce denial, but knew laughter was a release for the terror he felt because she'd been shot. He feared if he started laughing, he'd never stop—at least not until he killed someone.

"Did someone shoot at me?"

"No, Celie. It was an accident. No one would try to hurt you."

"It took me by surprise."

"It took us all by surprise. Are you in pain?"

"No. No. I hardly feel anything." She looked down at the bandage on her arm. "Did you do this?"

He nodded. "It wasn't much more than a scratch, but I wrapped it with a sizable bandage so you could boast about it to Lady Amanda."

She gave him a pained grimace. "How considerate of you."

He wasn't sure how he was able to keep a smile on his face while he looked at her, but even the fake humor he wore evaporated the minute he cast a glance at Hadleigh.

The duke sat on the other side of the room in the same spot where he'd been since Jonah had finished dressing Celie's wound. Amanda busied herself at the tea tray one of the servants brought in along with some pastries. She'd been uncommonly quiet since the shooting.

Jonah was glad she'd taken over the role of hostess, although he didn't know if she kept busy because she was too nervous to sit quietly or if occupying herself was the most inconspicuous way to avoid Hadleigh.

Whatever the reason, Jonah considered her decision to stay far away from the volatile duke a wise choice. The fierce scowl on his face matched a volcanic temper Jonah feared might erupt at any moment.

"I'd like to sit up," Celie said.

"No!" they all shouted at the same time.

"I think you should lie still a little longer." Jonah kept his voice soft. His gentle suggestion was an attempt to mollify everyone's explosive reaction. "You don't want to get up too quickly. You might faint again."

"Oh, for pity's sake." She lowered her head back to the pillow and dropped her hands to either side of her body. "It's nothing more than a scratch. You said so yourself. Besides, I feel fine now."

Jonah sat in the chair beside the sofa and took her hand. "But you fainted. That scared several years off my life."

"There's nothing to worry about now, though. I'm fine."

"Just lie there a few more minutes. Then you can get up."

"Oh, very well. Amanda!" Celie said her friend's name loud enough that Amanda put down the pot of tea and came to the sofa. "Watch the clock. I'll act the part of an invalid exactly five more minutes. Not one second more. I'm counting on you to tell me when my sentence is up."

"Very well, Celie. I'll begin—now."

As if Amanda's countdown were more than Hadleigh could tolerate, he bolted from the chair and stormed toward the door.

"Haywood, we need to talk. Now!"

Jonah knew this was coming. He expected Hadleigh to explode like a lit powder keg and couldn't blame him for his reaction. He'd feel just as angry if the roles were reversed. Unfortunately, Jonah didn't have any answers to calm the duke's anger.

He lowered his gaze to Celie's worried expression and smiled. "I'll be right back."

"He's angry, Jonah. Don't let him—"

"It's all right, Celie. Everything will be fine."

He followed Hadleigh out of the room, then gently closed the door behind him.

The two made their way down the hallway, and when Jonah reached a room far enough away from where Celie was, he stopped. His hope was that if—no, his hope was that *when*—Hadleigh raised his voice, the anger wouldn't reach where Celie was resting.

Jonah opened a door to the room his father had used as a study and entered. He barely had the door shut before Hadleigh's booming voice bellowed his first accusation.

"What the hell have you gotten yourself into? Do you realize that Cecelia could have been killed! So help me, if you're involved in something illegal, you won't have to worry about your enemies killing you. I'll do it myself!"

Jonah tried not to let the fury raging inside him get out of control but knew it wouldn't take much to lose his temper. He had to remind himself that Hadleigh was angry out of concern for Celie. He decided it was best to let him get the rage out of his system so they could sit down and rationally discuss who might be responsible for shooting at them.

He walked past Hadleigh to the side table and poured two generous glasses of whiskey. When he finished, he placed one on the fireplace mantel near Hadleigh's tightly clenched fist and took the other one with him. Without answering Hadleigh's accusations, he sat in one of the dark leather wing chairs in front of the mammoth desk that had been his father's and lifted his glass to his mouth.

He'd barely taken a sip when there was a knock on the door. Bundy entered.

"What did you find?" Jonah asked.

"You can see where the blackguard kept his horse. The grass is eaten short as if whoever it was waited a long time for you to arrive."

"So it had to be someone who knew we were coming?"

"Yes, Cap'n. That would be my guess."

"But we only decided to make the trip ourselves two days ago. That's hardly time for too many to find out about it. And I didn't see anyone last night to tell them. Did you, Hadleigh?"

"Of course not! What are you accusing me of?"

"Nothing. I'm simply trying to discover who might have known we were coming."

"That's easy to answer," Hadleigh said. "Gossip travels from one house to the next through the servants. Any number of people could have discovered we were traveling today, both here and in London. The greater question is, what enemies have you made who are desperate enough to see you dead and are willing to take the lives of anyone who associates with you?"

Jonah's temper snapped. "I don't know! I can't think of anyone—except you!"

"You bloody bastard!" Hadleigh rushed from where he stood by the fireplace toward Jonah.

Jonah jumped to his feet. He readied himself for the fight he'd looked forward to having for more than three years.

He anticipated any excuse to beat Hadleigh to a bloody pulp. He ached for an excuse to release the years of pent-up anger and frustration he'd endured for the hell Hadleigh had put him through. He was finally going to get his wish.

He rushed toward Hadleigh with his fists ready to smash into Hadleigh's face. He would enjoy the feel of his knuckles grinding against the duke's soft flesh. Of the crunching of Hadleigh's bones, of cartilage shifting in Hadleigh's face. He pulled back his fist in anticipation and—

"Stop it right now! Both of you!"

Hadleigh stopped before he came close enough for Jonah to strike him with the leverage it required to do any damage.

With a sigh of frustration, Jonah lowered his fist.

"How dare you both behave like candidates for Bedlam! How dare you try to solve anything with violence! How dare you—"

Before Celie could get her final sentence out, she staggered and reached out a hand to steady herself.

Jonah and Hadleigh raced to her, but Jonah reached her first and swept her in his arms. Once he had her safely in his grasp, he carried her to the sofa and laid her down.

"What are you doing up?" Jonah reached for the cover on the back of the sofa and draped it over her.

"How could I stay down when the two of you were getting ready to kill each other?"

"What kind of friend are you to let her up?" Hadleigh bellowed at Amanda.

"*You* try to stop her from doing something when she's made up her mind to do it! She's as obstinate, bullheaded, and stubborn as you are, Your Grace!"

Hadleigh looked at Lady Amanda as if she'd sprouted three heads. It was obvious that she was the only one of them who'd struck a stunning blow.

The expression on Hadleigh's face was so filled with disbelief that Jonah wanted to laugh. He looked at Celie and saw that she had her hand over her mouth, no doubt to stifle a giggle that wanted to escape.

Unfortunately, they were the only two who found humor in the situation.

"Sit down, Hadleigh," Jonah ordered. "Bundy, bring the ladies some tea and something to eat."

Jonah waited until everyone sat, then gathered Hadleigh's glass as well as his own and refilled them. He handed Hadleigh's glass back to him, then sat in the unoccupied chair next to Celie. The four of them comprised what would have, under normal circumstances, been an intimate setting.

Considering the anger and hostility still emitting from Hadleigh, Jonah thought such close proximity might be dangerous. Especially for Hadleigh and Lady Amanda Radburn.

It didn't take long before the servants brought in a tea tray as well as a variety of small pastries and cakes. Lady Amanda poured, and they ate in relative silence.

When Jonah couldn't take the tension any longer, he set his plate down with a determined thud. "For as much as I hate to admit this, you make an excellent point, Hadleigh. The shot that was fired was more than likely intended for me."

"We don't know that," Celie stared to argue, but Jonah held up his hand to stop her.

"Yes, we do, Celie. There is no reason for anyone to want to harm any of you. If there were, they wouldn't have needed to come here to find you. I'm the only one they could be certain would be here."

No one could argue with him.

"So what do you suggest?" Hadleigh set his glass on the table next to Jonah's. "We can hardly sit around and wait for whoever it was to try again."

"My guess is that there won't be another attempt. Not here, anyway."

"How can you say that?"

Jonah released a heavy sigh. "The only reason the shooter got so close was because they had the element of surprise on their side. If we'd been watching for them, they'd never have risked coming so near the house. They know we're watching now.

"In case I'm wrong, though, I'll have Bundy post guards to keep watch. Someone will make rounds from now on to make sure nothing looks suspicious."

He was relieved that Hadleigh, at least outwardly, seemed satisfied with his reasoning. "In the meantime, I think it would be best if you took the ladies to Hadleigh Manor as soon as possible."

"I'm sure we're perfectly safe here, Jonah," Celie started to argue.

He stopped her again. "I'm not. Even though I have no idea why someone would want to shoot at me, I can't pretend it was a mistake. And I can't take the chance that they won't try again. Until I know what this is about, I won't risk either your safety or Lady Amanda's."

He studied the determined look in her eyes and knew she thought his precautions were unnecessary, but he didn't care. He wouldn't risk anything happening to her. He'd come to care for her entirely too much to risk losing her. If something happened to her, he'd lose someone who'd become very important to him. He didn't want to have to find out if he could live the rest of his life with such a loss.

"Don't worry, my lady. I won't make any major decisions on the house without first consulting you. Hadleigh can bring you over every day to check the workmen's progress and make sure everything is proceeding as you think it should."

Before Celie had time to argue, Hadleigh intervened. "I think Haywood's plan is excellent. I won't take any risks with your safety, either. You've already given me enough of a scare. I refuse to relive this afternoon's events."

"Very well. But you will not eat your evening meals here, Jonah. It is only a ten-minute ride to Hadleigh Manor. Dinner will be served at eight each evening. We will set a place for you."

Jonah smiled. "How kind of you, my lady. It will be my pleasure to dine with you and your gracious company."

They visited a little while longer; then Hadleigh indicated it was time to go. "Are you sure you're well enough to travel?" her brother asked.

"Would you allow me to stay if I said I weren't?"

"Absolutely not. And don't even mention that Lady Amanda would stay with you. Your friend hardly qualifies as a chaperone."

Lady Amanda's eyes narrowed before she answered. "I appreciate your confidence, Your Grace. It's ever so reassuring to realize you hold me in such high regard."

With a lift of her chin, Amanda rose to her feet and walked to the door. "I'll wait for you in the foyer, Celie."

Without taking time for anyone to come to open the door, she exited the room with a lift of her chin and a swish of her skirts.

Hadleigh made a sound Jonah couldn't quite distinguish. If he were asked to describe it, though, he'd have to say it sounded strangely like a growl.

"Your brother is right to be concerned," he said as he helped Celie to her feet. "Are you sure you're well enough to travel?"

"Of course. You know what I received is hardly worth even being called a scratch." She lifted her arm to prove she wasn't minimizing her injury, then smiled at him. "Thank you for your concern, though. Your attention is very flattering."

Jonah presented her with a slight bow. "You're very welcome, my lady. The pleasure is mine."

He held out his arm, and she took it. When they reached the front door, Lady Amanda was waiting with her cloak on.

Jonah draped Celie's cloak over her shoulders, then clasped the loop beneath her chin. He couldn't bring himself to release her for a moment or two but looked into her eyes and held her gaze.

"If I were you, Lord Haywood, I wouldn't make your feelings so obvious. Celie's likely to become used to such fawning and will expect it forever."

"Then it will be my pleasure to provide it. I can think of nothing I'd rather do."

Hadleigh cleared his throat. "Enough, Haywood. You've made your point."

Lady Amanda clasped her hand over her heart and looked at Hadleigh in feigned disillusionment. "How disappointing, Your Grace. Instead of taking lessons for future use, you seem intent on crushing any display of affection. How coldhearted of you."

Hadleigh glared at Lady Amanda with unmerciful disdain, but Jonah wasn't sure the lady noticed. She'd already turned her back on them and walked out the front door unescorted.

Jonah and Celie followed, and Hadleigh walked close behind them.

When they reached the carriage, Jonah handed the ladies inside, then watched as the conveyance drove down the lane. The minute they were out of sight, he called for Bundy.

"Show me what you found, Sergeant."

Chapter 15

For more than a week, Jonah labored alongside the workers as they made repairs to Haywood Abbey. Other than concerns over the astronomical debt mounting from the cost of labor and supplies, every day's improvements were amazing. Hadleigh had been most insistent concerning the progress he wanted to see before they returned to London, and Jonah was confident that he would find no complaints when they took a final tour through the Abbey.

He placed his hands on his hips and stretched the muscles of his shoulders and back, then took a final look around the room. This was the last room of the suite that would be Celie's if she agreed to become his wife. This would be her sitting room. The room where she would entertain close friends. Her special sanctuary.

Only moments ago, the workmen had finished reattaching the molding around the ceiling, then replaced the furniture—a beautiful writing desk and a burgundy, black, and gray floral sofa with two chairs of complementary upholstery. Two small tables flanked either side of the chairs, and a low table that had been in the Haywood family for generations stood before the sofa. Celie could discard or add whatever she wanted in order to make her room more comfortable, but he didn't want her to see it barren the first time she entered. Furniture gave the room a warmth he knew she'd appreciate.

He took one more look around the room and smiled in satisfaction. He couldn't wait to see the expression on her face when she walked through the door the first time.

He turned to the door and stopped short when he saw her. The warmth of the glow on her face contained everything he'd hoped to see.

"It's beautiful, Jonah. I love it."

A gentle warmth wrapped around his heart. "I'm glad, my lady, since hopefully this room will someday be yours."

"Then I will be perfectly content here. It's lovely."

He looked at the sincerity in her eyes and knew she meant every word. His blood heated as it rushed through his veins. "Would you like to see the rest of the house—at least the rooms that are finished?"

"That's why I've come."

"Good. Is Hadleigh with you?" He looked toward the doorway. "I can't imagine him dawdling behind if Lady Amanda is within a stone's throw."

She laughed. "No, Hadleigh didn't come. Neither did Amanda."

His eyebrows shot upward. "Hadleigh let you come alone?"

"He left early this morning. He had important business with his steward he said would take most of the day. He promised to join us for dinner."

"And Lady Amanda?"

"She had a headache."

He crossed his arms over his chest and looked down his nose at her. "Why do I have a feeling Lady Amanda's headache improved the minute you left the house?"

Her face lit with feigned innocence. "Because you realize how quickly Amanda recovers from any malady?"

He rolled his eyes heavenward. "And why do I have a feeling Hadleigh has no idea you're here?"

"Because you're a very mistrusting person?"

"No, my lady. The reason is because I know your brother better than most and know he would never give you permission to come here without coming himself as your chaperone. He would, at the least, consider it dangerous. As do I."

Her lips formed a pert little pout. He couldn't stop from reaching out to wrap his arm around her shoulder and pull her toward him. "What excuse did you give him? That you intended to stay with Lady Amanda until she felt better?"

She tipped her chin upward. He knew she wanted to look him in the eyes, but couldn't. She knew he'd see through the lie she was about to tell. She attempted her bluff anyway.

"Do you honestly think Hadleigh would believe I'd stay with Amanda for such a minor malady as a headache?"

"Yes, my lady. He'd believe anything you said because he considers you incapable of telling him one thing and doing another."

"And you?"

He pulled her closer to him and hugged her. "I realize you're as creative as Lady Amanda in your schemes, and equally as capable of getting into trouble."

"I see." She worried her lower lip in a disconcerting manner. "That could eventually be a problem."

"I have no doubt it will be. You'll find I'm not nearly as trusting as your brother."

"That's most distressing, my lord."

"It's meant to be. Your brother assumes Lady Amanda is the mastermind behind all your mischief. If I were to hazard a guess, I'd wager a large portion of the money I don't have that you share equal blame."

She pulled back from his grasp. "I'm shocked, my lord. That you believe I'm capable of such deceit surprises me."

"I'm certain in the next several years I'll find many more things to be shocked over. And I'll learn to be impressed with your creativity."

She tipped her chin upward and smiled. "I certainly hope so."

He pulled her back into his arms and met her smile with one of his own. He felt himself sink into the depth of the magnificent blueness of her eyes and knew without a doubt there was no escape from the love he felt for her.

"I wish Hadleigh hadn't made you promise to wait before formally asking me to marry you."

"He only wanted you to have time to be sure you wanted to marry me. And he wanted to make sure I intended to make the extensive repairs needed for Haywood Abbey to be a fit home for his sister."

"To which you agreed?"

"Of course."

"Weren't you afraid I might be swept off my feet by another suitor during that six months and you would lose me?"

He pressed a kiss to the top of her head. "No. I considered it a wise request. I want you to be certain, too. I don't want you to feel I rushed you into a marriage you aren't sure you want."

"Weren't you afraid I might not love Haywood Abbey and refuse to make it my home?"

He chuckled. "No. That thought didn't enter my mind. If you didn't like the Abbey when you saw it, I'd simply build you another home. One of your own choosing."

"You'd do that?"

"Of course." He pressed another kiss to the top of her head. "I'd do anything for you, Celie. All you need do is ask."

"Oh, Jonah." She lifted her chin and looked at him. "Then I would like to ask a favor."

"How can I refuse you anything when you're so enticing?" He lowered his face until his lips were only inches above hers. "What favor would you ask?"

"Would you please kiss me?"

"Kissing you isn't wise."

"I know. But since you already assume my scheming abilities rival Amanda's, I think I'll prove you right. Please, kiss me."

Kissing her was one favor she wouldn't have to ask twice. He lowered his head until his lips touched hers.

Their meeting was soft and gentle, their contact stimulating. He didn't want their kiss to get out of hand. He didn't want the passion he felt when he held her to pass the point where he couldn't control the outcome. She knew the rules as well as he. The last thing he wanted was for her to feel forced into a marriage because of what they'd done.

She pressed closer to him, and he wrapped his arms around her to keep her near him. She wended her arms around his neck and matched the intensity of his kisses with a passion of her own. Again and again, she drew from him, deepening her kisses until the rapid rise and fall of their breaths matched the fury of his need.

Dear God, but he wanted her. He wanted her in his arms, in his bed, in his life. He wanted her for his wife, for his mate, for a lifetime, then beyond.

He deepened his kisses and met her demands with demands of his own.

He opened his mouth atop hers, and she accepted his assault with an eagerness that increased the passion that was growing beyond control. She raked her fingers through his hair as she battled his assault. The feel of her against him tested his resolve, and his determination to keep their passion from getting out of hand suddenly died.

He wanted her. Oh, how he wanted her. But he couldn't. He wanted her to have a choice without the guilt of what they'd done clouding her judgment. If she chose someone else as her husband, he wanted her to go to her marriage bed a virgin.

Without giving himself time to consider what he was doing, he lifted his lips from hers and held her in a warm cocoon.

"No, Jonah. Don't stop."

Her labored breaths brushed across his cheeks. She looked at him with a glaze of passion in her eyes. Her frantic touch caressed him with a need that increased his desire even more. Before he could stop her, she wrapped her arms around his neck and brought his head downward. And kissed him again.

"Love me. Make love to me," she begged through rasping breaths.

"We can't."

"We can," she whispered softly.

The sound of rushing feet brought them to their senses, and they separated with a jerk.

"I was afraid this is what I'd find," Amanda said, entering the room almost at a run. "What's the nearest way out to the garden?"

Jonah stepped away from Celie and straightened his shirt collar. He doubted he looked presentable and realized from the frantic look in Lady Amanda's eyes he needed to look in control.

"What's wrong, Amanda?" Celie asked as she made an attempt to straighten her hair.

"You brother is right behind me. We need him to find us anywhere but here!" She pointed to the bed.

Jonah led the way out the door and down the back stairs. Once on the lower level, he escorted the two ladies to the library, then out the French doors and onto the terrace. A table was already set up, and they each took a chair.

"Did you need something, my lord?" Bundy asked from the doorway.

"Yes, Bundy, tea. And some of the cake, if Cook has any left from lunch."

"Right away, my lord."

"And four cups," Jonah added.

"Yes, my lord."

Amanda cast an accusing look in Celie's direction. "I thought you said Hadleigh would be gone all day," she gasped, trying to catch her breath. "He arrived not fifteen minutes after you left."

"He told me he wouldn't be home until dark," Celie said in defense.

"Well, he changed his mind." She paused. "Or he set a trap, and we walked into it."

Jonah sat back in his chair and smiled. It was a rare treat to see the two connivers spar over a failed deception.

Before they had time to make any more accusations, Hadleigh's heavy footsteps indicated he was on his way.

"His Grace, the Duke of Hadleigh," Bundy announced.

Jonah rose to his feet. "Hadleigh, please, join us. We were just about to have tea."

Hadleigh ignored Jonah's invitation and focused his glare on his sister. "I thought you told me Lady Amanda was feeling under the weather and needed to rest, Cecelia. I hardly call this resting."

"The fault is mine, Your Grace," Amanda stated, but Hadleigh cut off the remainder of her sentence with a slash of his hand.

"The fault is *always* yours, Lady Amanda, but I keep hoping that eventually my sister will realize she has to stand up for herself and not give in to your every misbegotten scheme."

"Now, just wait—"

The situation was about to become explosive. Before it did, Jonah realized he had to step in. "Your sister wisely thought a little fresh air would be best for Lady Amanda, and they went for a walk. We're neighbors, after all, and they stopped by to see how the work was progressing."

Hadleigh gave him a hostile glare.

"Sit down, Your Grace. I've ordered tea. It should arrive any moment."

Hadleigh hesitated, then took the chair between Celie and Lady Amanda. Celie poured the tea when it arrived, and the conversation calmed to talk of the weather and the conditions of the farmland.

Jonah breathed a sigh of relief. Perhaps it was possible to have a normal conversation with Hadleigh in attendance.

They were nearly finished with their tea when Bundy arrived with a tray. Jonah took the letter and opened it.

"It's an invitation," he announced. "It seems there's going to be a dance in one week's time and we're all invited."

"Oh," Celie said with a smile on her face. "How exciting. I haven't been to a local event since I was young."

"Neither have I," Lady Amanda chimed in.

"In a week?" Hadleigh asked. "I'd hoped to return to London within the week."

"We can't, Your Grace," Celie said. "The locals have no doubt planned this event to coincide with our being here. They'd never forgive us if we left before that night."

Hadleigh's shoulders sagged, and Jonah could see his disappointment. He didn't want to stay for another week, but then, he hadn't wanted to come in the first place.

Talk at the table turned to the upcoming event, and Celie listed some of the people she knew would be there. Since Lady Amanda wasn't familiar with their neighbors, she considered it her duty to catch her up on who would most likely be in attendance.

That left Hadleigh and Jonah to converse with each other.

Neither said anything.

Chapter 16

Jonah climbed down from the scaffolding they'd erected to paint the ceiling in the entryway. When he reached the bottom, he rolled his shoulders to ease the aching muscles, then looked upward at the beautiful scene the artist had painted on the domed ceiling.

He felt a sense of accomplishment. He'd made good progress today.

Celie hadn't been to visit for two days. He couldn't wait until she visited so she could see what the workmen had accomplished since the last time she'd been here. She would approve. He knew she would.

He walked down the long hall and opened the door to the room that had been his mother's sitting room. This was the room where his mother entertained visitors when they came to call—which was often.

Celie would approve of this room, too. It was bright and cheerful, in several shades of yellows and greens. He put his hands on his hips and smiled.

"The house looks wonderful."

He turned to see Celie standing in the doorway. She was alone.

His heart leaped in his chest. She was the most beautiful woman he'd ever seen. Even though it had only been two days since she'd last been here, he'd missed her terribly.

"Do you like it?"

"How could I not? How could anyone not like it? It's beautiful."

Jonah walked to where she stood and took her hands in his. Once he touched her, just holding her hands wasn't enough. He brought her to him and wrapped his arms around her. She went willingly.

"I didn't expect you today. Since the other day, I thought your brother would keep a closer watch on you."

She smiled. "He tried to work from his study, but there were certain matters he needed to check on before we left. And I'm glad." She paused. "I had to come. I missed you."

He kissed the top of her head. "I've missed you, too. Are you sure your brother won't come back to find you gone?"

"He went out with his steward, and I overheard him tell his valet that he wouldn't return until dinner."

"I don't like you traveling alone, though. I'm not sure it's safe."

"Of course it is. It's been weeks, and nothing has happened."

"I know, but—"

"Shh."

Celie lifted her hand and pressed her fingers against his lips to silence him.

"Show me what you've done to the house since I was here last."

"It would be my pleasure."

Jonah took her on a tour of the house, starting with the ground floor. The workers were concentrating on the rooms here, hammering and plastering and painting. The noise level was high as the pounding echoed in the empty rooms.

With his arm around Celie's waist, they walked around piles of lumber and stepped over debris that littered the floor. Celie greeted each workman they encountered as they made their way from room to room. They each greeted her in return. When they finished with the ground floor, he led her up the stairs. The rooms on the first and second floors were for the most part completed, but she hadn't seen them all. He couldn't wait to see her reaction.

"We'll start here." He opened the door at the end of the hall. "This was my mother's favorite room."

Jonah escorted her into the room, and she stopped short, then sighed.

"Oh, Jonah." She turned to look at the entire room. "It's beautiful. Simply beautiful."

"I remember, when I was young, only very special guests were put in this room."

"Did your parents have guests often?"

"Yes, they were both fond of entertaining. Mother loved people, and they loved her. It wasn't until she died that Father changed. He became a different man after she was gone."

"Is that when he lost interest in the estates?"

"Yes."

There was a small settee in the corner of the room. It sat back in a cozy nook shadowed by the flickering candles that dimly lit the room. Jonah led her to the settee and sat beside her.

"I think he loved her so much he simply couldn't go on after she died."

Celie leaned against him, and he placed his arm around her shoulders. "Do you think it's possible to love someone too much?" she asked, relaxing against him.

For several minutes, he searched for the right answer. Before he spoke, he took a breath big enough to lift his chest. "I don't think it's possible to love someone too much. I think the danger lies in loving someone so much that you let them become your reason for living instead of your reason to continue living."

"I think you're right," she whispered.

"That's what Hadleigh did with Melisande. He idealized her to such a level that he distorted his love for her."

"I'm not sure I'd call what he felt for her love. I think it was more a blind adoration. Everyone has faults, but he refused to see Melisande's imperfections."

"Has anyone told you how intelligent you are?" he said.

She smiled and leaned into him. "Yes, I believe you mentioned it before."

Jonah wrapped his arm around her shoulder and pulled her close to him. "It bears repeating, my dear. You have a special understanding of people. I admire that."

She lifted her head and locked her gaze with his. "I love you, Jonah."

"Only half as much as I love you," he whispered. Then he brought his mouth down over hers.

* * *

Celie matched the depth of his kiss with a fervor that equaled Jonah's. She fed her desperation for him and encouraged him to deepen his kiss.

His kiss was hot and demanding, not gentle and passionate like the kisses they'd shared before. He ground his lips against hers, then opened his mouth over hers and urged her to follow his lead.

She did.

His tongue invaded her mouth, and she pressed back against his arm. The sensation of having him so deeply within her startled her—excited her.

She adjusted to his demands, accepted the weight of his body pressing against her, and wrapped her free arm around his neck to hold him to her.

He kissed her again, taking as much from her as she was willing to give—and she realized there wasn't anything she wasn't willing to give him.

His hand reached between them and settled low on her stomach. Bright lights exploded inside her head and shattered with greater intensity. She reacted with a violence that shook her to her core.

"We need to stop," he whispered, lifting his mouth from hers.

"No, Jonah. Not this time."

She tightened her hold around his neck and brought his mouth down on hers again. Their kiss was as passionate as before, the need as desperate.

Celie felt Jonah's hesitation. Knew his mind lectured him with all the reasons he shouldn't make love to her, but she wouldn't allow him to heed those warnings. She needed him too badly. She wanted him with an urgency she couldn't explain.

He hesitated as if he could stop what they were doing before it was too late. But his mind didn't realize it was already too late.

"Love me, Jonah. Make love to me."

With a sigh of resignation, Jonah brought her to her feet and kissed her with greater determination. There was no going back, and she didn't want to.

The large four-poster bed sat in regal majesty on the other side of the room. She didn't know how they reached it, but they were suddenly next to it. His hands worked frantically at her buttons, at the delicate straps, at the silks and satins beneath the sprigged muslin of her day dress. Next, he worked on his own clothing.

Celie knew what she was doing. She wanted Jonah to make love to her. She *needed* him to make love to her. She loved him. She'd always loved him. He held a special place in her heart. A place no one else would ever inhabit.

From the time she was old enough to realize there were different types of love, she knew Jonah would be the man she would marry. The love she felt for him was worlds apart from the love she felt for her brother or her parents.

There were times when she feared she would never realize those dreams. Those were her darkest days—when her brother's hatred for Jonah was so all-consuming she knew in order for her dreams to come true she'd have to choose between her brother and Jonah. Then a miracle happened.

Jonah reentered her life, and her brother's bitterness and hatred seemed to lessen. Her hopes, her dreams for a future with him, suddenly seemed possible. She'd never been happier.

And she refused to lose him now that he was a part of her life again. Yet that was what she was afraid would happen. Hadleigh warned her again yesterday about becoming too infatuated with Jonah. Warned her that it was dangerous to be near him. Even hinted that she sever all ties to him.

Something about the way her brother talked—his tone, his words, the cold hardness in his eyes—hinted that he might possibly refuse Jonah's suit.

She wouldn't let that happen. She couldn't. She loved Jonah. Her heart would shrivel and die if she lost him.

She wrapped her arms around his muscular body and pulled him atop her. She kissed him again and let her kisses speak the demands of her heart. She would have him. She wouldn't let her brother's hatred ruin her future or her happiness.

Her fingers roamed across his flesh, touching him as he touched her, caressing him as he caressed her. She wondered if her touch set his flesh on fire as his did hers. She wondered if a whirlpool of molten heat swirled low in his body as it did in hers. Wondered if he was as desperate for something she didn't have a name for as she was.

He kissed her again—not her mouth, but her body. His hot kisses traveled over her flesh, setting every inch of her on fire.

"Are you sure?" he asked, stopping his ministrations to her body.

"Yes. Oh, yes."

She pulled him close to her again and silently begged for him to complete the miracle.

She didn't care about the pain. She knew there would be that. Amanda had told her there would be. All she cared about was that, with this act, she was Jonah's, in body and soul. And he was hers.

She barely felt the pain as she rode the waves of passion. She soared until she could climb no higher. When she reached the pinnacle, she shattered like a bliss-filled rain shower and fell to earth.

Jonah moved above her, then dropped his head back onto his shoulders and cried out his release.

"Celie!"

She wept for joy when he cried out. The sound of her name on his lips at the peak of passion was the most wonderful sound she'd ever heard.

She caressed the light sheen of perspiration on his back, then held him close when he lowered himself to lie beside her.

She loved this man in ways she couldn't describe—the strength of his character, his intelligence, the teasing glimmer in his gaze, the safety and assuredness in his grasp, the way he considered her thoughts above his own. She loved everything about him. She felt safe in his arms.

Instead of becoming accustomed to the emotions that surfaced when she was with him, she was more in awe. She loved him more. Knew she would never want anyone but him.

She hoped he'd planted a babe inside her. Hoped she was already carrying his son or daughter. Hoped she could give him the next Haywood heir.

He stayed close to her for several wonderful seconds longer, then shifted his weight from her. He took her with him, cocooned her in his arms, and held her close.

She snuggled against him and pressed her cheek to his rapidly rising and falling chest. She loved the feel of his heated flesh against hers, the rapid thundering of his heart inside his chest, the strength of his breath against her cheek.

"Are you all right, Celie?"

"Of course. Are you?"

He laughed.

"I don't regret what we just did, Jonah. I'll never regret it. Please, I don't want you to regret it, either."

"You think I regret making love to you?"

His hands moved over her flesh, soft as a caress, gentle as a cloud, enveloping as a fortress.

"I think you already do. Not the act itself. I think you enjoyed that."

She looked up to meet his gaze when laughter rumbled inside his chest.

"Ah, yes. I most certainly enjoyed that," he said.

"I'm glad. Because I think you already regret that you weren't strong enough to wait until we were married."

"You don't regret not waiting?"

"No." She looked up again. "Does that make me a bad person?"

He pulled her into his embrace again and held her. "No, that doesn't make you bad. That makes you very passionate. And every husband wants a wife who is passionate."

She smiled as she snuggled closer to him. "I'll demand that Hadleigh announce our betrothal as soon as we return to London."

"Are you that anxious to be a bride?"

She tipped her head upward. "I'm that anxious to be *your* bride."

He kissed the top of her head.

"Are you anxious, Jonah? Or are you having second thoughts?" Her heart skipped a beat as she waited for his answer.

"No, Celie. I'm not having second thoughts. Especially not after what we just did. Hadleigh and I will have a discussion soon."

"I don't know if I can wait that long," she whispered. She tipped her head back and urged his lips toward hers. "Maybe we can—"

And they did.

Chapter 17

Four days had passed since he and Celie had first made love. Since then, she'd managed to get away from Hadleigh Manor three of the four days.

Tonight was the dance at the assembly hall, and tomorrow Celie would leave for London. Since there was still so much to do, he'd have to remain here.

Although he wasn't sure how he'd manage the days without her, he knew the separation was for the best. He had no self-control where Celie was concerned. If she weren't already carrying his child, it was only a matter of time until he got her pregnant.

Thinking of the child he and Celie would someday create filled him with unimaginable joy. Spending every day of his life with her caused his heart to leap in his chest.

He nudged his horse to travel faster and galloped the short distance to Hadleigh Manor.

He'd left earlier than he would have had to, but he was anxious to see Celie. Today had been the one day she'd missed coming.

When he thought of the risk he and Celie were taking, a niggling concern settled over him that refused to go away. He'd promised himself Celie would go to her marriage bed a virgin, but it was too late to worry about that now. Celie would be his wife. Their course was firmly in place—unless Hadleigh refused his offer. Unless Hadleigh refused to hand over Celie's dowry. If that happened, he didn't know what he'd do. He couldn't take her as his wife. He'd never be able to support her.

A painful weight settled over him. There was so much he had no power over. Such a large part of his future he couldn't control. And the frightening aspect was that the Duke of Hadleigh could manipulate the outcome of his future more than he could.

Jonah thought of the money he owed him for payment of the debts his father and brother had amassed, the mounting debt he was accruing in order to repair the dilapidated Haywood Abbey. If Hadleigh demanded payment now, there was no way he'd be able to come up with enough money to pay him.

A cold chill raced down his spine. He would lose more than everything. He would lose Celie.

He took in several deep breaths as he pushed his horse toward Hadleigh Manor. He needed to see her. Needed physical contact with her. He wasn't sure when such an intense emotion had overtaken him, maybe when he'd first realized he loved her. Maybe when he'd first made love to her. Maybe when he'd first seen her.

He only knew there was nothing he wouldn't do to spend the rest of his life with her.

He galloped up the long drive and dismounted in front of Hadleigh Manor. He handed over the reins to a footman and turned toward the house. He took one step and stopped.

"I've been watching for you," Celie said from the top of the steps.

Jonah rushed up the steps. "I'm early, I know, but I needed to see you. Are you all right?"

A smile lit her face. "I'm fine. In fact, I'm...wonderful."

Jonah reached for her hands and held them. He gave her fingers a gentle squeeze, then brought them to his lips and kissed her.

"You feel guilty about what happened, Jonah. Don't. Please."

Her voice came out in a hushed whisper that held a pleading quality he regretted she felt. "I love you."

Her eyes filled with moisture and her jaw quivered; then a huge smile lit her face.

"Greetings, Lord Haywood."

Jonah looked up to find Lady Amanda standing in the open doorway.

"We've been expecting you."

"Have you?" Jonah said, escorting Celie into the foyer. "If I'd have known my presence was anticipated with such eagerness, I'd have arrived sooner."

"Not everyone is eager to see you," Hadleigh's harsh voice said from the center of the foyer.

"Oh, Your Grace," Lady Amanda said with a smile on her face. "I am in awe."

"Amanda," Celie warned.

"No, Celie. I am truly in awe of your brother's talents."

Lady Amanda turned her attention to the Duke of Hadleigh, and Celie's fingers tightened around Jonah's forearm. He waited to enjoy the verbal sparring. The Duke of Hadleigh had found his equal in Lady Amanda.

"You never cease to amaze me, Your Grace. How ever do you manage it?"

"Manage what?" Hadleigh asked. The question seemed innocent enough, but the sound was more a hiss that came through Hadleigh's clenched teeth.

There was a hesitancy in his voice that Jonah agreed was a wise reaction. Danger loomed ahead, and Hadleigh realized it as well as Celie did. Unfortunately, things were proceeding at such a speed it was impossible to stop them.

"Your persona. Your facade."

"Facade?"

"Yes, how ever do you manage it to such perfection? The sarcasm in your voice, the scowl on your face, your haughty demeanor. It is amazing. Is this something you practice?"

"Amanda," Celie warned again.

"No, Celie. You think I am being disrespectful. I am not. I am truly impressed." She turned back to Hadleigh. "Do you find such a guise works to your advantage, or are there times when you find it necessary to fall back on your true nature?"

Hadleigh stood speechless. Jonah wanted to laugh out loud. Hadleigh had been confronted countless times by a countless number of adversaries, but none had been such a worthy adversary as the small female facing the ferocious duke.

A cavernous silence engulfed the entryway as the two opponents stared at each other. Relief came as Hadleigh's butler opened the door to one of the salons to allow two maids, each carrying trays.

"Oh, good, tea is ready," Celie said, rushing to Lady Amanda's side and literally pulling her away from Hadleigh and into the room. "Amanda, sit here beside me," she said, leading Amanda into the chair farthest away from Hadleigh.

Celie poured the tea, and when she handed Jonah his cup, she rolled her eyes in frustration.

Jonah wanted to laugh but knew that would only fuel an already volatile situation.

Tonight promised to be very interesting. He hoped they'd all survive the experience.

* * *

Celie had never met two people more destined to hate each other than her best friend and her brother. If the two of them survived the evening, their success threatened to rival one of the seven wonders of the universe. Amanda obviously didn't realize how her comments affected Hadleigh or how they threw him off balance. He was a duke, for heaven's sake. He was used to the respect and deference that accompanied his position. People guarded their words when they spoke to him. Instead, Amanda seemed to go out of her way to shock him with her outspokenness.

Jonah, at least, attempted to ease the tension as they made their way to the village assembly room where the dance was to be held. He and Amanda carried on a pleasant conversation. Her brother, however, wasn't helpful. The sullen expression on his face prevented either Jonah or Amanda from trying to include him in their discussions.

Not that either of them tried. There were times when she thought Jonah was as bent on fueling their ongoing feud as Hadleigh was.

Celie's gaze rested on Jonah as he conversed with Amanda. Every time she saw him, or thought of him, or stood close to him, her heart swelled inside her breast. She remembered what they'd shared the past week and the love she felt for him intensified.

"Do you anticipate a crush at the event?" Amanda asked Celie. "I know if the locals at home held an event like this, everyone for miles around would attend."

"It will be the same here. I think we'll be fortunate to find each other if we venture too far apart."

Amanda's smile brightened. "Tonight sounds more enjoyable all the time. Don't you think so, Your Grace?"

Hadleigh answered her with a grimace. Celie noticed, however, his gesture couldn't be called a smile. Every time he was forced to speak to Amanda, he wore a glowering frown that refused to go away.

"If you say so, Lady Amanda. You're about to find out. We've arrived."

The carriage stopped, and a footman rushed to open the door. As soon as the steps were lowered, Jonah stepped out and turned to assist Amanda to exit. Celie followed, and Hadleigh disembarked last. Celie knew it was cruel of her, but she stepped toward Jonah and took the arm he offered. That left Hadleigh to escort Amanda into the assembly hall.

The furious glare on his face told her he didn't appreciate her maneuver, but Celie didn't care. She wanted to walk in with Jonah.

The street in front of the assembly hall was crowded with wagons and carriages and horses tied to posts. The line of partygoers stretched from the entrance of the building, down the walk that led to the building, and around the corner. The guests included elderly matrons who needed canes for assistance, middle-aged married couples, and several young adults who came in groups of four and more. The laughter that rang out put everyone in a festive mood.

Excitement built inside her until she felt giddy with joy. She felt like she was attending the opera or the theater on opening night of a new performance. “Look, Hadleigh,” she said, watching the growing crowd make its way toward the building. “Everyone is here. And more are coming.”

In unison, they turned to watch as more carriages unloaded their passengers.

Celie wasn’t sure who noticed whom first, but her gaze stopped when she saw one particular couple coming toward them.

The rage in the woman’s eyes was frightening, the fury in her steps a warning. She marched in agitated steps with her husband in tow. Celie experienced a dread she wasn’t prepared to handle.

“Step behind me,” Jonah said, extending his arm to push her back.

“No, Jonah—”

“Yes.”

Celie cast a second startled glance at Melisande’s mother and realized that Lady Kendall was going to cause a scene. Even after all these years, Melisande’s parents hadn’t recovered from her death. At least Lady Kendall hadn’t. The fiery hatred in her eyes intensified as she stopped in front of Jonah and glared at him.

“How dare you show your face in polite society,” Lady Kendall said. Her voice was loud enough that everyone near them stopped to listen. "You should have been hanged for murder."

"Margaret," Lord Kendall said in a soothing voice, "let's return home."

"I prayed each night you were at war that you wouldn't come back alive. I asked that God would just give me that. But He didn't. He let you survive."

"Come home with me, Margaret," Lord Kendall said again. "You're only upsetting yourself. There's nothing you can do." This time he placed his arm around his wife's shoulder and turned her away from them.

"You deserve to die," she hollered over her shoulder as her husband escorted her to their carriage.

Her hateful words echoed in Celie's head even after the couple disappeared and the Marquess of Kendall's carriage was out of sight.

"Are you all right?" she heard Jonah ask.

She looked up and saw the deep frown on his face. She tried to answer him, knew she should be worried about him instead of him worrying about her—but she couldn't. She was trembling too badly to find her voice. And if she could find her voice, she wouldn't be able to form the words. Her teeth chattered too violently.

"Do you want to go home, Celie?"

"Do you?" she finally managed.

He shook his head. "I have to face this. Running will only fuel the gossip."

"Then I will stand at your side and face it with you."

He tightened his arm around her shoulder, and his strength traveled through her.

Jonah turned to Amanda. "Would you like to return to Hadleigh Manor, Lady Amanda?"

She laughed. "I should hope not. The evening has just begun. I've come to dance, and I can hear the orchestra from out here. They sound more than passable. It should be quite enjoyable."

That left only her brother, and they all seemed to focus on him at the same time.

"Well, Your Grace, have you decided with which camp you will toss your lot?" Amanda asked.

Hadleigh bristled visibly. His eyes narrowed when he lowered his gaze to meet Amanda's and his shoulders stiffened in determination. "Yes, Lady Amanda. I have decided what I am going to do."

Hadleigh didn't exactly step closer to where Amanda was on the narrow walkway, but it seemed as if he had. He raised himself up to his full height and towered over her like Celie had seen a vulture hover over its prey. "Someone is required to take responsibility for my sister, and if I leave, you would be that person. I shudder at the thought."

For the first time since Celie had known Amanda, her friend seemed at a loss for words. She recovered quickly, but not before Celie noticed a look of satisfaction on her brother's face.

"Your kindness never ceases to amaze me," Amanda said, fluttering her fan as if Hadleigh's words were a compliment instead of an insult. "Shall we go inside, then? The night is getting away from us."

Celie gave Jonah's arm a reassuring squeeze, then entered the assembly room with a smile on her face. This was the same as it was three years ago when Hadleigh had turned his back on Jonah, and society had followed suit. Except this time the outcome would be different. This time Jonah wasn't alone. This time she was with him.

Jonah escorted her through the room, and Celie recognized some childhood friends she'd grown up with. With her arm linked with Jonah's, they made their way to speak with them.

At first the tension in the room was uncomfortable. Conversations seemed stilted; people stared. But as the evening progressed, the scene outside lost importance.

Celie danced one dance with Jonah; then Squire James asked for the next set, and Robbie Benson, whose father owned the Keg and Ale, asked for the next. Amanda didn't lack for partners, either, although Celie noted that Hadleigh wasn't one of them. Jonah was monopolized the entire evening by several groups of townsmen who were interested in the improvements he was making to Haywood Abbey.

The evening was progressing much better than it had started.

"I haven't had a chance to be with you all night," Jonah said from behind her. "Would you care to step outside?"

Celie turned. The second she saw Jonah's captivating smile, a surge of warmth radiated through her. "I'd love to. I was afraid you weren't going to escape Vicar Redling and Mr. Hawthorton until the party was over."

"The thought crossed my mind, too, but Mrs. Hawthorton complained that her husband had only danced with her once, so to keep peace at home, he led her to the dance floor."

"Wise man," Celie said as they made their way out a side door and down the stairs that led to the lawn. Several other couples had the same idea and were walking through the little park the town had made surrounding the assembly hall.

Jonah led her to one of the few vacant benches placed inside the fenced-in park and they sat.

"I didn't get a chance to tell you how beautiful you look tonight. I'm sure all the other females are green with envy."

"I doubt it," she said with a smile on her face, "but I thank you for saying so. Have you noticed that Amanda hasn't lacked for admirers tonight?"

"Yes, I noticed. She was talking to the Conroy brothers when we left. Bertie Franklin was with them. All the young bucks here tonight are trying their hardest to make a favorable impression on her."

"Everyone except Hadleigh." Celie sighed. "Have you ever seen two people so opposite each other in your life?"

"They do seem to inspire the worst in each other. I'll say that for them."

Celie paused. "Have you recovered from the confrontation with Lady Kendall?"

"Yes, have you?"

"Me?" Celie placed her hand atop Jonah's. "I wasn't the focus of her tirade. You were."

"Yes, but she reminded everyone of Melisande's death three years ago. That couldn't have been pleasant for you."

She gently squeezed his fingers. "Nor for you."

His eyes closed briefly and he shook his head. "It's as if what happened that night will never go away. No matter how many years pass or how hard I try to distance myself from the events of that night, something or someone resurrects Melisande's death."

"Rumors have circulated about Lady Kendall's mental stability for quite some time. But I didn't realize she was so ill." Celie was suddenly struck by a frightening thought. "Jonah, you don't suppose Lord Kendall was responsible for shooting at us the day we arrived?"

He shook his head. "That thought occurred to me. I asked around about Kendall tonight, but Brandon Ransdell told me Lord Kendall didn't arrive at Kendall Park until the day before yesterday. He would know. His nephew is in charge of the stables at Kendall Park."

Celie experienced a sinking feeling. "If it wasn't Lord Kendall, who do you think it might have been? Are you sure there's no one else who might want to harm you?"

Jonah placed his other hand atop hers. "I don't know. Maybe what happened was an accident. Perhaps there was a hunter nearby and his shot went wild."

"You don't believe that, and I know it."

He smiled at her, but his smile wasn't sincere. "No, but it does no good to concentrate on the questions I can't answer." He gathered her hands in his. "I'd rather talk about us. Is Hadleigh still determined to leave for London in the morning?"

"Yes. Will you return with us?"

"No. I have too much to oversee here. But I'll be there in the morning to see you off. As soon as I finish here, I'll come back. I can't stay away from you too long, you know."

Jonah wrapped his arm around her shoulder and brought her closer. Celie went willingly. She remained in his arms for several wonderful moments before he spoke.

"We'd better go back inside," he said, kissing her lightly on the forehead. "I'm surprised your brother hasn't come for you already."

Celie rose with Jonah and walked back inside. She wished she could convince her brother to stay a few more days at least, but knew that was unlikely. She was glad he agreed to stay long enough to attend tonight's affair.

When they stepped inside the assembly room, the musicians were just starting a country dance, and Jonah led her onto the floor. They did the steps, weaving in and out of the line of dancers. Each time they came together, their gazes locked and he looked down on her with a smile that warmed her entire body.

Celie would always remember this night and how deeply she was in love with the Earl of Haywood.

* * *

The carriage came to a halt in front of Hadleigh Manor, and they disembarked. The ride home from the assembly dance had been pleasant, primarily because Amanda and her brother avoided talking to each other.

Celie attributed their lack of combative natures to the fact that Amanda had enjoyed herself so much. And to the fact that she'd danced so much she was exhausted.

Celie wanted to laugh. The difference she saw in her friend here compared to how she behaved in London was remarkable. It was as if she were determined to leave her mark on the male population, whereas in London she was determined to avoid being noticed. Celie couldn't help but wonder why.

Jonah bid them all a good night, then left to return to Haywood Abbey. When he was out of sight, she entered the manor house with Amanda and Hadleigh.

"May I speak with you a moment before you retire, Cecelia?" Hadleigh said when they'd given their cloaks and gloves to the butler.

"It can't wait until morning, Hadleigh?"

"No. It's important."

"Very well."

"I'll bid you both a good night, then," Amanda said as she walked up the stairs to her room.

Celie followed her brother into his study and sat in the chair in front of his desk. He closed the door, then sat in the chair that used to be their father's and now belonged to her brother.

"Is something wrong, Hadleigh?"

"Yes, Cecelia, something is wrong."

Her brother pushed around some papers on the desk, then leveled her with a serious expression.

"I received some disturbing news today that you need to be aware of."

"I assume this news involves Lord Haywood."

"You assume correctly."

Before she could inform him she didn't want to hear anything negative about Jonah, he raised his hand and stopped her.

"I already know you probably won't believe anything I have to say, but I couldn't live with myself if I didn't at least make you aware of what I discovered."

Celie sighed loud enough that her brother couldn't miss her frustration. "Very well, Hadleigh. What have you discovered that I need to know?"

"I received a message from my solicitor today informing me of the astronomical amount of money Haywood has spent to restore Haywood Abbey."

"Why does that surprise you, Hadleigh? You knew he intended to make major improvements to Haywood Abbey."

"He's using *your* money, Cecelia."

"Of course he is. He's using money from my dowry to make improvements to Haywood Abbey because it will be my home when we marry."

"*If* you marry. Haywood hasn't asked for your hand yet."

"He will. You know he will."

"I know nothing of the sort. What disturbs me even more is that he has charged all the bills for the repairs to his home to me!"

Celie stopped. "To you?"

"Yes, to me! Instead of putting the bills in his name so he can pay them with the money from your dowry, he expects me to cover them. I know you don't understand what this means—"

"Yes, Hadleigh," she interrupted. "I understand what this means. It means that if he doesn't ask to marry me, or if you would refuse his offer, he won't get my dowry. If that happens, *you* will be responsible for paying for the repairs to Haywood Abbey."

"Yes, Cecelia. That's exactly what it means."

Celie felt her world shift beneath her. "Why did the merchants think you would cover Jonah's debts? Why didn't your solicitor refuse them?"

"Because of you, Cecelia. Because all of London knows Haywood has been courting you. Everyone already believes the two of you will marry and he will get your dowry. Not only every merchant in London, but my solicitor as well. He didn't consider that there was anything inappropriate about the bills, since he knew I would want the house you lived in after your wedding to be in the best condition possible."

For several moments, Celie couldn't move. Her mind spun with possibilities for what had happened. One question refused to go away. Why did Jonah expect her brother to pay for the improvements to Haywood Abbey? What made him think Hadleigh would cover his debts? He knew how much Hadleigh disliked him. He knew what Hadleigh's reaction would be when he discovered what Jonah had done. But by then it would be too late. How would Hadleigh look if he refused to assist the man who was courting his sister?

Celie broke out in a sweat. Hadleigh would appear like a miserly bully when society discovered that he wouldn't loan money to the man his sister intended to marry when in time he'd receive her dowry and be able to pay him back.

She couldn't believe Jonah would do something so horrible, but he must have. Hadleigh wouldn't lie to her.

"I'm sure Haywood has a valid reason for putting his bills in your name, Hadleigh. We'll ask him when he arrives in the morning."

Her brother shoved the papers to the side of his desk and looked at her. "I sincerely hope so, Cecelia. I sincerely hope so. Now, go to bed. It's late and we want to get an early start in the morning."

Celie rose on shaky legs and walked behind the desk to kiss her brother on this cheek. "I know there's a reason, Hadleigh. There has to be."

Celie bade her brother good night, then went to her room. She would go to bed, but she knew she wouldn't sleep.

Why would Jonah have done such a thing? What possible reason could there have been?

She couldn't wait until morning to discover what he had to say. But the doubts grew larger with every step she took.

Chapter 18

Jonah rode up the lane to Hadleigh Manor and took in the sight before him. The servants were busy loading trunks onto a wagon for their return trip to London. In front of the luggage wagon was a cart to transport the staff members traveling with them. In front of that was the carriage emblazoned with the Hadleigh crest.

Jonah smiled when he thought of the return trip to London. He was glad he wouldn't be confined with both Hadleigh and Lady Amanda. He was certain that one of them would be charged with murder by the time they reached London.

Jonah dismounted near the house and handed the reins to a footman. Hadleigh's butler held the door open, and he went inside. Loud voices assaulted him the minute the door closed behind him.

He walked to the morning room and leaned a shoulder against the doorjamb. The conversation inside was too humorous to interrupt, so he waited quietly so as not to give away his presence.

"I think you've said enough, Amanda."

"But, Celie, you've heard His Grace say more than once that if I were *his* sister, he'd purchase a ticket for me on the next ship leaving England. He's never had a more perfect opportunity to make good on his threat."

"She's not serious, Hadleigh." Celie glared at Amanda. "Amanda, behave yourself."

"Very well, if you insist." Amanda crossed her arms over her chest and sat still. "I'll just sit here and make out my last will and testament. Take your time, Your Grace."

The Duke of Hadleigh gave Amanda the most scorching look Jonah had ever seen him give anyone. Perhaps if Lady Amanda would just look a little contrite, his expression might soften. But she seemed unaffected by his glare.

"May I be of assistance?" he said, stepping into the room.

"Lord Haywood," Celie greeted with a smile. "You've arrived."

"Just in time, from the sound of it."

Jonah greeted Lady Amanda with a nod, then moved to Celie and took her hands in his. He released her hands when he noticed the smile on her face fade. "Is something wrong?"

"I need to speak to you."

"Very well. We can go—"

She shook her head. "Later."

He nodded, then walked to the fireplace.

A low fire burned in the grate. Even though it wasn't terribly cold at this time of year, the rooms in the larger homes still needed a fire to take the chill from the air.

He leaned an elbow against the mantel and lifted his gaze to where Hadleigh stood opposite him. The expression on his face looked murderous.

"Am I interrupting something, Hadleigh?"

The narrowing of his eyes didn't bode well.

"Don't patronize me, Haywood. I've taken all the verbal abuse I'll tolerate for one day."

"I see you and Lady Amanda have been discussing politics again."

"The lady doesn't discuss. She preaches. And criticizes. And insults. The arguments in the House will seem calm after the tumultuous time I've spent in the country."

Jonah shifted his focus to Celie. It was obvious she was as upset as her brother.

"I assume, then, that you're ready to depart."

Hadleigh pushed away from the mantel. "Yes. We were waiting for your arrival."

Jonah walked to the sofa and helped Celie to her feet, then assisted Lady Amanda. He escorted them to the foyer where they readied themselves for the several hours' trip to London.

He knew Celie intended to allow Lady Amanda and her brother to leave first so they would have a moment of privacy. He stayed with her on the veranda while her brother and Amanda walked down the steps.

Before they reached the bottom, a bullet shot past them and slammed into one of the stone columns near where he stood.

Hadleigh pushed Lady Amanda back up the stairs and toward the house, but before he could make his way up the steps, a second shot hit the bricks to his right. He halted halfway between Jonah and the gunman.

"No one move," Jonah said, then pushed Celie and Lady Amanda behind him.

He looked to the side of the steps where a small, fragile-looking lady dressed in black mourning garb stood. Even though a dark netting covered her face, he knew immediately it was the Marchioness of Kendall. The blood in his veins ran ice cold.

He should have realized the night of the assembly ball that grief had robbed Lady Kendall of her grasp on sanity, that she was the one who had fired at them when they'd arrived.

He knew why she was here. He knew there would be no reasoning with her. She wanted someone to pay for her daughter's death. And that someone was going to be him.

Hadleigh stepped forward. "Lady Kendall? What a pleasure to see you."

"I've come to do what you promised you'd do, Your Grace. And have not."

She waved the gun in her hand, and Jonah attempted to push Lady Amanda and Celie closer to the house. He needed to protect them. He needed to protect Celie.

Hadleigh held out his hand in an effort to intervene. "You don't want to harm anyone, Lady Kendall. Why don't you come inside and rest for a few minutes? We can have tea and—"

"Liar!"

The color left Hadleigh's face. "Please, Lady Kendall. If you'll come inside, you and I can talk about this. I'm sure you'll feel better once you hear what I have to—"

"No! You promised you'd make him pay for killing my Melisande. You promised you'd ruin him! You lied!"

"I didn't lie to you, Lady Kendall. Melisande's death will be avenged. I promise you it will."

"No, it won't. You've already forgotten her." She waved the gun. "He killed her, and you promised on her grave you would ruin him!"

"I will! It will happen!"

"I thought you loved her. But you didn't. No one loved her as I did."

"I did!"

Hadleigh's voice rang out with heartache and pain. The raw agony of his words shattered the quiet country air, as if Melisande's death had occurred yesterday instead of three years ago.

At that single moment, Jonah knew any indication that Hadleigh had recovered from Melisande's death had been an act. He'd tolerated Jonah's presence to give him a false sense of camaraderie. He'd given him a deceptive impression of goodwill so Jonah wouldn't realize he had set a trap to ruin him. And Jonah had walked into it without hesitating.

The unrestrained anger in Hadleigh's voice told him what a fool he'd been. The hostile expression on Hadleigh's face outlined the bitterness that still ate away at him three years after Melisande's death.

With those two words, Hadleigh revealed his plan for revenge.

The plan was brilliant. As perfect as any plan he could have devised. And he'd used the one person Jonah would never suspect as the pawn to lure Jonah to his destruction.

A pain more intense than the near-fatal wound he'd endured in the war sliced through his body, then lodged in his heart. He thought of the hurt Celie would endure. The betrayal. All at her brother's hands.

He inched back, praying she and Lady Amanda were close enough to get inside. But when Lady Kendall noticed him move, she lifted her hand and pointed her gun to where Celie stood.

"Lady Kendall." He lifted his hands in surrender and took a step toward her. "I'm the one you want. Let Hadleigh and the ladies go inside. You and I can—"

Her laughter startled him. It wasn't the humorous sound of someone enjoying a good joke or the easy sound of someone conversing with friends, but the demented cackle of an individual far beyond the fringes of sanity.

"You think I want you, Lord Haywood? You think your death will make up for my Melisande's death? No! I want you to live your life after you've lost someone who's important to you."

"No!" Hadleigh's bellow startled them all to silence. "No! You can't mean this!"

Lady Kendall lifted her hand and pointed the gun at the center of Hadleigh's chest. "This is your fault, Hadleigh. If you would have kept your word, I wouldn't be forced to take matters into my own hands."

"I haven't gone back on my word. This is all part of the plan."

"Liar! You promised you'd exact revenge on Haywood for murdering my Melisande. You promised when he had the most to lose, you'd take it all! But what have you done! You've rewarded him for killing my Melisande! You welcomed him back into society! You paid his debts! Instead of taking anything away from him, you're giving him your sister to be his wife!"

"No! I'd never let him marry Cecelia. I would have stopped it before it came to that!"

Jonah saw where this was going. Hadleigh's words only confirmed what he already suspected. Hadleigh had never intended to let him marry Celie. Hadleigh didn't intend for him to use the money from Celie's dowry to fix Haywood Abbey. He wanted him to spend the money; then he would demand payment. When Jonah couldn't repay the money, Hadleigh would take everything he owned away from him.

Except Jonah wouldn't be the only one destroyed. Celie's life would be ruined, too.

Somehow, though, there'd been a gap in communication, and Hadleigh's plan was backfiring. He'd failed to inform Lady Kendall what he'd intended to do.

Melisande's mother had waited three long years for the man responsible for her daughter's death to pay. She'd waited three years for Hadleigh to make good his promise to take everything away from him. And she thought the land, his estates, Haywood Abbey were what mattered most.

They weren't. Oh, maybe they were before he met Celie, but how could anything be more important than she was? How could he love anything more than he loved her?

"What are your plans, Lady Kendall?" Jonah took one more step away from Celie, toward Melisande's mother. "To kill Lady Cecelia?"

"Yes! Hadleigh promised me that when you had the most to lose, he'd take it from you! Instead, he offered you his sister so you could save everything."

Jonah's heart thundered in his chest. He couldn't let anything happen to Celie. He had to do something to save her, had to convince Lady Kendall that Celie wasn't important to him. He'd lose her if he succeeded, but at least she would be alive. At least he wouldn't be responsible for her death. "Do you honestly believe Lady Cecelia means that much to me?"

"Of course she does. The two of you are lovers. I've watched her visit you at Haywood Abbey almost every day this whole week. Do you think I don't know what you were doing?"

Jonah heard Celie's soft cry from behind him, but he didn't dare look at her. If he did, he'd see the hurt, the humiliation, the regret, and it would be his undoing. Instead, he had no choice but to add more hurt to the pain she was already suffering.

Hopefully, Lady Amanda's arms would be comfort enough to support her. Because what he intended to say would devastate her. He had to make his words so believable Lady Kendall would abandon her plan to kill Celie.

He braced his shoulders and erected a sturdy wall around his heart. Then he separated himself from his emotions, from the love he felt for Celie. It was the only way he would survive what he had to do.

"If you think killing Lady Cecelia will cause me regret, I'm afraid you will be disappointed. Hadleigh wasn't the only one with an agenda. I had one, too."

Jonah took another step toward Lady Kendall. "Did you think I would accept everything Hadleigh did to me three years ago without avenging myself? Without avenging my family?" He forced a laugh. "Do you know how difficult it was to hold my head high three years ago when everyone in society turned their backs on me? Do you know how many miserable days and nights I spent in the Crimea formulating my plan of revenge? It was Hadleigh's fault I nearly got killed while there. Hadleigh's fault I wasn't at my father's and brother's sides when they died. Hadleigh's fault I wasn't here to bury them." He threw his arms out from his side, praying Lady Kendall would pull the trigger. At least her bullet would stop his tongue from saying anything more to hurt Celie.

Melisande's mother didn't seem convinced. The hand that held the gun trembled more uncontrollably. And Jonah was forced to continue.

"Taking the lady's virtue was all part of my plan. Ruining her for anyone else was always my goal. My intention was *never* to marry her."

"No, that can't be!"

"Oh, but it was."

He laughed. He wasn't sure how he could manage to laugh when the lies he spoke ripped his heart from his chest. He wasn't sure how he would survive another day knowing the hurt he'd caused her. Yet what choice did he have?

"Hadleigh bought into my plan from the start. Did you know that? He thought I intended to marry his sister." He laughed again. "As if I'd consider marrying the sister of the man who'd ruined my life. What a fool he was." Jonah gave Hadleigh a look he prayed held all the fury and revulsion he felt at the moment.

"From the beginning, Hadleigh's offer of his sister's hand was too good to be true. From the start, I knew he had set a trap to destroy me." Jonah paused long enough to give his words emphasis. "I was determined to best him. And I did!"

Jonah wasn't sure, but he thought he heard a whimper from behind him. If he looked, he knew he'd find Lady

Amanda with her arms around Celie's shoulders. But he didn't think the soft cry had come from Celie. She was too strong, too noble, too proud to show him or her brother how much they'd hurt her. No, the whimper had no doubt come from Lady Amanda. Only a dear, dear friend would feel such anguish on Celie's behalf.

"So, my lady, if you want to exact revenge for your daughter's death, kill Lady Cecelia if you want. Her death won't matter to me. The only person who will regret her passing is her friend. And perhaps her brother—if he cares for her even a little. Although I'm not sure he does if he'd conspire to use her like he did."

Lady Kendall's hand shook even more. She lifted her arm and changed where she aimed the gun—to the middle of his chest. The path of the bullet would go through him before it reached Celie—through his heart.

He was glad. He couldn't imagine living the rest of his life without Celie in it. And she wouldn't be. His lies had been too convincing to think she'd ever believe him if he told her he hadn't meant any of the words he'd said.

"But my Melisande is dead! Dead!"

"If you think my death will take away the pain of your loss..." He lifted his arms, praying she'd be satisfied with taking his life in exchange for losing Melisande.

She pointed the barrel of her gun at the center of his chest, and Jonah waited. Her hand shook and the frown on her forehead grew more intense.

He held his breath, knowing it could be his last. He waited for Lady Kendall's next move. Then, out of the corner of his eyes, a figure approached. It was the Marquess of Kendall. Jonah prayed the marquess had come to stop his wife and not assist her.

"Margaret? I've looked for you everywhere. You didn't tell anyone you intended to leave the house."

Lady Kendall turned to face her husband. "Kendall, I've found the man who killed our Melisande."

"I need you to come home with me, my dear. We have company."

"Company?"

"Yes, the boys. They've come for a visit and missed you when you didn't come down for lunch. They're out searching for you."

A wide smile lifted the corners of Lady Kendall's mouth. "Are they? How sweet." She turned back to Jonah and refocused her gun to the center of his chest. "But I found the man who murdered our Melisande. I told you I would."

"Yes, I know you did. Don't concern yourself over him any longer. I'll take care of him—later."

"You will?"

"Yes, dear. I will."

"Very well. I'll leave the matter to you. I need to hurry home to see my boys. I'm sorry I caused them concern."

The Marquess of Kendall stepped close to his wife and placed his arm around her shoulders. "Yes, we need to hurry now."

"Of course, Kendall. We can't keep the boys waiting."

"No, we can't, sweetheart. Perhaps you can rest a little before lunch. Everything will be better once you've rested a while."

"Yes, I think you're right. I am terribly tired."

"I know you are. You've worked too hard this morning. You need to rest."

"Yes, I do." She looked up at her husband with an adoring smile. "I don't know what I'd do without you to look after me."

"I know, Margaret." The Marquess of Kendall turned his wife away from Hadleigh Manor. "Is that my pistol you have?"

She looked down at the weapon in her hand and shrugged. "It must be. I wonder how it got here."

"Why don't you let me have it?"

"Of course, Kendall. I certainly have no need of a gun."

"No, you don't." He took the first step with his wife, then turned to look over his shoulder. "I'll take care of her, Hadleigh. This won't happen again. You have my word."

Jonah didn't move until the Marquess of Kendall and his wife were out of sight, then turned to look at Celie.

But she'd already left him.

Chapter 19

Jonah walked to the closed door and turned the handle.

Locked.

Celie had locked him out of her life. She'd made it evident that she wanted nothing more to do with him. And he knew how hopeless it would be to try to convince her that his words had all been lies. He knew he didn't stand a chance of convincing her that he really loved her.

He turned back to where Hadleigh stood at the bottom of the steps and was filled with rage. He bounded down the steps and, before Hadleigh could move, pulled back his fist and drove it into his jaw.

Hadleigh landed in a heap on the ground, but Jonah couldn't stop there. "You bloody bastard!" He kicked Hadleigh in the ribs, then mounted his horse and rode like hell back to Haywood Abbey.

When you have the most to lose, I'll take it all.

He should have known Hadleigh would never allow him to marry his sister. He should have known he'd never lift a finger to help Jonah repair the dilapidated Haywood Abbey. He should have known Hadleigh wasn't above using his own sister to exact his revenge. If only he'd seen it coming before it was too late.

Jonah raced through the meadow, taking chances he wouldn't ordinarily take, riding at a pace he knew wasn't safe for himself or his horse. When he reached Haywood Abbey, he bounded to the ground and stormed through the front door.

Bundy must have heard him ride up and was waiting for him.

"Is everything all right, Cap'n?"

Jonah couldn't stop the demented laughter that escaped from somewhere deep inside him. "No, Sergeant. Everything is not all right."

His breath caught. Without Celie, he'd lost the only thing that was important to him.

"Has the lady left for London?"

"Yes, Sergeant. She's gone."

When you have the most to lose, I'll take it all.

Jonah tried to think through the rush of fear and devastation crashing through him.

"Have you and the lady had a misunderstanding, my lord?"

Jonah looked into Bundy's anxious expression. "Yes, Bundy. A misunderstanding."

"Shouldn't you try to work it out, then, Cap'n?"

Jonah shook his head.

"You can't mean to let her go, Cap'n. She loves you. You love her."

A sword as lethal as the blade with which the enemy had struck him down on the battlefield pierced him, only this time the blade sliced through his heart instead of his side.

Jonah nearly doubled over from the pain of the unexpected punch he took to the gut.

When you have the most to lose, I'll take it all.

Bloody hell! Bloody damn hell! Hadleigh had made good on his threat. Hadleigh had taken everything away from Jonah. And Jonah hadn't seen it coming.

Jonah staggered across the foyer and into his study. He dropped into the nearest chair and sat with his forearms propped on his knees. He stared down at the floor for several long, torture-filled minutes.

"What are you going to do, Cap'n?" Bundy finally asked.

Jonah knew Bundy wanted an answer, but it was too late for any solutions. He'd walked into Hadleigh's trap with both eyes open and he was about to lose everything.

No. He'd *already* lost everything. He'd already lost Celie.

"Is there something you need, sir?"

Jonah looked up, but it wasn't Bundy he saw. It was Hadleigh. Hadleigh laughing. Hadleigh congratulating himself. Hadleigh toasting his success. It had taken him three long years to exact his revenge, but he'd accomplished it in spades.

It wasn't the money Jonah minded losing. It was Celie. Hadleigh had used Celie to accomplish his revenge. The bastard had used his sister to destroy Jonah. And he hadn't realized it wasn't the money that was most important to him. It could never be the money. Not when he had something worth so much more. Not when he had Celie's love.

Jonah thought of the huge amount of money he'd already spent making repairs and improvements to the Abbey. He thought of all the debts Hadleigh had paid. All the money Jonah now owed. Money he'd never be able to repay.

A picture of Hadleigh toasting Jonah's demise flashed before his eyes. Oh, how Hadleigh must be enjoying himself. How much more he'd enjoy himself when he demanded Jonah repay his debts and he couldn't.

How much more he would enjoy his success when he realized it wasn't the money that Jonah couldn't live without. It was Celie.

Jonah sat straight and took a painful breath. If only he'd realized what Hadleigh was doing before it was too late. He should have known there were strings attached to his demand to pay Jonah's father's debts and repair the Abbey. He should have known Hadleigh had no intention of letting Jonah improve the lives of the Haywood tenants who'd gone without for so long. He should have known Hadleigh wouldn't do anything that might benefit anything Jonah owned. He hated him too much.

Jonah raked his fingers through his hair in an angry gesture, then halted. It was too late for him. He'd already lost everything that was important to him: the Abbey, the estate, the land, and Celie. But that didn't mean everyone who depended on him needed to lose everything. The Haywood tenants had gone without too long. They deserved something good to happen to repay them for their loyalty and devotion.

Jonah rose to his feet and faced Bundy. "I want a list of the supplies it will take to repair every tenant's home and fix their outbuildings, Sergeant."

"Yes, sir, but—"

"Then I want each of the tenant's wives to choose something they want. I don't care if it's a new bed, a new table, enough cloth for six new dresses. I don't care. Something that's important to them."

"What?"

"And I want the list before dark."

"Don't you think you should go after—"

Jonah slashed his hand through the air to stop Bundy from finishing his thought and paced back and forth across the room. "First thing in the morning, I want you to send some men to London to get any supplies we might need to finish repairing Haywood Abbey and bring them back. Tell them to make sure the bills for everything get sent to the Duke of Hadleigh."

"Are you sure, Cap'n?"

"Yes! Now, move! We don't have much time."

"But Lady Cecelia, she's no doubt on her way to London. Don't you think you should…?"

Jonah's knees weakened. He wanted nothing more than to go after Celie, but it wouldn't do any good. Not yet. She was too angry with him, too hurt. He needed to give her time before he went after her.

"I want you to send one of the local lads to the village to hire as many workers as he can find. And not only men. Women, too. They can do some of the lighter chores."

Jonah donned the determined expression he'd used so often when issuing orders during the war. It was an expression he'd perfected that left no doubt as to his seriousness and hid his fear. "Go, Bundy! We've got to get everything we need before it's too late."

Jonah almost choked on the words. A pain more severe than anything he'd ever suffered stabbed through his heart.

Celie had left him, which meant he'd lost the one thing that was most important to him. He'd lost everything.

But that didn't mean that everyone on his estate had to go without any longer. The Haywood tenants deserved decent roofs over their heads and at least one luxury they'd only dreamed of having.

Jonah headed for the door almost at a run. Hadleigh may have destroyed him, but he refused to go down without a fight. He hadn't endured the horrors of war without learning some of the skills it took to survive.

He would think of himself later, when everyone else who depended on him had been taken care of. Then he'd let himself think of how much he loved Celie. And he'd let himself think of how impossible it would be to live without her.

And he'd do everything in his power to get her back.

Chapter 20

Jonah sat behind the massive mahogany desk in his study with his booted feet propped on the corner of the desk, a nearly empty whiskey bottle in one hand and a more than half-full glass of whiskey in the other. This was the third day since he'd returned to London.

It was the third time he'd gone to see her. His third attempt to convince her that he hadn't meant anything he'd said.

The third time he'd been turned away at her door.

He lifted the glass but stopped halfway to his mouth. The thought of taking another swallow of the vile liquid turned his stomach.

Bloody hell, he couldn't even manage to do a proper job of getting drunk.

He set the glass on the desk and dropped his head back onto the cracked leather. The entryway was finally quiet for a little while.

Since the Duke of Hadleigh had let it be known that he would not cover the astronomical bills Jonah had amassed, Jonah had been besieged with creditors and bill collectors.

For a while, he thought he might not survive with his flesh intact, but as the man he'd trusted to cover his back during the war had done so often before, Bundy had come to his rescue in this as well.

He wasn't sure what scheme his sergeant had concocted to clear his home of the scores of creditors threatening his life, but it had worked. His town house was peaceful for the first time since he'd returned.

He closed his eyes and prayed that, for at least a little while, he would be allowed a few restful minutes when he wouldn't be tortured with the fact that he'd lost Celie. He prayed that the hurt and the agony that ate at him night and day would ease for just a moment. But he knew that wasn't possible.

Jonah thought of the lies Hadleigh had told him and cursed himself over again. He thought of the pain Celie felt, believing the two people who loved her most had betrayed her. He knew her whole world had been destroyed and she was left with nothing stable to hold on to.

Jonah rose to his feet and placed another piece of wood into the burning flames, then sat in his chair and propped his feet on the corner of the desk.

In his mind, he relived the scene with Lady Kendall. If only there had been another way to keep Celie safe. If only he'd been able to avoid saying the words that had destroyed her love for him.

If only she hadn't found out how little Hadleigh thought of her that he'd use her as a pawn to gain revenge.

That wouldn't have saved him, because the condemning lies had come from his own mouth, but perhaps she wouldn't realize her brother thought so little of her he'd used her to exact his revenge.

Hadleigh's threat came back as a roaring warning that echoed with the force of a violent thunderstorm.

When you have the most to lose, I'll take it all.

And he had. He'd taken Celie away from him.

He reached for the bottle he'd left beside his chair, but stopped when he heard voices out in the entryway.

Bloody creditors!

He pulled the stopper from the bottle, then paused midway in pouring more liquor into his glass. The door flew open and Lady Amanda Radburn stormed into the room with Bundy on her heels.

"I'm sorry, Cap'n, but the lady insisted."

"Lady Amanda," Jonah said, not bothering to pour the liquor into his glass but tipping the bottle to his mouth. "Why doesn't your persistence surprise me?"

"Are you drunk?" She placed her hands on her hips and glared at him.

Jonah laughed. "Unfortunately, no."

"Good."

His guest evaluated him for a second, then came into the room and sat in the chair facing Jonah's desk.

"Bundy," he said, sitting up in his chair, "see if Cook has something to serve with tea."

Lady Amanda held up her hand. "That's not necessary, Bundy. I won't be here long enough for tea."

"You shouldn't be here at all." Jonah sat back in his chair and placed the bottle on the corner of the desk. He needed to keep it within reach. He'd already decided if Celie's friend had come here to chastise him for breaking Celie's heart and call him every name Celie had been too upset to use, perhaps the whiskey he hadn't finished would come in handy. "So, why have you come?" He tried to look bored.

"To hear the truth instead of the lies you told Lady Kendall."

Jonah felt the air rush from his body. "What makes you think I lied to Lady Kendall?"

"Because I have the advantage of watching the players in this drama from an objective viewpoint. I just left Celie and—"

"How is she? Is she all right?"

Lady Amanda slashed her hand through the air. "No, she's not all right. She's hurt. She's miserable. Her heart is broken, and she's certain it will never heal again."

She leveled him with an evaluative glare. "Do you care?"

"Of course I care." Jonah dropped his feet to the floor. "No one should have to endure this kind of pain. No one should be submitted to such cruelty, especially from the two people she thought loved her most."

"Are you talking about yourself and Hadleigh?"

Jonah felt a heavy weight drop to the pit of his stomach. "Yes. Me, because I took everything Hadleigh said at face value. Because I didn't realize there was an ulterior motive to his machinations. Hadleigh, because he used his sister without caring that she would be hurt."

"I'd like to know what happened."

"Why?"

"Because I think you truly love Celie." She kept her gaze focused on him and didn't let it waver. "*Do* you love her?" she asked. "And I want the truth. If you dare lie to me, what Hadleigh did to you will be nothing compared to the hell Celie and I can put you through."

"Yes, I love her. I'd be a fool not to. She's the most amazing woman I've ever met. And..."

"Yes?"

Jonah swallowed. "I'm not sure I can live the rest of my life without her."

"That's all I wanted to know." Lady Amanda slid back in her chair and folded her hands in her lap. "Now, how did you and Celie get yourself into such a mess?"

Jonah took a deep breath, then told Celie's best friend how Hadleigh had paid all of Jonah's father's debts. He repeated Hadleigh's demand that Jonah begin work repairing Haywood Abbey and his promise to cover the expenses until he received Celie's dowry.

When he finished, Lady Amanda slammed her fists on the cushioned arms of the chair and bolted to her feet.

"That conniving bastard!" She stormed across the room like a raging hurricane. "He had no intention of allowing you to marry Celie. No intention of you ever getting the money from her dowry. He used her to ruin you."

Jonah blinked several times at the very unladylike expletives that came from Lady Amanda's mouth. "It won't do any good to accuse Hadleigh of anything," he said. "He'll only deny he intended any such thing. Besides, he still holds the trump card."

Lady Amanda lifted her eyebrows. "And what is that?"

"He must approve Celie's choice of a husband. If we marry without his approval, I won't get even one pound of her dowry."

"You would not take Celie without her money?"

Jonah leaned forward. "I am destitute, my lady. Considering Hadleigh's well-conceived plan, I'll be lucky if it takes even a fortnight to be shunned by all of society again. What kind of life could I give Celie? Without her dowry, I couldn't *allow* her to become my wife, even if she wanted."

"Maybe if we—"

Jonah held up his hand to stop her words. "I've already considered every conceivable possibility. There's no way. Nothing short of murder."

For several seconds, neither of them spoke. Celie's friend had a faraway look in her eyes, as if she were contemplating something that required a great deal of thought.

With a slow nod of her head, she lifted her gaze and focused her attention on Jonah.

"I would like to invite you to tea, Lord Haywood."

Jonah shook his head. "I'm sorry, Lady Amanda, but I'm not—"

"Neither am I." She held up her hand to stop him. "The tea I'm inviting you to will be held at my residence in exactly one hour."

"Will Celie be there?"

"Yes. As well as the Duke of Hadleigh."

Jonah smiled. At least the corners of his mouth lifted in what he hoped would pass for a smile. "I'm afraid the Duke of Hadleigh will not welcome me anywhere near him."

"That's not your concern." She waved her hand as if it were possible to brush away the Duke of Hadleigh when talking about him.

"Are you sure you can convince Hadleigh to come?"

"Oh, yes. Hadleigh will do anything in his power to make amends with Celie. She's refused to see him since she returned to London. After how he used her, he's truly afraid that he may have lost her forever."

Jonah shook his head. "I don't think there's anything you can do, my lady. I applaud you for making the effort to help me, but—"

"Do you have a plan to get the woman you love back? Or don't you love her enough to try?"

Jonah's temper rose. "I've even considered murder, my lady, and I'd do it if I thought I would end up with Celie and not a hangman's noose. Yes, I want her enough. My blood turns to ice at the thought of having to live the rest of my life without her."

Jonah rose to his feet and walked from one side of the room to the other in long, angry strides. "I can't believe what a fool I was not to see this coming! I should have known Hadleigh hadn't given up on his vow to exact revenge for Melisande's death. Instead, I allowed a friendship I thought still existed between Hadleigh and myself to control my judgment, and I am paying for my stupidity."

"Hadleigh's purpose was to take advantage of you, and it's a point to your credit that you didn't realize what he was doing. It means that you're not as coldhearted as he. It means your mind is not as twisted with hatred as his."

Jonah stared at Celie's friend for several long seconds. There was something quite pretty about her, and he wondered why she hadn't been spoken for. Or if she had, why she hadn't accepted anyone's offer.

"Why are you doing this?"

She looked at him as if he'd just asked the most ridiculous question imaginable. "Because Celie is my best friend and I can't stand by while my best friend is miserable and not try to do everything in my power to help her."

He caught an evasive look in her eyes before she quickly hid it. "And the other reason is?"

"There is no other reason, my lord," she said with a laugh.

"I think there is. Another reason that is equally as important to you as trying to keep your best friend from suffering."

Lady Amanda tugged on her gloves as if preparing to leave. "If there is," she said, avoiding looking him directly in the eyes, "it is a reason I intend to keep to myself. Now, if you will kindly make yourself presentable, I will go to invite the Duke of Hadleigh for what I pray will be his downfall."

Jonah watched Lady Amanda Radburn walk from his room, then went upstairs to shave and dress for tea.

Chapter 21

You what!

Celie stared at her best friend as if she'd lost her mind. "You can't be serious!"

"I've never been more serious in my life. Lord Haywood should arrive momentarily. And so should your brother." Amanda reached over and clasped both Celie's hands in hers. "There are some things you don't know—important things. And you need to be aware of them."

Celie shook her head. "I've heard all I need to. You don't know what it's like to realize you were nothing more to your brother than a pawn he could use to ruin the man he hated. And"—she took a shaky breath—"you don't know what it's like to find out that the man you've always loved only pretended to love you to destroy his most hated enemy." She felt a fresh onslaught of tears fill her eyes.

"If that were true, I wouldn't lift a finger to help Lord Haywood get you back, and you know it."

Celie looked at the serious expression on her friend's face. "How can you think Jonah loves me? You heard him. He only used me to get even with Hadleigh for everything he'd done to him after Melisande's death."

"And you don't think he could have been lying?"

Celie shook her head. "I've always known Jonah couldn't love me. But I'd loved him for so long I let myself believe he could."

"Then you need to hear the truth with your own ears. You need to hear how your brother used not only you but Lord Haywood to achieve his revenge. That's the only way you'll ever trust Haywood."

"What makes you think Hadleigh will come once he finds out Jonah will be here?"

"Because he doesn't know—yet." Amanda smiled when she heard a commotion at the front door. "But he will soon."

Celie recognized her brother's voice and looked up as the butler admitted him into the room.

"Cecelia." He rushed to the sofa where she was and sat beside her. He turned toward her and clasped her hands in his.

She pulled her fingers out of his grasp and rose to her feet.

He rose to stand beside her. "Please, allow me to explain. Nothing is what you think. You have always been the most important person in the world to me. I would never have let anything hurt you."

"Wouldn't you have?"

"No. You don't understand. It was Haywood. I had to—"

Jonah's voice echoed from the foyer, and his sure footsteps thudded as he made his way toward the drawing room. Her heart thundered in her breast.

The door opened, and he stepped inside the room.

His gaze focused on her first, but that wasn't a surprise. They were so attuned to each other it wasn't uncommon for her to realize the precise moment Jonah walked into a room. Or for him to find her the minute he arrived. She didn't know what it was, but it had been that way between them from the beginning.

"What the hell is he doing here?" Hadleigh bellowed.

"I invited him, Your Grace."

"Then you can uninvite him! I don't want him anywhere near my sister!"

"If Lord Haywood's company is so disagreeable, you are welcome to leave, Your Grace. But if you do, I'm afraid you will never see your sister again."

Her brother opened his mouth to speak, then closed it. Celie kept her gaze focused on where Jonah stood near the door.

"Celie?"

This was the man to whom she'd given her body. To whom she'd given her heart and her soul. The man who'd rejected everything she'd offered him. Who'd stomped on her heart and ground it beneath his heel.

She should hate him. She told herself over and over that she should, but the part of her heart he possessed refused to turn away from him. He held too tight a grip on her emotions for her to let him go.

"Are you all right?"

She shook her head. She wasn't all right. She doubted she would ever be all right again. "I..."

She'd convinced herself that now that she knew the truth she wouldn't feel the same about him. But she did. She still loved him. She still missed him. And she still wanted to run into his arms and have him hold her.

"Do us a favor," her brother interrupted, "and leave Cecelia alone. You've done enough damage."

"This is my home, Your Grace, and I would like Lord Haywood to stay. I, for one, would like to hear what he has to say."

"Well, I wouldn't!"

Amanda's mouth curved upward. Celie couldn't believe it. She was smiling.

"No, Your Grace. I don't imagine you would."

Her friend, the one person in all the world who'd stood at her side even when it would have been to her advantage not to, stepped close to her and placed her hand on her shoulder. "You need to hear everything, Celie."

Jonah ignored Hadleigh's hostility and took a step into the room. "I need to talk to you for a moment."

"No!" Hadleigh crossed the floor in long, angry strides. "Get out! You have nothing to say to my sister."

"Your Grace." Amanda lifted her hand and stepped in front of Hadleigh. "Don't you think it might be best if you allow Lord Haywood to explain? After his admission to Lady Kendall, I'm sure there's nothing he can say to sway your sister's opinion of him. But it's evident he won't give up until he tries one last time."

"He's done enough damage. He admitted he deceived Cecelia. That his only intent in asking her to marry him was for her money."

"That's only partly true," Jonah said. "I needed your money, Celie. I've never denied that. But there's something I want you to know before I leave."

"You can't believe a word from this murdering liar, Cecelia. You know you can't."

"Murderer, Your Grace?" Amanda said, taking an obvious step away from Jonah. "I had no idea Lord Haywood had committed murder."

"Of course he did."

Hadleigh glared at Jonah, and Celie saw a look of hatred in her brother's eyes she thought had lessened in the three years since Melisande's death.

Amanda clasped her hand to her throat. "No wonder you believed his admission so readily. What I don't understand, though, is why you considered allowing Celie to marry him in the first place."

"I allowed it because..." Hadleigh halted in midsentence.

In the flash of an eye, Celie realized that if her brother had finished his thought, she would have heard something she wasn't sure she was strong enough to handle.

"Wouldn't you like to boast of your success, Hadleigh?" Jonah dropped his shoulders as if admitting defeat. "I mean, what satisfaction is there in victory if no one is aware of the plan you orchestrated to achieve your triumph?"

"Shut up, Haywood. There was no plan."

"Of course there was a plan. And I played into your scheme perfectly."

Amanda wrapped her arm around Celie's waist, and Celie braced herself for what she was about to hear.

She knew that whatever was about to unfold wasn't a secret to Amanda. Amanda already knew what Hadleigh had done and thought it was important for Celie to know it, too. And tragic enough that she expected Celie would need her support.

"What plan is Jonah talking about?" she asked.

"There was no plan. You're listening to the ravings of a desperate man." Hadleigh turned his hostile glare in Jonah's direction. "Get out!"

"I will, as soon as I congratulate you."

Jonah moved slightly. Celie's heart raced. There was a warning look in her brother's eyes that frightened her. There was a determination in Jonah's she'd never seen before.

"I underestimated you, Hadleigh. When you issued your threat that you'd wait until I had the most to lose, then take it all, I thought you meant earthly possessions. But you didn't, did you?"

"Shut up. You deserve to lose everything. You deserve to rot in hell."

"Did your sister know what you intended? Was she involved in your scheme? Or was she just the pawn you used to trap me?"

Celie shifted her gaze to her brother. "What plan? What is Jonah talking about, Hadleigh?"

"There was no plan! He's only trying to make trouble. He's desperate. That's all."

"Someday, you'll have to ask him, Celie. But when you do, be prepared."

"Out!" Hadleigh bellowed. "Get. Out!"

"No, Hadleigh." Celie knew if she was ever going to hear the truth from her brother's mouth, she had to force the issue now. "I would like to hear what Jonah has to say."

"Cecelia," her brother said in a stern voice, "I don't know what you hope to prove by such defiance. Listening to this scoundrel's lies will do nothing except force you to relive how he used you to exact his revenge against me. Don't you realize that he'll only tell more lies in his attempt to convince you that what he admitted to Lady Kendall wasn't true?"

She turned her focus on Jonah. "Were they true, Lord Haywood? Were the things you said to Lady Kendall true?"

Jonah paused, and she knew then that he considered lying to her. When he spoke, the pain inside her chest hurt more than she thought she could bear.

"Yes, Celie. In part, they were all true."

Amanda wrapped her arm around Celie's waist when she staggered.

"See, Cecelia! I told you Haywood was nothing but a blackguard from whom you needed protection."

Jonah ignored Hadleigh's outburst. "I meant it when I said how much I hated your brother when he turned his back on me that first time and all of society took their cue from him. I spent many hours considering what I could do to regain my acceptance. But I knew nothing would force society to welcome me back.

"And every night, when I fell asleep on the cold, frozen ground in the Crimea, with little food in my belly and only the rags on my back to keep me warm, I planned what I would say and do the minute I stepped back on English soil.

"And when I received word that my father and brother were dead, I blamed Hadleigh. I deceived myself into believing that if I had been here with them, I could have made them realize the destructive path they were traveling and changed the outcome of their lives. And if not, at least I would have been here to bury them."

Jonah held out his arms in surrender. "But all my plans were nothing more than that—idle imaginings. Ramblings of loneliness. And self-pity. And helplessness.

"I didn't act on any of them. And I would never have done anything to hurt you."

He took a step toward her.

"I couldn't, Celie. I would never do anything to hurt you—because I love you."

"Liar!"

"I said the words I knew Lady Kendall wanted to hear—*needed* to hear. I took the blame for Melisande's death even though I didn't cause it. I told a grieving mother that I was responsible for everything that happened that night. And I did my best to convince her that your death wouldn't affect me. I needed her to believe I didn't care for you. I would have said whatever was necessary in order to save your life. Because I couldn't imagine a life without you in it."

"No!"

Her brother's loud denial blasted through the silence.

"He doesn't love you, Cecelia. He's incapable of the emotion. Don't you realize how great a fool you made of yourself by thinking he could ever love you?"

"That's not true, Celie. I love you. No matter what you think of me, or how much you believe you hate me, I want you to know that I love you. I have from the first day I saw you again."

She didn't know what to believe. Her roiling emotions couldn't make sense of what her mind told her.

"Jonah, did you only want to marry me for my dowry?"

Jonah stopped, then closed his eyes and shook his head. "No, Celie. I wanted to marry you because I loved you. I've always known that Hadleigh controls your dowry."

Celie felt the bottom fall out of her world. "Hadleigh controls my dowry."

A frown deepened across Jonah's brow. "You didn't know?"

She shook her head.

"Oh, Hadleigh." Jonah's voice brimmed with disbelief. "Was there *no* limit to your deceit? Wasn't it enough that you used your sister to achieve your goal? Did you trust her so little that you needed to keep the terms of her dowry from her?"

Celie swayed and was thankful Amanda was there to steady her.

"I didn't use Cecelia," he answered with a hateful glare. "I *saved* her."

"*Saved* her!" Jonah took a step closer toward the duke. "Did you once ask yourself if your sister would be of the same opinion when she found out what you'd done?"

"I didn't need to ask her. She would have answered with her heart and been miserable for the rest of her life."

Jonah's eyes opened wide. "You fool! You arrogant fool!"

The muscles on either side of Jonah's jaw knotted as the noticeable anger etched on his face intensified. His breathing became harsh and labored, and Celie knew that whatever her brother had done was meant to destroy her love for Jonah.

A numbing fear ate away inside her and she was frantic for answers.

"Jonah, explain what happened," she pleaded, praying that he'd ease her fears.

She wasn't sure what had transpired between Jonah and her brother, but she knew that Jonah wasn't responsible for the damage that had been done. Her brother was.

Jonah took a step toward her and smiled. "Everything will be all right, Celie. Just remember that I love you. I will *always* love you. I have from the first night I saw you."

"No, Celie," Hadleigh bellowed. "Don't believe him. He sought you out that first night to anger *me*! To antagonize me because he knew I was unable to stop him."

"Celie knows why I approached her. I explained my reasons a long time ago. I have always been honest with her. Which is more than I can say for you, Hadleigh."

"That's a lie," Hadleigh bellowed.

Jonah took another step closer to her. "When you are ready to hear everything that was done to destroy our future, you will have to ask your brother to explain it to you. You need to hear what he intended from his lips, not mine."

Celie spun to face her brother and she knew in that moment that he had been behind everything that had happened to her. "What have you done?"

"I saved you! I kept you from ruining your life! And I intend to prevent this blackguard from destroying anyone else's life ever again."

Celie took in a gasping breath. She moved her gaze from the angry look on her brother's face to the resigned expression on Jonah's.

"Jonah?"

"None of this was your fault, Celie." He took a step toward the door. "Always remember that. What happened wasn't your fault. It was mine. It was all…mine. And your brother's."

Celie watched Jonah turn. He was going to leave her. If she didn't do something soon, she was going to lose the only man she would ever love.

"Where are you going?"

Jonah stopped. "I'm going home—for as long as I have a home." He walked to the door, then paused. "You'll be pleased to know that the creditors you sent line the entryway of my home, Your Grace. It won't be long and I will have lost it."

"You deserve to lose it. You deserve to lose everything. Just like I did."

Celie heard the anger in her brother's voice and felt her world shatter around her. What had he done?

Jonah's bitter laughter startled her.

"The house? The Abbey? You can have it all. They mean nothing to me."

"You'll lose it all! I've made sure you will!"

Jonah's shoulders lifted, then fell. "So be it." He reached for the handle on the door. "Without Celie to share it with, it means nothing."

Jonah pulled open the door, and Celie realized he was going to leave her. She had one question she needed to ask before he left. "Jonah?"

He stopped. "Yes?"

"Did you send the bills to repair Haywood Abbey to Hadleigh without his knowledge?"

Jonah smiled. "Is that what your brother told you?"

She nodded, and his smile broadened. "Oh, Hadleigh. Was there no limit to your lies?"

Celie's world trembled. Her brother had lied to her. She looked away from him and back to Jonah. "Wait, Jonah. I'm coming with you."

"No!" Hadleigh yelled, clasping his fingers around her upper arm to stop her.

"Jonah!"

He turned to face her. "You can't come with me, Celie. I have nowhere to take you."

"That doesn't matter! Nothing matters as long as we're together."

Celie saw Jonah's body stiffen as if her words had been attached to the end of a whip and cut through his flesh.

"It matters," he said, then turned away from her.

The second before he disappeared from sight, he stopped and turned. But it wasn't to her that he looked, but at her brother. And the glare in his eyes was the vilest, most hate-filled look she'd ever seen.

"I will grant you a few moments of satisfaction, Your Grace. You have accomplished what you intended. I have lost it all. I have lost Celie. But so have you."

For several long, agonizing seconds, Jonah didn't move. Then he slowly opened the door and took his first step away from her.

She wanted to run after him to stop him, to go with him, but there was nothing to be gained by begging him to stay. Or by going with him. She needed to find out everything her brother had done and undo what she could to save the Abbey.

Celie listened to the ominous sound of the door as it closed behind Jonah and felt her heart plummet to the pit of her stomach.

A fury unlike anything she'd ever felt before exploded inside her and she turned on her brother.

"What have you done?"

Chapter 22

"What have you done?" Celie demanded again, angrier than she'd ever been in her life.

Her brother's shoulders lifted in indignant righteousness. "I've saved you from having to spend the rest of your life with a man who is incapable of loving anyone. He would have destroyed you just like he destroyed everyone who was foolish enough to care for him."

"Are you talking about Melisande?"

"Yes! Because of him, she's dead!"

Celie stepped back and stared at her brother. His pain over losing Melisande was plain. It hadn't lessened, as she'd assumed, but had grown even stronger.

"Jonah didn't have anything to do with Melisande's death, Hadleigh. She ran out onto the street and was hit by a carriage."

"Because she was running away from him! Because she loved me and Haywood wanted her to run away with him!"

"You fool! Melisande didn't love you. She didn't love anyone but herself."

"That's not true. We had an understanding. We were going to marry, but Haywood wanted her for himself. He was forcing her to leave with him."

"If anyone was forcing someone to do anything, it was Melisande no doubt trying to convince Jonah to marry her."

"No!"

Celie looked her brother in the eyes. "You always had Melisande on such a high pedestal you couldn't see her for the person she really was."

"I know what she was. She was the most beautiful person who ever lived. She was—"

"Spoiled to the point of revulsion," Celie cut in. "She'd been pampered her whole life and allowed to do anything she wanted. She'd gotten by with the unthinkable."

"No!"

"Yes! Her parents were as blind to her faults as you were. She was cruel and heartless. She belittled every other female with whom she came into contact and reveled in their shortcomings."

"No!"

Celie slashed her hand through the air to stop her brother from defending Melisande.

Hadleigh was silent.

"She did. Because ridiculing everyone made her feel superior. Laughing at them made her feel more important."

Celie couldn't believe that someone as intelligent as her brother had been so completely taken in by Melisande's beauty that he'd been unaware of the kind of person she was inside.

"You never liked Melisande, Cecelia. I always knew the two of you could barely tolerate each other."

"*No one* liked Melisande, Hadleigh. If you had been able to see past her stunning beauty, you wouldn't have liked her, either."

"Stop it! You're only saying such horrible things because Melisande was in love with the man you were foolish enough to give your heart."

"Melisande may have been in love with someone, but it certainly wasn't Jonah."

"You didn't see them that night. She was begging Haywood, pleading with him to leave her alone."

"No, she wasn't, Your Grace," Amanda said from behind them. "She was begging Haywood to take her to Gretna Green so they could marry."

Both Celie and Hadleigh turned to look at Amanda.

Amanda had been so uncharacteristically quiet since Jonah left that Celie had almost forgotten she was there. Hadleigh must have, too, but she'd gained his full attention at the mention of Gretna Green and marriage.

"That's not true. Melisande and I were going to marry. Melisande's father and I had come to an agreement years ago. Besides, Haywood wasn't even titled then. He was the second son of a man destined to lose everything. Why would she want to marry him?"

"No doubt to pass off the child she was carrying as Lord Haywood's babe."

Several seconds passed before Hadleigh spoke. When he did, his reaction was as violent as the eruption of an exploding volcano.

"Lies! Who told you such vicious lies?"

Amanda stepped closer and faced Hadleigh as if he were a servant instead of the duke he was.

"They're not lies, Your Grace. For your sake, I wish they were, but I know for a fact that Melisande was carrying a child."

"How can you know such a thing? That was a story no doubt started after Melisande's death by some jealous females."

Amanda shook her head. "I'm not sure if you'd ever heard Melisande talk of Mrs. Crumpert, but—"

"Crumpert? Of course. Melisande called her 'Crumpy.' She was Melisande's nurse, then her nanny, and eventually, she stood in for a chaperone when Melisande needed someone to accompany her."

"Melisande's mother dismissed Mrs. Crumpert without a reference after Melisande died because she was the only person other than Lady Kendall who knew Melisande was with child. Lady Kendall thought she could stop any rumors from circulating if she used the excuse that they'd come from a disgruntled former servant who had been dismissed. Without a reference, Mrs. Crumpert was desperate. She came to Lillian, my oldest sister, because she'd held a position with our family before leaving Father's employ to go to Lady Kendall. Lillian, of course, took her in. She's nursemaid to her two babes even now."

Hadleigh shook his head as if he needed to clear it. "That can't be. It can't."

"It is, Your Grace. Melisande was carrying another man's babe, and she was desperate to find a husband before you announced your engagement. She wisely feared your reaction when you discovered you'd been duped. She chose Haywood because she considered him the most malleable of her acquaintances."

"He refused her," Hadleigh whispered as if talking to himself.

"Yes, because he didn't love her. And he knew you did. Unlike you, he refused to betray your friendship."

"But I thought—"

"You thought of no one but yourself and your need to exact revenge on an innocent man." Celie faced her brother. "A man who'd once been your closest friend."

"But Haywood didn't deny it when I accused him of trying to steal Melisande away from me."

"Would you have believed him?"

Hadleigh opened his mouth to say something, undoubtedly something to indicate that he might have, then closed his mouth and sank into the nearest chair.

"Dear God, what have I done?"

Celie might have felt sorry for her brother if he hadn't been the cause of so much pain. "I want to know what you did, Hadleigh. I want to know *everything*."

For several long minutes, Celie didn't think her brother was going to admit anything, but eventually, he turned his gaze to Amanda.

"You know, don't you? That's why you brought Haywood here, because you know."

"Yes, I know. So you'd best tell your sister yourself, because my version of what you did won't be nearly so sympathetic."

Hadleigh nodded in acquiescence, then lifted his hollow gaze to face her. Celie braced herself for the pain she knew would follow.

"I never meant to hurt you, Cecelia. Never."

"But you have. You've hurt me more than I ever thought I could be hurt."

Hadleigh's shoulders sagged. "It's just that I hated him so. I'd hated him for so long that destroying him was all I thought of. Do you know what that's like?"

He paused. "Of course you don't know. You're so good. So kind. The only person in the world who's done nothing to deserve this. But I didn't think it would go this far."

"How far?"

"I didn't think you could ever love him. I didn't think you would ever love anyone."

Celie was glad she was sitting. If she hadn't been, she feared her legs would have buckled beneath her. "Why did you think I'd never love anyone?"

"Because you refused every suitor who asked for your hand. Because you never showed interest in anyone. I thought you loved as I did. I thought you loved someone who couldn't return your love. I thought you'd chosen to live your life alone rather than marry someone you could never love."

"I had, Hadleigh. You were right—in part. I was in love with someone—Jonah. I'd loved him for as long as I could remember."

"But I didn't know that. That was why I used you to ruin Haywood. Because I was certain you'd dismiss him as swiftly as you dismissed every other suitor who'd asked for your hand."

She glared at him, a riot of tumultuous emotions attacking her from the inside out. "What did you do? Tell me everything. Everything, Hadleigh. Every single detail."

She was angry. None of this was Jonah's fault. Her brother had orchestrated the entire affair, and both she and Jonah had walked into the trap without realizing how desperate her brother was to exact his revenge.

She glared at her brother. He sat in the chair with his arms braced on his knees and his head downcast. He didn't resemble a duke. He possessed none of the confidence and authority he usually wore. He looked defeated. A shadow of his former strength.

"My plan was brilliant. I knew Haywood wouldn't be able to refuse."

"What did you tell him?"

He hesitated as if he didn't want to say the words that would tell her how desperate he'd been to ruin Haywood. How easily he'd used her to achieve his goal.

"I covered his father's and his brother's debts, then offered him the one thing I knew he couldn't refuse—the money necessary to save Haywood Abbey and bring it back to its former grandeur. The ability to provide for his tenants and give them a better livelihood. I knew he regretted how his father's lifestyle had forced the Haywood tenants to go without. How little his father had provided for them. I knew he'd go through hell itself to make things better."

"So you offered him the money to make the improvements to Haywood Abbey?"

"Yes. I told him that when you married the amount of your dowry would cover the money I'd loaned him. That I expected him to repay every pound of the money it took to repair Haywood Abbey. But I had no intention of ever letting him get his hands on your dowry. I never intended to allow him to marry you."

Celie sat for several agonizing moments, then slowly rose to her feet. The room closed in around her, the heavy air impossible to breathe. She reached out to grasp any piece of furniture that would steady her as she made her way to the window.

The sun shone. A gentle breeze moved the trees in soft, flowing waves. It was peaceful on the other side of the glass. Totally unlike the turmoil and tragedy that was happening on this side. Her brother's voice shattered her escape and brought her back to the present.

"I didn't for an instant think you'd be receptive to his suit. You'd never shown interest in any man's attentions before. In fact, far from it. You spurned every man who gave you a second glance. I had no doubt you'd do the same with Haywood's suit."

"Instead, I..."

She couldn't continue. The pain of reliving those first few nights when Jonah walked back into her life. Her fear that her brother would give him the "cut direct" and force society to do the same. The relief she felt when he didn't and Jonah took his rightful place. The elation that first night when he sought her out on Lady Plimpton's terrace, when he asked for her help, invited her to ride with him the following day—and the days after.

"I was so sure he'd leap at the chance to get the money I dangled in front of him that it didn't once occur to me that he might not."

"He refused the money?"

"He tried, but I told him I wouldn't agree to allow you to marry him without a decent roof over your head. I demanded that he take the money if he was serious about courting you."

Celie clasped her hand to her mouth to stop a small cry of joy from escaping. "He only accepted the money because you forced his hand."

"Bloody fool. He almost ruined my plan." Hadleigh walked to a small table where several crystal decanters sat with various liquids and poured some of the liquor from one of them into a glass. He took a long swallow, then faced her. "I thought his estates, his tenants, and repaying his father's debts were most important to him. I intended for him to make major improvements to his homes from the money he assumed would come from your dowry, and when he was so deeply in debt he'd never see his way out, I'd tell him you wouldn't agree to his marriage proposal. By then he would have spent thousands of pounds he'd never be able to repay and his creditors would tear him limb from limb."

"Instead," Celie said, walking to where Hadleigh sat and standing in front of him, "I not only accepted Jonah's attentions, I told you I intended to accept his offer of marriage."

"Why, Cecelia? Why him when you'd never shown interest in another man?"

"That's hardly the point. The question is, how could you have used me like that?"

Hadleigh's chest rose, then fell before he answered. "I didn't consider what I was doing as using you. I knew..." He paused to swipe his hand over his face. "I was *so sure* Haywood was responsible for Melisande's death. I wanted revenge in whatever way I could."

"So you used me as the bartering chip. You offered him the money to improve the lives of the Haywood tenants. And all the while, your objective was to destroy him."

"I was desperate! I knew to save his property he'd have to marry someone who came with a sizable dowry. When he came home a war hero, it was only a matter of time until someone trapped him for her husband."

"So *you* trapped him." Celie tried to ignore the pain in her chest. "For me."

The pain of knowing if it hadn't been for her brother, Jonah probably would never have had anything to do with her was nearly unbearable. "You must have laughed yourself silly each time you thought of the money Jonah was spending to make me happy."

"No, Celie! Far from it."

Her brother bolted from his chair and stepped closer to her.

"I thought I had everything planned out so perfectly. I never thought you would accept his proposal. I didn't think you would want to marry him."

"But I did…because I love him. I've loved Jonah my whole life. I've loved him with my whole heart. How could I consider marriage to anyone else?"

Her brother looked up with heart-wrenching anguish in his eyes. "Nothing went the way I intended. I didn't anticipate that the two of you would get along. I didn't expect to see you gaze at each other the way you did and laugh together at things that only people who were becoming friends found humor in. And I never thought to see you fall in love with Haywood. Or him fall in love with you."

Celie was shocked. "Are you listening to yourself, Hadleigh? Do you hear what you're saying?"

Celie's brother, the powerful Duke of Hadleigh, sank into the nearest chair and dropped his head to his hands. "Unfortunately, I do. And it makes me sick."

"It should!" She glared at him. "You thought of no one but yourself and how you could destroy a man you thought had taken something away from you. And not once did you think of me!"

She stomped across the floor in quick, angry strides and railed at her brother with all the hurt and disappointment he'd caused her. "You didn't care that I would live the rest of my life thinking that the man I loved didn't love me. That he didn't want me." Celie took a step closer to her brother. "Do you care that little for me, Your Grace?"

"I love you, Celie. You are the dearest person in the world to me. I would undo everything I've done if I could, but I can't. I thought I had everything worked out so perfectly until..."

Hadleigh rose from his chair and stood tall before her. "What I did was unforgivable, and I'll do anything in my power to make it up to you."

Celie tried to compose herself. She tried to tell herself that her brother hadn't done something so heinous out of hatred toward her, but because he'd been so filled with the need to avenge Melisande's death.

She tried to rationalize his actions with the excuse that he hadn't been able to think clearly. But she knew it would take her a long time to get over what her brother had done to her.

Words weren't enough. She would need much more than an apology to make things right between Jonah and her.

"What can I do, Cecelia? Tell me what I can do to fix what I've done. Tell me how I can make this right."

She faced him with her fists on her hips and an angry glare in her eyes. "You will order your solicitors to bring enough money to cover the bills Jonah thought my dowry would pay. And tell them to hurry. You won't have much time."

Celie walked toward the door. She had to see Jonah. She had to do everything in her power to keep from losing him.

She reached for the door handle. She needed to get to Jonah as quickly as she could. "Then," she said, opening the door and taking her first step to go to the man who possessed her heart, "you can get on your knees and pray that the man I love will take me back after everything we did to him."

Chapter 23

❦

Celie disembarked from her carriage almost before the footman had time to lower the steps. She raced across the cobbled walk, up the three steps, then across the portico. The door opened, but Bundy stepped into the opening to block the entrance.

"If you've come to cause Lord Haywood more problems, my lady, then I'll ask you to come again another day. The cap'n doesn't need anything more to handle today."

"I haven't come to cause more problems, Bundy. I've come to remove some of Lord Haywood's calamities."

Jonah's loyal butler stared at her for several long seconds as if evaluating the truth of her words.

She was afraid he wasn't going to let her enter, but finally, he breathed a heavy sigh and stepped aside.

"Be prepared, my lady. There's a crowd of angry men inside who've refused to leave no matter how much I threaten them."

"I'll take care of them, Bundy."

She lifted her shoulders and entered the house as if she were the lady of the manor—because, in time, she would be.

"What's the meaning of this?" she said, scanning the men who lined the walls of the entryway.

"We're here to get our money," one of the men announced. "Word reached us that we was to collect our pay today for the goods and services Lord Haywood contracted to repair his estates, or we wouldn't get any money at all."

Celie lifted the corners of her mouth in what she hoped was a convincing smile. "Well, at least part of the message you received was correct. Lord Haywood knows how much each of you depend on the money for the goods he purchased, so he would like to take care of his debts immediately. What was incorrect in the message you received was where you were to go to receive payment. The Duke of Hadleigh will see to it that you are paid. He is waiting for you at Hadleigh House."

"Are you sure, ma'am? That's not what the note I received said."

"Do you know who I am, sir?"

"Of course I do. We all do. You're the Duke of Hadleigh's sister."

"No, sir," Celie said with an indignant air. "I am the Earl of Haywood's betrothed. I happen to be the Duke of Hadleigh's sister by an accident of birth. I am the Earl of Haywood's betrothed by choice."

"I'm sorry, my lady," the embarrassed merchant stammered.

"That's quite all right. I accept your apology. Your error doesn't, however, change the facts. *If* you want your money—and I'm sure you do—I'd advise you to move yourselves to Hadleigh House posthaste. His Grace's solicitors are waiting to pay you in full for your goods and labor."

En masse, the group of merchants and creditors to whom Jonah owed money exited through the door Bundy held open for them. Within seconds, the hallway was empty and the house quiet.

"That was mighty impressive, my lady," Bundy said, closing the door on the last of them. "Perhaps you'd best be gone, though, when they come back. They'll be heaps angrier then."

"No one will return, Bundy. His Grace will pay what's owed them."

Jonah's butler's eyebrows shot upward, indicating he wasn't convinced he could believe her.

"Where is Lord Haywood?" she asked, not caring whether Bundy believed her or not. She had more important things on her mind. And convincing Jonah that she wanted to be his wife was at the top of her list.

"He's in the library." Bundy nodded toward Jonah's favorite room, which was located at the back of the house.

"Thank you, Bundy. You and the rest of the staff may take the remainder of the day off. You won't be needed until tomorrow after luncheon."

"Are you sure, my lady?"

"Oh, yes. Quite sure."

Celie didn't wait to see the shocked expression on Bundy's face, but headed down the hallway to confront Jonah.

She didn't knock when she reached the library, but opened the door and stepped inside the room.

The man she loved with all her heart sat behind the huge mahogany desk with his back to her. He didn't turn around when she closed the door, but lifted the whiskey glass in his hand and took a long swallow.

"You must be serving them tea, Bundy. The house almost seems quiet."

"The house *is* quiet. That's because the lynch mob is gone."

Jonah spun around in his chair and bolted to his feet. "What are you doing here?"

"Where else should I be?"

Jonah shook his head. "You don't belong here."

"Really? Where do I belong, then?"

"With your brother. He can at least provide a roof over your head. I can't."

"Then you lied when you told me you loved me."

Jonah set his whiskey glass on the desk. "I didn't lie. I love you so much I'm not sure I'll be able to survive the rest of my life without you. But that doesn't change anything. I'm about to lose everything."

Jonah stepped around the side of the desk and walked to the window on the far side of the room. "Did you happen to miss the score of men that lined the entryway when you arrived? Each one of them wants money that I don't seem to have."

Celie crossed her arms over her chest and forced herself to stay where she was. Oh, how she wanted to go to him. How she wanted to wrap her arms around him and feel the warmth of his flesh against her. How she wanted to cup her fingers around the back of his head and bring his mouth close enough to kiss him.

Her knees turned weak and she gasped a shuddering breath.

"Oh, I counted far more than a score of men demanding payment for bills we accumulated. There were at least thirty, and I imagine by now my brother's army of solicitors is having quite the time trying to pay them all."

Jonah turned to face her. "What did you say?"

Celie walked across the room and sat on the corner of the desk. "I said that I sent all of them to Hadleigh. He's the one who created this problem. He can deal with it."

Jonah's eyes opened wide. "How did—"

"Amanda told him the truth about Melisande."

There was a wary tone in Jonah's voice when he spoke. "What truth?"

"That she was carrying another man's child. That if the two of you argued that night, like he says he saw, it was no doubt because she was trying to force you to marry her."

"How did she know that?"

Celie stood. She leaned forward until their bodies were so close she could feel the heat that radiated from him. "We can discuss that later," she said, wrapping her hands around Jonah's middle and pressing her cheek to his chest. "Much later."

"Celie, what are you doing?"

"Shh," she whispered, standing perfectly still. "I want to listen to your heart race in your chest."

A low, earthy moan echoed in her ear, and Celie smiled. "Do you think you could put your arms around me, Jonah?"

He moaned again, this time with a more agonizing tone.

"Try, Jonah. It won't hurt. I promise."

Jonah lifted his arms and wrapped them around her, and Celie knew it was possible she could die from the rush of emotions racing through her.

"Now, do you suppose you could kiss me?"

"I think it's possible, my lady."

He lowered his head and brushed his lips against hers. She wrapped her arms around his neck and pulled him closer.

"I told Bundy he wouldn't be needed any more today." She tipped her head to the side to give him better access.

"Did you?" He kissed her again. His fingers skimmed over her shoulder, then around her upper arm, then traveled inside the bodice of her gown to cup her breast.

Celie felt the flames of passion build inside her. She was more than ready for Jonah to make love to her, and she didn't want to wait one more minute.

"Jonah, kiss me."

A seductive smile lifted the corners of his mouth as he lowered his head and covered her mouth with his.

His kiss was hot and demanding and wildly intoxicating. She gathered him closer and met his demands. She was desperate to show him how much she loved him, desperate to have him make her his wife.

Jonah opened his mouth atop hers and took possession of her. He deepened his kisses until neither of them could breathe; then, in a movement that caused a sudden void, he lifted his head and broke their kiss.

"Jonah?"

"Not here, Celie. Not like this." He brought his mouth down on hers and kissed her once more.

"I want to make you a promise," he said, brushing the backs of the fingers of one hand down her cheek while he held her close with his other. "I swear that you will never want for anything. I can't promise I can provide all the luxuries you enjoyed under Hadleigh's roof, but you will never go without. I will spend the rest of my life doing everything in my power to provide for you."

"Do you think I will demand so much, Jonah?"

"I think you *deserve* that much. You are the rarest jewel in the world, and I am the most fortunate of men to have found you."

Jonah's face blurred before her and a warm tear of joy spilled from each eye to run down her cheeks. He wiped them away with his fingertip, then lowered his head and kissed her again.

"I was serious when I told your brother he could take whatever he wanted from me and it didn't matter. Anything except you. I couldn't have survived if I had lost you. I love you too much to live the rest of my life without you."

Tears filled Celie's eyes and Jonah's tall figure blurred before her.

"I will give you a lifetime to show me how much you love me."

"Only one lifetime?"

Celie swallowed the lump that formed in her throat. "No, I love you so much it will take a second lifetime to use all my love up. And maybe a third."

"Then we'd better not waste a minute of the time we've been given," Jonah said, and carried her up the stairs to the room they would share for the rest of their lives.

About the Author

❦

Laura Landon taught high school for ten years before leaving the classroom to open her own ice-cream shop. As much as she loved serving up sundaes and malts from behind the counter, she closed up shop after penning her first novel. Now she spends nearly every waking minute writing, guiding her heroes and heroines to happily ever after. She is the author of more than a dozen historical novels, and her books are enjoyed by readers around the world. She lives with her family in the rural Midwest, where she devotes what free time she has to volunteering in her community.